CRASH INTO ME

K.M. SCOTT

Crash Into Me is a work of fiction. Names, characters, places, and events are the products of the author's imagination. Any resemblance to events, locations, or persons, living or dead, is coincidental.

ISBN 13: 978-0-9891081-5-7
ISBN 10: 0989108155

Published in the United States

DEDICATION

Thank you to all the wonderful people who have been there for me. This couldn't have happened without you.

One

"You're going to be late!" Jordan yelled from the kitchen in her usual bellow.

She didn't have to remind me. As I stood checking out my look in the mirror that hung on the back of my closet door, I cringed at the idea that people were going to actually see me in my outfit in just minutes. I looked more like a waitress than a junior assistant to an art gallery owner. A short black skirt and white button down blouse? I might as well be serving pasta down the street at Mama Leone's. Or serving drinks at some gentleman's club. Why my boss thought this was appropriate for an art gallery was beyond me.

Smoothing my light brown hair that fell to just below my shoulders, I leaned in close to the mirror and saw that the tawny eye shadow and the darkest black mascara did their best to make my blue eyes pop. I stroked a final coat of plum lip gloss over my lips and put on my best supermodel face.

Too bad everything below my neck ruined all my hard work.

I made my way down the hallway, stopping by the kitchen to give my roommate a look at my getup. She'd seen it before, but some things never got old.

"And here she is, Miss America," I sang.

Jordan put her glass down on the counter and brought her hands up to her face to cover her smile. A pretty blonde with knockout green eyes, she was my best friend and the only person who knew just how much I hated the outfit. "Oh, honey. At least you make that look good. Good legs make everything look better, and you have great legs."

"I think I've heard that," I joked. At least Jordan helped make me hate this outfit a little less. That is until I got the first sneer from some overly made up woman dripping with expensive jewelry looking down her plastic surgery perfect nose at me. Then I'd hate it again.

"I'm off to work. What are you doing while I'm moving up in the art world?"

"Justin and I are catching a movie."

"So you're doing Justin," I teased. She'd begun dating him a while back, but recently they'd gotten much closer, much to her delight. Jordan saw him as a possible "Mr. Right" and loved that he wanted to move toward more commitment.

"Don't hate," she said with a smile. "You'll be late, and then that nasty boss of yours will be all over you."

"Enjoy. I'm off to pay my dues again," I joked only slightly as I headed out the door.

I walked toward the subway with Jordan's words rattling around in my head, oblivious to the throngs of people heading out for the night. "Don't hate." In truth, I didn't hate the idea that she had found someone. I actually liked Justin. He wasn't an ass like a lot of guys, and he was pretty tolerant of having a third wheel when Jordan dragged me along with them to save me from a Friday night in. And he was just her type—tall, dark, and lanky. While I wasn't as convinced as she was that he was "The One," simply because I wasn't sure that even existed, I liked that she was happy.

It gave me hope that as she was always claiming good things did, in fact, happen to good people.

The crowd of New York art devotees far less knowledgeable about art than parties milled about the Anderson Gallery, champagne glasses in hand and noses in the air as they feigned appreciation for the work of a new artist that odds were would likely be a has-been by this time next year. The artwork wasn't bad, as far as modern art went, but I didn't have the time to stand around feeling unimpressed. As the lowest rung on the gallery's ladder, I was responsible for ensuring that the patrons were happy, full of alcohol and hors d'oeuvres, and convinced that the artist's work was the "next big thing," as Sheila Anderson, my boss and owner of the gallery that bore her name, had made quite clear in the pre-show meeting just hours before.

Her hand-picked outfit for me fit oddly, which was exactly the purpose. The black skirt was far too short and felt more like a big belt in the chilly, air conditioned room. God, my ass was almost hanging out! And the white, button-down shirt one size too small? My biggest fear that night was that a button would pop, fly from my chest, and take someone's eye out. But since my job was to be a "hostess," as Sheila liked to term my employment as her personal slave, this was what I had to wear. The only thing that made it even bearable was that she'd hired two other women to work that night, so at least I wasn't alone in my outfit of shame.

Four years of school and a degree in art history and I was handing out cocktail weenies. But it was a job that paid the bills. Well, barely paid the bills. No matter. I had bigger plans for my life than this, and I knew I needed to pay my dues before the good things showed up.

On nights like this, though, it just felt like I was paying more than anything else.

A tall, blonde standing near the floor to ceiling window at the front of the gallery lifted her glass to alert me she needed a refill, and away I went scurrying to provide her with the much needed champagne. Unlike most of the other gallery patrons, she was at least pleasant and gave me a nod of thanks. Hopefully, Sheila saw that.

In truth, this wasn't such a bad job. I told myself that all the time, and sometimes I even believed it. The best part about it was that I got to be around the art. That made all the awful jobs I was assigned tolerable. When all the people were gone and it was just me, my broom, and the artwork, I could honestly say I was happy. I'd stand in front of a sculpture from some unknown artist and let my eyes drift over the smooth lines and curves of the piece to imagine what may have been in the artist's heart as he or she lovingly molded their masterpiece. The Anderson Gallery didn't have work from the big names like Monet or Rodin, but it had art and that let me convince myself that years of studying hadn't been for nothing.

A crowd of people gathered near one of the paintings hung on the far wall. It was the best piece in the show, so it wasn't surprising, but from the sound of their voices, it wasn't the painting they were interested in. I moved toward them, curious for a distraction from standing around with trays all night. The group was mostly women, each one more beautiful than the next, and I suddenly felt self-conscious craning my neck to see what they were so intrigued by, as if I didn't belong. A few blondes, brunettes, and a redhead who all looked like supermodels and were dressed in names I only knew from magazines circled around someone, laughing and chattering about things I couldn't understand. Then one woman moved aside and I saw him.

He was stunning, even more gorgeous than the women that surrounded him. Over six feet tall with short dark hair, he wore a dark grey suit and black shirt that hung as if they were made especially for him, accentuating every well-built inch of his body. I edged myself closer, drawn to him, and saw his eyes. Deep chocolate brown, they looked as if they had seen all the things I hadn't in this world. He was wealth, opulence, and excess.

A beautiful brunette hung on his arm, an appropriate accessory for such a man, like fourteen caret gold cufflinks or a stainless steel Rolex. As I stood there gawking at him, I heard one of the women say his name.

Tristan.

In that moment, I wanted more than anything for the whole world to fade away until it was just me and him. I'd heard of love at first sight before and never believed in it, but as I watched him take up all the empty space in the room, I was in love.

No, not love. Lust.

He glanced over at me, and my cheeks flushed with heat. His gaze fixed on mine, brown eyes staring at me as if we knew each other intimately. As if he knew the deepest, darkest parts of me. My brain told me to look away, to break the connection, but the rest of my body rebelled. I wanted to feel those eyes on every part of me.

"Nina, what are you doing? I saw at least three patrons with empty glasses as I crossed the room. Chop, chop!" Sheila barked in my ear, tearing me out of my fantasy.

My boss marched away, and I watched as Tristan and his women moved on to another painting. Everything was as it should be with everyone in their correct place. Him with a group of gorgeous women and me with my tray of cocktail weenies. A few minutes later, I watched him leave, never even knowing his last name or what his voice sounded like.

As the show wound down and the sated art lovers made their way to other fashionable locations in SoHo, I began my post-show duties. Sheila had a look of pure happiness on her gaunt face as she said goodbye to her other help for the night, which could mean that she was high or pleased with how the show had gone. As she was coming my way, I'd know in a minute which it was.

Sheila was a touchy-feely person, so even before she got to me her hand was reaching out for my arm. Raking her long, bony fingers down my shirt sleeve, she purred, "Nina, except for that brief slip with the champagne, I think the show went off wonderfully." Turning to lock the gallery's front door, she waved her hand around the room. "You can leave a lot of this mess for tomorrow, or if you prefer to clean up tonight, you can have Sunday off. Your choice. I know you'll get it done. You're dependable."

She didn't bother to wait for my response before she grabbed her black cashmere wrap and traipsed out the back door. I was nothing if not reliable, so she didn't have to worry about whether I'd clean or not. By the time she returned on Monday, her gallery would be spotless.

As I swept up the last cocktail napkin and put the last champagne glass in the holder for the caterer, I thought about how my boss saw me. Dependable. God, that was an awful way to be seen! Garbage bags were dependable. Wrenches were considered dependable. A good car was dependable.

The only thing worse would be if she'd called me sturdy.

With that cheery thought in mind, I turned off the lights, tied up the garbage bag that shared my dependable nature, and headed toward the back door to drop it off and go home for the night. One last job and I was Brooklyn bound.

I threw the trash in the Dumpster behind the building and locked the gallery's back door. Lost in thought, I heard someone behind me say, "Nice show, huh?"

The sound of his deep voice nearly made me jump out of my skin, and I spun around to see him. The man from earlier. Tristan. He stood leaning against a black sports car, arms folded across his chest, still dressed in that grey suit and looking even more incredible than when I'd first seen him. As I stared at him, drinking in how gorgeous he looked, my brain switched from pure fear back to normal to ask the obvious question.

Why is he here?

"Yeah, it was great. The artist is quite talented," I lied.

"It was shit and you know it. Nice outfit, though."

Instantly, I was once again acutely aware of how silly I looked in my waitress getup. His remark stung, and I snapped back, "It's called working. Now unless I can help you with something, I have to go. Have a good night."

I checked the lock on the gallery door and turned to walk away. I hadn't made it two steps before he quietly said, "I didn't mean anything bad by that. You look nice."

Was that sincerity in his voice? I didn't know. I just knew I didn't want to feel embarrassed by my work anymore that night.

Turning around, I tried to get a feel for this guy, but he just stood there staring at me like I was the most important person in the world at that moment. "Thanks."

"What do you say we go for a ride?"

"A ride?" I was confused, but I probably should have been afraid. I was standing in a back alley with a strange man, no matter how incredibly sexy he was, and there wasn't anyone nearby. How the hell was it possible that in a city of eight million Tristan and I were the only two there at that moment?

"A ride," he repeated in a slow, silky voice that made my stomach flip. "At least I can give you a ride home."

"You don't even know my name."

He stepped away from the car and in two strides was in front of me just inches away. Looking down at me, he smiled. "You're Nina Edwards, you work at this gallery, and unless I'm mistaken, you don't live anywhere near here."

As much as I wished he wasn't right, he was. Sunset Park, Brooklyn was miles away. However, that didn't mean I should forget everything I'd been taught all my life, even if he was the hottest man I'd ever spoken to. And even if this was one of my fantasies come true.

"I don't even know your name," I lied again.

A slow smile spread across his perfect mouth. "My apologies. I'm Tristan Stone and I'd like it if you'd let me take you home."

He extended his hand and I shook it, noticing how powerful it felt as it enveloped mine. His very expensive suit coat sleeve rode up just enough to show his Rolex, and I smiled at the fact that I'd called it correctly earlier.

He probably had gold cufflinks just under those sleeves too. But where was the brunette?

As my mind raced with these ideas, I realized he knew my name. "How do you know my name? We've never met."

Placing his hand on my lower back, he guided me to the passenger side of his car. His touch was light, yet it was thrilling, making my head spin. As he opened the door, he stepped aside and let me sit down before he leaned in close and said, "I asked."

I watched him walk in front of the car while I enjoyed the lingering scent of his delicious cologne, and as he passed through the headlights, I noticed now that he wasn't flirting with me that he seemed to be frowning. He must have sensed I was looking at him because when he stopped and turned to face me, the smile reappeared, almost on cue.

He sat down behind the wheel and revved the engine. "Ready?"

I was nowhere near ready, but there was no turning back now. The sharp click of the car's doors locking signaled it was time to go, and with a deep breath, I pressed a nervous smile onto my lips and nodded. I just hoped this wasn't going to end up being the biggest mistake of my life.

Tristan flew through the streets of SoHo, weaving through traffic at sixty miles an hour as I covered my eyes and silently prayed for my life. Maybe this wasn't a good idea.

"Are you going to keep your eyes closed the whole time?"

I opened my fingers and peeked through just in time to see us swerve around a cab and quickly closed them again. "Yes. The whole time, which will probably be about another minute at this speed."

"C'mon, open them up. You're safe. I won't let anything happen."

Slowly, I lowered my hands to my lap and worked hard not to dig my fingernails into my legs. I wasn't usually this uncool, but then again, I wasn't usually racing through the city at top speeds in a car that likely cost more than Jordan and I combined made in a year.

Tristan's Jaguar rode like it was gliding on air. The body hugging black leather seat may have been more comfortable than any piece of furniture I'd ever sat in. A soothing blue glow emanated from the dash, which was full of knobs and buttons around a center touchscreen. I may not ever have cared much about cars, but even I knew this was top shelf.

"Nice car. Do you always drive it like you plan to wreck it?"

As he swerved to miss a car stopped in front of us, he said, "Drive it like you stole it, right?"

Looking around the inside of the car, I wondered out loud, "You didn't steal it, did you?"

Tristan let out a deep laugh that sounded like it came all the way from his toes. "You're funny, Nina. Nothing like you were back there during the show."

"Back there I was working. My boss pays me to be serious." I stopped and chuckled. "Well, actually, she pays me to be like her personal slave."

"I knew there was something more to you than the pretty girl who served the drinks and disgusting little hot dogs."

God, he was sexy! There was something about the way words slid from his mouth when he spoke that made me want to beg him to stop the car so I could press my lips to his.

I turned to look at him and his strong jaw caught my attention. Even from the side, he was gorgeous. Relaxed for the first time since the car had begun moving, I joked, "I'll have you know those cocktail weenies are a big hit."

He turned his head and smiled a sexy grin. "I bet they are."

While my gaze slid down over his torso and I noticed how perfectly his shirt lay on his body, out of the corner of my eye I noticed a road sign as we sped past it. I-95? "Uh, I think you're going the wrong way. The Cross Bronx Expressway doesn't go anywhere near my house."

He shifted into third gear and hit the gas, pushing me back against the seat. "Guess you should have been paying attention instead of hiding behind your hands."

Fear raced through my body. Was he serious? "Are you kidnapping me? I mean, this feels a little bit like kidnapping since you obviously aren't taking me home."

That I sounded ridiculous and a man like him probably didn't have to kidnap women didn't occur to me in my fear. Women likely pleaded with him to take them anywhere.

"I don't think they'd call this kidnapping," he teased. "Maybe if you were tied up or at least had a gag in your mouth."

"Please take me home, Tristan. We're nowhere near my house and you're scaring me."

My hands began to get sweaty at the real fear that I had made a terrible mistake. I didn't know this man, and no matter how infatuated I'd been with him just hours before, he had total control of me at that moment, something very frightening.

Still speeding toward God knows where, he took his hands off the steering wheel and held them up in front of him. "If you want to go home, take the wheel and turn the car around."

I frantically grabbed the wheel and the car jerked to the right, racing off to the side of the road. I panicked, turned it to the left, overcompensating, and screamed in terror as we began to spin out. Then everything before my eyes went black.

The car rolled to a stop on the shoulder and I heard him say my name in a soft voice. "Nina. Nina, it's okay. We're okay."

I looked around at the car and him and saw he was telling the truth. We hadn't crashed and I was still alive. Adrenaline coursed through my body, and my hands began to shake uncontrollably. Suddenly, I was overcome with emotion and lashed out at him as tears began to roll down my cheeks. "You're crazy! You're fucking crazy! You could have killed me!"

My crying startled him, and for just a moment he didn't possess that cool exterior he'd worn since the first moment I'd seen him. His brows knitted, as if he were in pain, and he leaned in toward me to press his forehead to mine. He cradled my face in his hands, instantly exciting me. Closing my eyes to mask my discomfort, I heard him say, "We only know how precious life is when he come close to death, Nina."

He sat back in his seat, and I turned to look at him, my emotions all a jumble. "Why did you want me to come with you tonight? Why did you come find me? I'm not like those women who were around you at the show. Why me?"

"Those women don't interest me. If they did, I could have any one of dozens right now."

Oddly, that made me jealous. I didn't even know this man, but the idea of him with anyone else bothered me.

Fighting back my insecurities, I said, "Maybe they like it when you nearly kill them, but I don't. Most ordinary women like me don't."

He stared straight ahead into the night and started the car again. "Don't underestimate yourself, Nina. You're anything but ordinary."

In truth, I didn't think I was ordinary, but it was nice to hear from someone other than yourself sometimes. My cheeks warmed at his compliment, making me happy the inside of the car was dim. He didn't need to think I was as infatuated with him as I already was.

Full of fake bravado, I said, "You have no idea what I am. And where the hell are we going?"

"I want to show you something. This is going to take a few, so why don't you enlighten me as to what you are," he said with a smile that made an ache form in the pit of my stomach.

"Isn't it a little presumptuous of you to think I have no plans? It is a Saturday night."

He didn't seem bothered by the idea that I had plans or even had a boyfriend. I had neither, but he couldn't know that.

Turning his head to face me, he looked at me with those soulful brown eyes. "Do you have plans?" he asked with an innocence that made me smile.

I didn't want to admit that I, a young, available, attractive New York woman, had no plans whatsoever on a Saturday night. I mean, I could have had plans. There were men interested in me. Just not anyone I was interested in being interested in me.

But he didn't need to know that.

"I did have things planned, if you need to know," I lied with enough attitude to hopefully hide my fib.

He chuckled and pushed down on the gas, again throwing me back in my leather seat. He never asked what my plans were and obviously didn't care. Talk about ego! As if I had nothing better to do than speed up the Taconic.

We traveled in silence with the ghostly outline of the trees and the white line on the side of the highway rushing by making me dizzy. The mood felt awkward, but I didn't know what to say. Here I was racing toward some unknown place with a man I barely knew in a car I'd only seen in ads in magazines and movies.

I only hoped I would be alive at the end of whatever this was.

As if he read my mind, he said, "Nina, relax. I don't plan to kill you and leave bits and pieces of you along the side of the road."

Terror raced through my body. I turned in my seat to face him, tugging the seatbelt away from my neck. "Who says that kind of thing? Jesus! Now I'm worried you're actually going to do that. And how do you know what I'm thinking?"

Once again, he laughed at what I said. "Tell me about what you do when you aren't hosting art shows."

Slumping back in my seat, I tried to calm myself. "I guess that's supposed to make me relax?"

He turned to look at me for a moment and then turned back to face the road. "No. It's supposed to tell me what you do when you're not hosting art shows."

"I like to read, hang out with my friends, and paint."

And there it was. The truth of my life in one short sentence. I sounded like some lame teenage girl who really spent her Saturday nights crocheting booties for her cat.

"What do you paint?"

"Whatever I'm feeling."

"Are you a good artist?"

"That's usually in the eye of the beholder."

He arched one dark eyebrow and looked over at me. "Then I'll have to judge your work for myself sometime."

Why was he talking like we were a couple or moving toward being that? We'd spent all of an hour together and now he was making plans to see my artwork. Yet he hadn't made any effort to even hold my hand or kiss me.

What was with this guy?

"Are we almost there?" I asked, uneasy about this entire thing.

"Almost."

As if my question had been a cue, he took the next exit and in minutes we were in the middle of pitch black nowhere. If I was worried before, now I was almost terrified. Scenes from every horror movie I'd ever seen flashed through my mind, all leading to the same ending. Me murdered and in pieces along an isolated country road and my sister devastated because I had forgotten the one thing she'd always told me not to do—get into cars with strangers. Ever since her house was broken into and ransacked, she'd been nearly paranoid about strangers, which I'd thought was a bit of an overreaction, but now I was thinking she had the right idea.

"Can I ask a question and have you answer with more than one word or one sentence that really says nothing?"

He stopped the car at a stop sign and turned to face me with a devastatingly sexy grin on his face. "Yes."

I couldn't help roll my eyes. He was either the most insufferable person I'd ever met or one of the funniest. I couldn't decide which. "Where are we going and can you promise me you're not going to do anything awful to me?"

"That's two questions, Nina."

The car began to roll again, and I let out a heavy sigh, hoping his dry humor was an indication that I wasn't going to be killed anytime soon. "Okay, can I ask you two questions and get straight answers?"

"Of course. You can ask whatever you want and I'll answer."

"I'd like straight answers."

His mouth hitched up at the corners into a sly smile. "As straight as you want."

"Where are we going?"

"To see a house I'm planning to buy."

"Really?"

He turned his head to look at me. "Do you want that to count as your second question?"

And after being scared shitless and almost killed, then confused and finally frustrated by his vague answers, I had to laugh. "No."

"Then what's your second question?"

"Are you going to do something awful to me out here in the middle of nowhere?"

Without a word, he stopped the car and put it into park. Then he leaned over, nearly touching my cheek with his lips, and pointed out my window. "That's the house, and I have no plans to do anything you wouldn't like or even love. What do you think of it?"

He was so close and smelled so delicious that I couldn't think clearly. I turned my head slightly and his lips brushed my skin, sending a jolt of electricity straight to between my legs. Pressing my thighs together, I turned toward the window and pretended to look up at the house on the hill.

"It's nice."

"It's twelve million dollars."

Holy shit! In my mind, I counted the number of zeroes on a check for twelve million dollars. Then I imagined what I could buy for twelve million dollars. And even all that probably wouldn't fill the house I was looking at.

His breath drifted over my neck, and I leaned back slightly, wanting so much for him to kiss me or touch me with his hand. He did neither, though, even as he remained there so close.

In my ear, he whispered in a voice that hit me somewhere deep inside, "See? Nothing bad."

Just when I was sure he would do something, he sat back in his seat and began driving back toward the city. My mind and senses were reeling. Never before had I wanted to feel the touch of a man's lips on me so badly, but he never made a move. The experience left my emotions raw, and I feared saying anything more as I was sure I would embarrass myself, so I sat silently as he drove toward Sunset Park, speaking only when he asked me where I lived.

When he finally pulled the car up to in front of my building, my feelings were all a mishmash. I felt happy about the fact that he hadn't killed me, but it seemed that he never had any plans to do that or anything else, including anything sexual. I couldn't be sure, but it seemed like he just wanted company. I guess I had been that, but my infatuation had secretly made me want so much more.

"Thank you for coming to see the house, Nina."

"Okay. Thank you for not killing me out in the middle of nowhere, I guess," I said with a smile, sad our time together was over, likely forever.

"I'll watch you get in."

"Thanks."

I waited a long moment just in case he wanted to lean in and kiss me, but he simply smiled and stared into my eyes, making me feel intensely insecure. Finally, I blurted out, "Goodbye," and got out.

Crossing in front of the car, I forced myself not to look inside at him. Whatever this had been, it was over, and I needed to get over it. I felt his stare on my back as I stepped onto the sidewalk, but I told myself to not turn around.

Then from behind me I heard the car window lower and he said my name. Turning around, I was struck by how lonely he looked in that car all by himself. I waved and smiled, and he said quietly, "Nina, be careful getting in cars with strange men. You could get hurt, and I wouldn't want anything bad to happen to you."

He drove off, leaving me more confused than before. Frustrated and baffled by my time with Tristan Stone, I hurried into my building.

Two

Sundays were always the best day of the week, as far as I was concerned. My father had never been a very religious man after my mother died, so my sister and I had never done the Sunday church thing. For us, the last day of the weekend meant sleeping in and then a late breakfast of pancakes and waffles smothered in butter and maple syrup and lovingly made by my father.

I'd continued this tradition as often as possible, even while I was in college, and now that I was out on my own, I loved Sundays even more. Granted, there were no pancakes or waffles usually, but there was sleeping in.

Beautiful, luxurious sleeping in.

Jordan thankfully shared my love of Sunday mornings, so our apartment was like a tomb often until early afternoon. The former best friend of my college roommate, she had been the opposite of Alyssa, who acted like weekends were her own personal version of boot camp. Jordan had joined with me to refuse to rise and shine at the crack of dawn one snowy February Sunday in freshman year, and we'd been friends ever since. We liked to say that it had been in our rebellion against the dawn and Alyssa that we'd become friends.

She hadn't been home when I returned from my bizarre time with Tristan, so I was eager to tell her about it all and get her opinion. But even crazy guy stories didn't warrant waking up before noon on a Sunday.

I rolled over and saw on my alarm clock that it was just about that time, so it was fair game to head down the hall and hope she was awake. Dressed in my usual shorts and a t-shirt I liked to sleep in, I padded barefoot toward her room only to find it empty. She had been getting more serious with Justin lately, so I assumed she'd spent the night at his place. Disappointed, I shuffled back to my room and flopped down on my bed once again.

The discussion of Tristan Stone and his sexiness would have to wait.

That didn't mean he was leaving my mind anytime soon. Even if we hadn't spent any time together, he'd still be rambling around the corners of my brain. I was infatuated, so the memory of his gorgeous face would stick with me for a while.

Clicking on the television, I stared at the show on the screen while I daydreamed about the events of the previous night. Why had he come to find me if all he wanted was someone to drive upstate with? He had many friends, I imagined, so why seek out a stranger who was so unlike him?

Just admitting to myself that I wasn't of his social level made me wince. I hadn't grown up around money, but my father had always made sure my sister and I were taken care of, so money was never a real issue. We weren't wealthy, but we weren't poor. The idea that someone's income would make them better than someone else was foreign to me, but in my time living in New York, it had become very clear that my feelings on money weren't everyone's.

Tristan Stone was very wealthy and far above my place in the world, even if I still counted myself as the middle class person I'd always been before living on my own. This made his actions the night before even less understandable.

I scrubbed my hands over my face in frustration. I wanted him to like me as much as I liked him. I wanted him to be lying in bed thinking of me. Even better would be him lying in bed alone thinking of me. But just thinking of me would be nice.

Who was I kidding? He was likely in bed with the brunette or the group of women he'd attended the show with. A stab of jealousy pinched at me as I imagined what he looked like out of that grey suit and naked in bed...with other women.

Get over it, Nina. It was some kind of game he was playing and it's over.

I silently repeated that a few times trying to convince myself to forget him and the time we'd spent together. I knew I should.

I just couldn't.

He filled my mind, and I loved it. Inhaling deeply, I still could smell his cologne, either as a wonderful memory or because of some fragment remaining inside my olfactory system. Masculine and powerful, it would forever remind me of him. I closed my eyes to imagine his face. The deep brown eyes that spoke volumes even when he didn't. The perfectly shaped mouth and the lips that had lightly brushed my cheek for just a moment, sending my body into overdrive. The masculine jaw of a man who looked like a man, not a boy.

What did he look like when he was just lying around on an early Sunday afternoon? Did he wear boxers or boxer briefs? Or did he sleep naked? I wanted to know what he looked like under his clothes. He had stood at least half a foot taller than I, probably more if I wasn't in those ridiculous three-inch heels Sheila made me wear to shows. He had appeared imposing, but I couldn't say if he was a big man or lean.

All I knew is that I wanted to know.

I let my mind drift back to the house he'd shown me. I fantasized about how he'd look standing in the doorway of one of its enormous rooms dressed in a suit much like the one he'd worn on our ride. In my mind's eye, he looked perfect. He wore a midnight blue shirt and matching tie that he fussed with. I saw myself there with him, straightening that tie as I stood in front of him admiring how truly stunning he was.

The sound of the front door slamming yanked me out of my daydream, and I heard Jordan yell, "Nina! Even I don't think you should be sleeping this late on this gorgeous day!"

Before I could get out of bed, she was standing in my doorway, all smiles. "Good morning, sleepyhead. What are you still doing in bed?"

Her happiness was catching, and I smiled. "Just hanging out. Where were you? Justin's?"

Her smile grew even bigger. "Yes. He and I have moved to me staying over, so you get to have the apartment all to yourself on nights like last night. Tell me you took advantage of that and didn't just come home after slaving away for Shitty Sheila and her crappy art show."

I didn't say anything, but my cheeks grew hot and my blush signaled that I had something to tell her. "Well, there was something. It's probably nothing, but..."

Jordan squealed. "Ooooh! I'm going to get a drink and you need to meet me in the living room to tell me everything. Get up and start talking!"

I loved that she was willing to listen to my silly ramblings about what would likely amount to nothing. Some friends only wanted someone to listen to them but weren't there for you when you had some juicy details, or in this case, wishful juicy details. But that wasn't Jordan.

By the time I made it out to the living room, she was planted in her favorite comfy chair with a glass of diet soda in front of her. "I'm ready, so hit me with the details."

I took a seat across from her and folded my legs under me. For a second, embarrassment rushed through my body. I was twenty-four years old and no stranger to dating. It's not like I was a virgin either. Suddenly, I felt silly about making a big deal out of my time with Tristan.

"Well?" Jordan asked impatiently.

"I met someone, sort of," I said, struggling to describe exactly what had happened.

"Nina, you never like the guys we meet. He must be something pretty damn good."

I screwed my face into a grimace. "I like some of them," I protested half-heartedly, knowing she was probably more right than wrong.

"Uh-huh. Name one."

I couldn't name one. They were all perfectly nice, I guess, but none of them really got me going. It never took long for me to fall out of like with them.

"That's not the point."

"No. The point is that you met someone you actually like. Tell me everything!"

"His name is Tristan. Tristan Stone. He..."

Just as I began to tell my story, Jordan's green eyes grew wide and she leaped out of her chair, nearly knocking over her glass. Marching over to the table by the window, she rifled through the half dozen newspapers she bought every day on her way to work downtown. When she turned around, she held up one in front of her. "You mean him?"

I craned my neck to look at a picture of a couple at some gala event. She walked a few steps closer, and I saw the man in the couple was Tristan. The woman on his arm didn't seem to be any of the women I'd seen surrounding him at the gallery the night before, though.

"What day is this from?"

Searching for the date, Jordan said, "Tuesday. Now tell me what happened with someone so famous that he ends up on Page Six regularly."

Stunned, I sat back in my seat, unsure what to tell her. I didn't know him like that. "What do you know about him?"

"Nina, you're the one who met him. I've only read about him in the gossip page."

God, I felt stupid! He wasn't just some good looking guy with a great car. He was someone famous. Now I was sure last night hadn't meant anything to him.

"I don't know anything about him like that. I saw him at the show and then he showed up at the gallery later on."

Jordan sat down and shook her head. "What do you mean he showed up later on? To buy something? I bet Sheila loved that."

"No, he was waiting outside the gallery in the alley way after I locked up."

"What do you mean? Had you spoken to him during the show?"

I shook my head. "No. He was there with a bevy of hot women and never even spoke to me."

"So what happened? You're killing me here! I swear you tell stories like my students."

To be compared to a group of fourth grade Catholic school kids wasn't helping, no matter how exclusive Jordan's school was. I wrinkled my nose and smirked at her. "Thanks."

"Neen! Give up the details!"

"He was waiting behind the gallery when I was leaving and asked me to go for a ride with him in his Jaguar. He offered to take me home, but instead we ended up driving upstate to see a house he said he was thinking of buying."

"Shut up!" she squealed. "Is he as stunning in person as he is in the papers?"

I reached out my hand to take the newspaper from her. "I don't know. Let me see." She handed me Page Six and there he was, just as gorgeous as he was last night. I secretly wanted to keep this picture so I'd always have him near me.

"So? Is he?"

Tearing my gaze from the newspaper, I nodded. "Yeah. Maybe even more, although I didn't see him dressed in a tux. He wore only a suit to the show."

"Did you sleep with him, Nina?"

"No!"

Jordan knitted her eyebrows. "Stop acting like it's 1952. Sleeping with a hot guy is permissible these days."

"I know all about feminism, Jordan. I just don't choose to jump into bed with every guy I meet."

Pointing to the newspaper I'd stuffed down in between the sofa cushions next to me, she said, "You see the woman in that picture with him? That's the fifth or sixth different one I've seen him with this month. The rumors are that he sleeps with a different woman each night."

I raised my eyebrows more in despair than disgust. "Really? You believe everything you read in the papers?"

"No, but you know how celebrities are. And if the pictures are any indication, he likes tall brunettes who look more like stick figures than humans."

I looked down at my less impressive five foot seven frame and what I liked to call a "healthy" body. I was in pretty good shape, but I was definitely not a stick figure.

"I'm sorry, Nina. I didn't mean to say he wouldn't like someone like you. He'd be damn lucky if he did."

Jordan's sympathetic smile made me feel better and worse at the same time. The reality was that if he was a man who slept with a different woman every night, no matter what type of women he preferred, he hadn't wanted to sleep with me. He hadn't even wanted to kiss me.

"It's okay. I've never had a problem not being a stick figure," I joked.

"So, if you didn't sleep with him, what did you do with Tristan Stone?"

I wasn't sure how to explain it, so I chose to go with the boring truth. "We hung out. Nothing more."

"Nothing?" she asked, her voice sing-song.

"Nothing."

Jordan looked confused. I understood her confusion. I still had no idea why he'd come to find me and then never even really touched me.

"Any plans to see him again?"

I tried to tamp down my disappointment. I didn't want pity now. "Not really. It wasn't much of anything, Jordan, so there's no reason to believe he'd want to hang out again."

"This sounds like a mystery to me. Why would he come find you and then not want to see you again? What was the conversation like while you were heading upstate?"

"Monosyllabic."

"You or him?"

"Him. I spent most of my time worried he was going to kill me and leave me on the side of the road."

Jordan sat back in her seat and chuckled. "Don't be silly, Nina. Wealthy people don't kill people. They hire people to do that."

Rolling my eyes, I mumbled, "Funny. I'll keep that in mind if I ever see anyone who might look like his butler or driver near here."

"Seriously, though. What do you plan to do about him? You obviously like him."

Even though Jordan knew me as well as anyone in the world, I didn't want to admit what I planned to do. It's not like I could coincidentally show up where he spent his time. We lived in two different worlds, and I likely couldn't afford the cover charge to get into that life. What I could do was click around online and find out about him.

Some might call that stalking. She'd likely call it stalking. I liked to think of it as research for my fantasies.

"There's nothing to do about him. We'll stay in our separate areas of the world and that's that."

"Oh, that's so tragic and romantic! It's like that Julie Roberts movie where she's like Cinderella. What's that movie?"

"Holy shit, Jordan! Pretty Woman? I'm not some poor prostitute in fuck-me boots!"

She waved my protests off and walked toward the kitchen with her glass to refill her drink. "You know what I mean. Two people from two different worlds. It's so romantic."

"Like Romeo and Juliet," I yelled toward her.

She peeked her head out of the kitchen doorway. "Now who's being scary? Romeo and Juliet? You do remember from high school that they both die at the end, right?"

Nodding, I chuckled. "Yeah. This is no more like Pretty Woman than Romeo and Juliet. Whatever it was, it isn't anymore."

I ran my fingers over Page Six in the seat next to me. Before Jordan returned, I quickly pulled the newspaper out and stuffed the folded page into my shorts. "I need to get going. Can't spend all Sunday lying around."

Jordan smiled another sympathetic smile as I walked past her. "Okay. Hey, Justin and I are going to be hanging out at The Last Drop Tuesday night. Want to come?"

My spidey senses told me this was a setup. A dating setup in the making. "You and Justin and your third wheel? Or will there be a fourth?"

Her look turned sheepish. "I think you might like him, Nina. Alex is pretty good looking, has a good job, and he doesn't seem like a loser."

"A ringing endorsement if I ever heard one," I joked and continued walking. "I'll think about it."

"At least it'll be a night out. We'll have a few drinks, shoot some pool, and maybe have a few laughs," she yelled as I closed my bedroom door behind me.

I sat down on my bed and opened my laptop, content to spend my afternoon looking up information on Tristan. While my computer turned on, I examined the picture of him with his girl du jour at some gala. His face was expressionless and he seemed more like a statue of himself than the real thing. The woman, however, looked like she was thrilled to be there with him, clinging to his arm and smiling a huge, toothy grin for the camera.

Raising the picture to look at it more closely, I studied it for any sign of the person who'd smiled and laughed as he'd driven to the middle of nowhere the night before. He didn't seem to exist in this person.

Setting the paper aside, I typed my first words into the search bar. "Tristan Stone." I figured I might as well start with the obvious and go from there. It didn't take long to see that Jordan had been right. The pictures I saw showed him with a different woman every time, but he was the same cold figure in each one. The soulful brown eyes that had looked at me were nowhere to be found. Neither was the genuine smile that he'd so freely given, even if it had seemed like he was laughing at me more times than not.

Once I'd looked at enough pictures of him to truly make me feel like a stalker, I began reading and found out the real details on him. He'd inherited his father's luxury hotels along with other businesses that included an internet startup company and some company that had to do with real estate.

I sat transfixed on the words as they stared back at me from the screen. Tristan, the man who'd come to find me just for company, was a millionaire many times over. Maybe even a billionaire. The car was his. The Rolex was his. He was the kind of man women dreamed of, and he'd wanted to spend time with me.

And now I would never see him again.

Closing my laptop, I flopped back on the bed and groaned. I needed to stop thinking about Tristan right now. He was something unattainable, and I needed to accept that. It didn't matter that he had looked happier in the short time with me than he ever looked with all those women at all those fancy parties. None of that meant anything because of the simple fact that even if he'd been happy, he'd made no effort to get my number, kiss me goodnight, or even find out much about me.

I covered my eyes with my arm and tried to push all thoughts of him out of my mind. If I kept this up, I'd end up becoming obsessed over a situation that was doomed never to be. He was where he belonged and I was where I belonged.

Life was as it should be, no matter how disappointing that fact was.

Three

Tuesday night came, and I chose to accept Jordan's offer to hang out with her, Justin, and Alex at the bar. Monday's work at the gallery had made it difficult to stop thinking about Tristan, but I had done my best to talk myself out of my infatuation. In truth, I probably hadn't really succeeded, but the human mind is an interesting mechanism and very susceptible to delusion. Regardless of whether I was lying to myself or not, I headed out to The Last Drop and promised myself I'd keep an open mind about Alex.

The Last Drop was the one place in Sunset Park that could be picked up and dropped back in my home town in Pennsylvania. It was just a bar, what was traditionally called a "hole-in-the-wall" back home, with a couple pool tables, some dart boards, and a back room with booths and another pool table. Jordan and I had found it soon after moving into our place, and Tuesday night had become our night out each week. It wasn't much, but it was fun.

She'd told me everything she knew about Alex as we waited for him and Justin, and when I say everything, I mean everything. She must have compiled some kind of dossier on him because she knew his height, weight, where he went to school, what he did for a living, how much money he earned, in addition to dozens of other details I probably could have done without. I mean, should a woman really know about a potential boyfriend's favorite sexual position—cowgirl—before she even meets the guy?

As I hadn't heard anything to necessarily turn me off, I figured staying wouldn't do any harm. Worst came to worst, at least I'd occupy my mind with some friends, a few beers, and a few games of pool while I crossed another male off my list of potential boyfriends.

"Nina, I hope you like him," Jordan said as she leaned across the table to talk over the blaring of the music from the jukebox. "We could all go out if you do."

I nodded and smiled my agreement. By the time the song had ended, Justin and Alex had arrived and I got my first good look at the man Jordan had chosen for me. Tall, with dirty blond hair and blue eyes, he was certainly attractive. My suspicious mind immediately went to the question of why he'd be single, but I told myself to give this a chance. I was single and there wasn't anything profoundly wrong with me.

"Hi, Nina. I'm Alex. Nice to meet you."

Good masculine voice, nice looks, seemed intelligent. Maybe Jordan hadn't been wrong.

A few beers and two games of pool later, I had impressed him with the few things that made me stand out amongst the millions of women in New York—my down-to-earth way and ability to shoot a mean game of pool. Why this was so intriguing to men had always baffled me, but I'd learned over the years to make it an asset. I wasn't supermodel gorgeous and I wasn't heiress rich, but I could wield a stick like nobody's business and oddly enough, it was one of the few games men didn't seem to mind losing at.

Crouching down to collect the balls for another game, I looked up to see Jordan's eyes grow as wide as saucers as she looked my way. I hadn't had too much to drink yet, so I figured she wasn't giving me the "Holy Fuck!" look because of something I'd said. Standing up, I gathered all the balls into the wooden rack and positioned the top ball on the break spot. I looked up to see if Alex was ready and saw Jordan still with the wide eyes and pointing slyly in my direction, urging me to look.

I turned around and there was Tristan standing behind me near the entrance of the bar and sticking out like a sore thumb in a suit and tie. Tristan looked around as if he'd never seen the inside of a bar, his expression a mix of curiosity and focus. I watched as he scanned the bar area and then turned his attention toward the back room where I stood stunned to see him.

His gaze met my surprised stare and he smiled that same smile he'd given me nights before as I'd tried to get him to give me a straight answer. Jordan said something behind me about pool or something, but the sound of my heartbeat pounding in my ears drowned much of it out. I stood as if my feet were nailed to the ground and unable to move as I watched him walk toward me in a way that made him look like he was gliding across the floor.

By the time he reached me, I had forgotten there were even other people in the room. He was that mesmerizing.

"Nina."

True to form, he said little but his eyes spoke volumes. As I struggled to form a coherent sentence in my mind, I looked into those gorgeous brown eyes of his and saw a flicker of apprehension. Everything else about him appeared calm and confident, but his eyes hinted at some kind of fear.

Was he afraid I wouldn't talk to him? Why?

"Tristan. What are you doing here?"

"I'm here to see you."

I couldn't help but chuckle. "I figured that. I can't imagine you're acquainted with anyone else in this bar."

His gaze never wavered from me, and he asked quietly, "Can we talk somewhere?"

He wanted to talk more. Okay. Smiling, I found the ability to move my legs again and guided him toward one of the wooden booths on the far side of the room. We sat down across from one another, and I realized I hadn't even said anything to Jordan or Alex. No matter. She'd understand, and I'd apologize to her later.

"How did you know I'd be here?"

He settled his gaze on me. "Do you come here a lot?"

"Every Tuesday. But that doesn't answer the question of how you knew I'd be here."

"There's a billiards tournament in Las Vegas every year that I sometimes play in. You should come with me next time. It's late summer. We could make a week of it."

With every word he spoke, I grew more confused. Why was he talking like we were a couple? Now we were taking trips together? Shouldn't we at least have dinner first? Or maybe sex? God, just the thought of it made me squeeze my thighs together in sweet agony.

"Tristan, what do you want?"

"You."

My stomach dropped and a rush of excitement hit me between my legs. He wanted me.

"You want me for...?"

"You were an art major in college. You'd know a lot about what pieces I should buy, wouldn't you?"

My excitement fizzled back to confusion. "Yes, I majored in art history. I minored in painting. What do you want me for that has to do with that?"

"Why don't you come for a walk with me?" he asked, more as a command than a question as he stood from the booth.

My curiosity was piqued, even if my ego was dinged. I would have likely said yes to anything he asked, so I walked over to where Jordan was standing and quickly whispered, "I'll be back. He wants to go for a walk."

Pulling me aside, she leaned in and asked, "Is everything okay? What does he want?"

"I don't know. I'm thinking maybe he wants someone to help him pick out paintings, maybe for his office or something. Maybe for that house he's buying. I don't know. I have my phone on me, so if anything goes wrong, I'll call."

Jordan hugged me and in my ear whispered, "Be careful. Remember, wealthy people hire people to do their work. I doubt he's here for a decorator."

"I will. And don't worry. I'll tell you all the details when I get home," I teased.

Squeezing my arm as I moved away from her, she said, "You better!"

Jordan and I were breaking the best friend code's first rule: Never let your friend leave with a strange man. He wasn't a strange man, per se, but she couldn't have stopped me even if she thought he was. With each step I took toward Tristan, an excitement began building in me. I hoped he wanted me like I wanted him, but if all he wanted was someone to help him pick out art, maybe he'd pay me enough so I could begin to build up my savings. Whatever it was, at least I'd be spending time doing something with art.

The night air was unseasonably chilly for May, so my little sundress and sweater weren't going to do much to keep me warm. I hadn't planned on walking very far that night, so my shoes weren't really right for what he wanted to do either.

Tristan remained his quiet self as we made our way one block and then two away from the bar. Unable to contain my curiosity, I asked, "What did you want to talk about?"

Glancing at me, he said, "You."

"That's the second time tonight you've answered that way. What about me?"

"What made you decide to live in this section of Brooklyn after college?"

I stopped dead and stared at the back of him as he continued walking. After a few steps more, he noticed I wasn't next to him any longer and stopped to turn around. "Nina?"

"How do you know so much about me, Tristan?"

"I asked."

"Asked who?"

He closed the space between us and stood no more than six inches from me. That gentle smile spread across his lips again. "People who'd know. I like to know about the people I surround myself with."

"What are you talking about? Do I have to ask you to do the straight answer thing again?"

He cocked one eyebrow and then finally said, "You make me smile, Nina. I can't say that about most people."

"That's nice. It's not a straight answer, though."

His hand clasped mine, sending a jolt of electricity straight up my arm. "Let's keep walking so you don't get cold. Your place is near here, isn't it?"

I felt like I was dealing with a madman. It was like we were having two different conversations, neither of which was very satisfying. And now he was holding my hand and appeared to be directing me back to my apartment—a place he'd only been once. I didn't know whether to be flattered he had made the effort to find out about me and remembered where I lived or concerned that he was some kind of scary stalker.

The fact that I had done a little of my own stalking of him didn't escape me either. We made one interesting couple.

"Tristan, please just tell me what you want. I know you're probably used to women who love this mysterious Bruce Wayne-Batman behavior, but I'm just an ordinary soul who likes straight answers."

"Why do you always think you're so ordinary?"

I yanked my hand from his and shook my head. "No more! You show up out of nowhere in the alley behind the gallery, force me to go for a ride, and now you show up at a bar I hang out at. Are you some kind of scary stalker guy or do I owe your company for some kind of bill and you're here to collect? Either way, you're driving me crazy!"

I hadn't meant to sound so emotional, but there it was. The truth. I barely knew this person and already he drove me nuts.

Instead of looking surprised like I thought he would, he just smiled. Not that it wasn't a gorgeous smile, but something about it just sent me over the edge. I stalked away toward home, frustrated enough not to care whether he liked it or not.

I heard his footsteps behind me as he walked quickly to catch up with me. It felt good knowing he wanted to talk to me, even if all he said sounded like damn riddles!

"Nina, I'm sorry. Stop and let me talk for a minute."

Spinning around, I was nearly knocked over as he took a step right into me. His much larger and muscular body crashed into mine, and I went tumbling backwards. Thankfully, he caught me before I landed on my ass.

There I was, in his strong arms, staring up into those dark eyes as he gazed down at me. "You want to talk? All you say are one syllable words and sentences that make no sense. I'd love it if you'd talk, but you don't."

"I'm not usually much of a talker, but you seem to want to hear what I have to say, so let's talk."

He released me and I stood up, smoothing my dress over my thighs. "About what?" I didn't mean to sound so exasperated, but the man had a way of bringing that out in me.

"Art."

More one syllable words. If it wasn't no or yes, it was art with this guy. "Art? What about it?"

"Why do you work at that gallery if you went to school for art history?"

Talking about work wasn't talking about art. Deflated, my shoulders sagged under the disappointment that he seemed once again interested in hearing about my job as personal gopher to Sheila Anderson.

"Because even though I possess more knowledge about the art world in my little pinky finger than my boss does in her entire body, I also only possess a bachelor's degree in art history. To be a curator or someone who deals with exhibitions, you have to have experience in the gallery world, which is what my slave labor job is."

"It's too bad you don't know anyone who owns their own art gallery."

Blowing the hair off my face, I said in frustration, "Yes, it is."

We stood there at that odd point in the conversation looking at each other like neither one of us had understood the other one's language. To be honest, I was beginning to think he was from some other planet by the way he behaved, but since he hadn't grown tentacles or extra heads and was getting more gorgeous by the minute, I still liked him, as bizarre as that seemed to someone like me who prided herself on good judgment.

"You could work at one of mine."

And with those seven words my spirits were buoyed once again.

"You have more than one art gallery?" I asked in stunned amazement, jumping over the obvious first question about him having even one art gallery.

"In some of my hotels. The one here in the city might work, wouldn't it?"

He was sounding decidedly clear, which made me think I must have slipped into some dream dimension or lost my mind. "You have an art gallery in one of your hotels in New York and you want me to work at it? As what?"

If he said anything that even remotely sounded like the job I had at the Anderson Gallery, I was going to punch him right in that beautiful mouth.

"I have a curator, but would assistant curator work?"

I understood the words he was saying, but my brain seemed to have short circuited because I was unable to form an answer. Would assistant curator work? Hell, yes!

He was all smiles, but I wasn't so sure. Putting my hand up, I said, "Wait. This all sounds too good to be true. What hotels do you own?"

With a sense of pride, he answered, "Richmont. I assume you've heard of them."

"And you want to offer me a job as an assistant curator at the Richmont in Manhattan?"

"Yes."

"And what do I have to do for this job?"

"Whatever an assistant curator does."

I looked up into those beautiful eyes and wondered if he was just playing dumb or if it was possible he was really that obtuse. "You know what I mean. What do I have to do to get that job?"

Then I waited for it. There was always a catch. As my father always said, "If it sounds too good to be true, it probably is." Tristan's response certainly wasn't what I expected, though.

"You'll have to pass one test. After that, the job is yours."

"What kind of test?" I asked, wary of where he was going with this. I didn't mind taking tests, but something told me he had something else in mind than a paper and pencil exam.

"I want you to tell me what picture I should put up on the wall in my home."

"The one all the way upstate?" I asked, praying that I didn't have to take that drive again tonight. The buzz from the two beers I'd drunk earlier had worn off, and the thought of speeding to the middle of nowhere again didn't thrill me, even if it was with Tristan Stone.

"No. Come with me," he answered as he took my hand and led me to his car parked at the end of the block.

I went as he ordered and let him take me to the Richmont downtown. I'd seen the hotel from the street once or twice, but seeing it from the owner's point of view was an entirely different experience. A valet parked the car as we were shown into a private elevator lined with mirrors that traveled exclusively to the penthouse. I stared straight ahead at the mirror on the elevator door, my gaze drifting down over the figure standing next to me. I noticed he seemed bigger than I'd thought he'd been the other night, with the top of my head reaching only his broad shoulders. His face was placid, and even now as he stood silently staring at the mirror in front of us, he was beautiful with chiseled features and powerful body. But what made Tristan stunning were those deep, soulful eyes. Warm brown eyes the shade of melted milk chocolate I could have spent the rest of time getting lost in. I looked for any sign that the man from Page Six was there beside me, but the Tristan I got to see was still with me. Quiet, but gentle and drop dead sexy.

The elevator doors opened up to a penthouse unlike anything I'd ever seen. Tristan's home was something right out of a design magazine. I walked around with my mouth agape at the opulence of his place. He seemed almost disinterested in his own home, though, except for the one bare spot on the wall in his bedroom. That seemed of the utmost importance to him.

Pointing at it, he asked, "What do you think should go there?"

I stared at the wall as my mind quickly went as empty as the blank space. "Is this the test?"

"Yes."

"I don't know. I'd have to spend some time examining the rest of the decor. You don't want just anything hanging there. If that were the case, the poker playing dogs picture would work."

He chuckled but wasn't going to be put off. "All you must do is answer the question correctly and the assistant curator job is yours, Nina."

He stood so close that my mind went from blank to muddled. All I could think of was the luxurious feel of his suit as his arm brushed the back of my hand and the sexy smell of his cologne filling my nose. I turned away from looking at the spot to see him staring down at me. I could think of nothing, but I blurted out, "A Cooper," knowing in my heart that wasn't what he wanted to hear.

His expression showed his disapproval—or was it disappointment?—and he turned away, shaking his head. "No."

I had no way of disagreeing, but even now as I knew I'd failed the test and lost out on the dream job of my life, I still couldn't think of an appropriate choice. Dejected, I looked up at him and quietly said, "If you can just take me home, please."

He pulled his phone from his suit coat pocket and spoke into it in a flat tone. "I need a car downstairs to take a young lady to Sunset Park."

Whatever the person on the other end said I had no idea, but in seconds the elevator door opened and

Tristan ushered me toward the exit. He said nothing, and I got into the elevator, sad that I'd failed the test and lost my chance but also sad that I'd let him down. It was strange, but although I barely knew him, I was uncomfortable with him being unhappy.

The doors began to close, taking him away, and I pushed back the tears welling up in my eyes. Just before he disappeared from sight, I whispered, "I'm sorry."

And then he was gone.

If I could have called in sick from work on Wednesday, I would have. Just going to the gallery reminded me of him, and even more, it reminded me of how I'd utterly failed at my one chance to really do something in the art world. By the time the day was over, I was committed to spending the night in bed with ice cream and a sad movie so I'd feel justified in crying my eyes out.

Jordan had end of year conferences, so the apartment was all mine to mope around to my heart's content. It was strange, but I felt empty inside after what had happened with Tristan. I knew it should have been over the chance he'd given me, but it was because I'd lost him. But had he ever really been mine to lose? I had no idea. I just knew that as I walked around the apartment aimlessly I was missing him.

By seven o'clock, I had devoured a pint of mint chocolate chip ice cream and was ready for the DVD player to deliver enough sad love stories that I'd cry the memory of Tristan Stone right out of my heart. I needed true love separated by horrible circumstances and life changing romance.

A knock at the door just before the first movie began slowed my mourning, and as I padded barefoot down the hallway to the front door, I hoped it wasn't Alex, who'd called three times since the night before. I didn't have the answer no matter what the question was he wanted to ask.

I opened the door, and instead of Alex, there stood Tristan. My heart leaped in my chest at the sight of him. Dressed impeccably in a suit, as always, he was a sight for sore eyes. I knew I shouldn't be thrilled to see him, but I was.

"Come for a ride with me. I want to talk."

And with that everything that had happened between us came rushing back. All the confusion. All the frustration. And now, all the anger at how he'd toyed with me.

"Go back to your penthouse, Tristan. Find someone else to do your charity work on."

I threw every bit of power I had into slamming the door in his face, but he jammed his foot in the opening. It pushed back against my hands as he tried to stick his face in through the crack to speak.

"I just want us to talk. What can that hurt?"

"Go away. Your brand of talking just confuses me and then I feel bad after," I said as I pushed on the door to no avail.

"Please."

And there it was. The magic word. Please. God, my father's good parenting had come back to haunt me yet again. Something in the word please had a way of making any argument I had melt away.

I stopped pushing on the door and opened it up to see him staring at me with those brown eyes of his. As usual, they told me more than his words had, and now they were pleading with me to go with him one more time.

Even if I wanted to say no, which I didn't, I couldn't have. Whatever power he had over me I just couldn't fight it.

Hanging my head in resignation, I welcomed him in. "Give me a minute to get dressed."

As I walked to my room, I thought about how much I wished I could say no. It was no good that even before a man kissed me that he had this much control over my heart and mind. I couldn't imagine what he'd be able to do if we ever slept together.

He drove out of the city, and I knew where we were going. Back to the middle of nowhere, but this time my fear wasn't that he would kill me and leave me in pieces on the side of the road. No, this time I was afraid he'd already taken the most important piece of me and there was nothing I could do about it.

Four

We pulled up to the house he showed me the other night, and he turned off the car. He hadn't said ten words the entire way there, but now he turned to face me and said with a smile, "I didn't want things to end like they did last night."

His voice sounded sincere and made me want to make things better. "I'm sorry I didn't know the right answer."

"That's not important. The test was unfair. I'm the one who should be apologizing."

"Why did you bring me here, Tristan?"

"Let's go in."

As we walked toward the front door, he took my hand in his. His fingers enveloped mine and my hand seemed to disappear into his beneath his jacket. I felt small next to him now.

And then I looked up and what stood in front of me took my breath away. Massive white marble columns held up a front portico a full story high and flanked by the tallest evergreen trees I'd ever seen. A huge center section of the house broke off into a wing on the left and right sides, each the size of a full home itself. A second floor the same size as the main floor sat below a blue-grey color roof forty feet above the ground.

"Wow...your house is..." I stammered out as I stopped walking and craned my neck to take it all in.

Tristan smiled at me and my amazement. "I'm glad you like it. It's got twenty acres too. Come see the inside."

Just like his penthouse, the country house looked like something straight out of a magazine. A massive wrought iron and glass light fixture hung from the twenty foot ceiling in the wide entryway, and the beige marble floor gleamed beneath my feet. The walls were painted a cream color and looked like old world plaster. The entire room was simply stunning, and it was just the foyer!

Room after room unfolded before my eyes, each one unique and gorgeous. By the time he'd finished showing me the main area of the house, I'd seen four fireplaces already. Each room came with an explanation about how he planned to change it or what he wanted to keep, but I couldn't help but wonder what one person would do with all this space. I imagined him wandering through the rooms lonely and looking for someone to talk to.

He led me back to the main entryway where the home branched off into two wings. "Is anyone else here or will you live here alone?" Just asking the question made me sad.

He didn't seem bothered by it, though. "I have a man who handles things, a gardener who moved into the carriage house already, and a few other people who will be working for me here."

"Oh, so you won't be living alone?"

He didn't answer and pointed toward the left side of the house. "I want to show you that wing. I think you'll like it."

"Tristan, how many bedrooms does this house have?"

"Six."

Six bedrooms for one person? "Does that include rooms for the people who work for you?"

Shaking his head, he smiled. "No. They don't count."

He continued to talk about where he was taking me, and I wondered if he meant the bedrooms didn't count in the total or the people who worked for him didn't. After a hallway that left the main part of the house, we entered what looked like an apartment. Well, not an apartment like mine but one that someone like him would live in.

"Do you like it?"

I looked around at the bedroom, which was no less than four times the size of mine and decorated impeccably, and couldn't help but laugh. "I can't imagine anyone not liking it."

His voice turned serious. "I don't care if anyone else likes it. I want to know if you like it, Nina."

I was startled by his tone. What did it matter if I liked a room in his house? "It's very nice."

This was the thing that confused me about Tristan. He never seemed to act the way other people would. He'd taken me for a drive twice, and neither time we'd done much talking, as if sitting next to someone and not saying anything was normal. Now he'd showed me his house and seemed oddly concerned that I like it. Why?

I wanted to ask, but I doubted I'd get a straight answer anyway. That definitely wasn't his way.

He led me back to see the indoor pool, and I fell in love. Even if we only stayed whatever we were at that moment, I hoped I'd get to swim in that pool. It had been designed to look like an enormous Roman bath with a sixty foot pool and sauna. The back wall of the room was an exquisite mosaic tile design that portrayed Neptune riding in his undersea chariot led by a team of sea horses. Artistically, the varied shades of blue and white in the intricate mosaic were stunning. The other three walls of the pool area were filled with floor to ceiling windows along with four sets of double doors that I was sure flooded the area with gorgeous sunlight in the afternoons.

I looked down at the imported Italian tile on the pool's deck and then back up at him. "It's gorgeous, Tristan. Your house is beautiful."

The smile I received in return for my compliment was warm and sweet. "I'm glad you like it. Are you hungry?"

"No."

"Why don't we have a drink then?"

That was an idea I liked. Spending time around him made me nervous and uneasy, so hopefully a drink would calm my nerves. "I'd love a drink. Thanks."

He flashed another warm smile and took my hand to lead me to a large sitting room. Compared to the open and airy feeling of the pool area, this room had a darker vibe. Dark cherry wood moldings and ten foot tall built-in bookcases gave the room a heavier feel. As he poured us drinks, I looked around and noticed examples of fine artwork lined the walls. He had impeccable taste. Art hundreds of years old sat beside contemporary pieces perfectly matched.

So why the test at the penthouse the night before?

This was who Tristan Stone was. Contradictions on top of unanswered questions. And the more I knew about him, the more I wanted to know the answers.

He extended his hand to offer me a seat on the extra deep sofa and handed me my drink. I took a sip from my glass and felt the warmth from the liquor course through my body. Surprised by its almost instant effect, I looked at him and murmured, "Oh. What is this?"

"Scotch."

For the first time since I'd met him in that alley way, his body relaxed as he sat next to me. Maybe it was the double Lagavulin he had in his hand or maybe it was that we were finally getting to know one another. Whatever it was, he wore relaxed well.

By the time my glass was half empty, my drink had definitely relaxed me, and my curiosity got the better of me, along with my inhibitions. I looked at him sitting there in his white dress shirt and dark suit and without thinking, I asked, "Why are you always in a suit and tie?"

His eyes grew slightly wider for just a moment, and then he was that relaxed man again. "You don't like me like this?" he asked in a teasing tone.

"Oh no, I didn't mean that," I answered, afraid that I'd offended him. "I like you very much like that."

Now his smile wasn't that warm grin I'd seen just a few minutes earlier but a mischievous, almost devilish one. He took a sip of his drink and slid his tongue across his lower lip, making it glisten.

"Maybe you're right. It wouldn't hurt for me not to wear a tie," he said as he began to unknot it. Slipping it from around his neck, he let it slide out of his hand onto the table in front of us. "And no tie means I don't need the top button done either."

He opened his shirt and with just one button undone he looked like an entirely different man. His dress shirt sat crisply and the collar framed his strong neck perfectly. I had to fight the urge to lean over and press my lips to the part that had been covered by the shirt and tie and slide my tongue up over his Adam's Apple. What would his skin taste like, I wondered? Would it taste like the soap he used or the cologne he wore or would it have a hint of salt as a man's skin often did?

Nervous and needing a distraction, I leaned forward to take the deep blue silk tie off the table. Running it through my fingers, I asked, "How do you tie a tie? I never learned."

He placed his glass on the table and slid the tie from my hands. "Come. Sit between my legs and I'll show you."

I stood and turned to see him spread his legs wider to accommodate me. Nervous but suddenly desperate to be close to him, I sat down in front of him but on the edge of the couch, unsure of myself.

"Move back."

I did as he commanded and moved back until my shoulders touched his chest. Sitting ramrod straight, I waited for him to begin, anticipating how wonderful it would feel as his hands slid around my neck.

He leaned forward and moved my hair over to one shoulder. "The first thing is to make sure all of this is out of the way."

My neck was exposed, and as he spoke, his warm breath danced across my skin. I closed my eyes and willed my body to relax, hoping he couldn't hear my heart nearly pounding through my chest.

His voice was low and husky in my ear. "Lean back against me, Nina."

I slowly let myself fall back against him, feeling his hard chest against my back. His head was next to mine, his mouth positioned next to my ear so I felt every breath he took in and let out.

"The first thing to know is that there's only one kind of knot you need to master. The Windsor knot."

"Oh. I thought there were others," my voice squeaked out.

"Maybe for boys, but men tie the Windsor knot."

The way he said the word 'men' made my stomach flutter. In truth, I'd probably dated more boys than men, but Tristan Stone was definitely a man.

His arms came over my shoulders until he rested his hands near my collarbone, each one holding an end of the tie. "Now pay attention because I'm going to want you to show me you can do it after this," he whispered in my ear.

Unfortunately, the sensual timbre of his voice combined with the feel of his hands so close to my breasts made paying attention impossible. I thought he said something about the wide end and the narrow end, and he may have said something about looping, but I was lost in the experience and couldn't have cared less about the actual tying of the tie.

"Finally, tighten and you're done."

I opened my eyes and looked down to see his hands so big resting on the tie below a perfectly done Windsor knot, his large stainless steel watch heavy against me. My lower abdomen tightened at the feel of his fingers on my body, and a delicious ache settled into between my legs.

How wonderful it would feel to have those hands gliding over my skin, those fingers touching my body.

He slid the tie from my neck and undid all his work. "Now you show me what you learned."

I attempted to take the tie from his hand, but he pulled it away and whispered, "On me. Turn around and sit toward me."

Nervous fear shot through me as I stood up, and I hoped I'd be able to turn around without my legs giving out. The dress I wore only fell to the middle of my thighs, so when I straddled him, it was likely to ride up so far my panties would show. I didn't care about that so much as him knowing that I was already dripping wet just from sitting there pressed up against him.

Taking a deep breath, I turned around and climbed on top of his lap. He stared into my eyes, unnerving me, but something held me firm in his gaze. His hard cock pressed against the front of his pants and my damp panties. There was no way he didn't know how excited he'd made me.

I took the tie from his hand and slid it around his strong neck, even as my fingers trembled at the feel of him underneath them. Trying to hide my ignorance of my task, I wrapped the wide end of the tie around the narrow end, but it was no use. I didn't know what came next.

Dropping the two ends of silk, I looked down to avoid his gaze. "I'm sorry. I don't know how to do this."

"You didn't listen when I told you how to?" he asked in a voice that was as seductive as it was stern.

Shaking my head, I continued to look down at the untied ends of the blue fabric laying against his shirt. "I couldn't. You were so close, and it was impossible to pay attention to what you were saying."

He slid his hands down my back and cupped my ass to pull me into him, grinding my soaked panties into the thin fabric separating his cock from me. Kneading my flesh through my dress, he whispered near my mouth, "I love how honest you are, Nina. It makes me want to be honest with you."

I wasn't sure how to answer, but it didn't matter. As my head swum from the sensations he'd created in me, he pressed his mouth to mine and kissed me. His lips were soft yet demanding, and I eagerly kissed him back, seeking a release of that sweet ache, but his kiss only increased the feeling, making me want more.

He nudged his hips off the couch, sliding his cock over my sensitive clit, and I couldn't stop myself from moaning into his mouth. I didn't want him to think he had this effect on me so soon, but I was powerless. I wanted him so badly at that moment, I would have done anything to keep his hands on my body.

Unable to stop myself, I began to timidly move my hips to ride him, still fully clothed but needing so much to come. I didn't care that he wasn't inside me or even that I looked too eager. I wanted him to get me off, even if it was just rubbing against his cock through his pants.

He had other ideas, though. Pressing his palms against the tops of my thighs, he stopped me from grinding against him, and I moaned a needy sound into his mouth. God, I wanted him!

His thumbs slid under the bottom of my panties and touched my bare skin, making my thighs quiver in anticipation. Dragging the pads of his thumbs up and down over my pussy, he was careful to avoid my swollen clit, driving me mad with desire.

"Please don't tease me, Tristan," I whispered breathlessly next to the corner of his mouth.

"I want to make you feel good, Nina."

I so desperately wanted that too. Kissing his neck, I moaned my need into his warm skin, so soft beneath my lips.

"Sir, I have completed the task you assigned," a man's voice intoned from somewhere in the room.

Shocked that we weren't alone, I popped upright and looked around. "What was that?"

Leaning his head back, Tristan spoke toward the ceiling. "Rogers, thank you. That will be all for tonight." Facing me again, he smiled. "Maybe we should move this somewhere more private."

Torn out of the mood, I was disoriented. I'd thought this was private.

Tristan kissed me again and I knew instantly Rogers' interruption hadn't dampened his mood any. Lifting me off him, he stood and took my hand. "Follow me."

I did and he led me to one of the bedrooms. It was masculine, with dark woods and deep brick red decor, but I had no idea if it was the one he called his. The room appeared too perfect, as if no one had ever slept there before, but he seemed comfortable as he turned around to face me, still holding my hand.

"We won't be interrupted in here. Come."

He stood looking at me, his eyes tinged with the apprehension I'd seen earlier when he'd walked into The Last Drop. As if I'd deny him or myself the experience that was to come.

I wanted to look away, uneasy at what he might be thinking, but I couldn't. Was he unsure of his choice to bring me here? We were so different and from such different worlds. Maybe it was wrong.

Tristan slipped out of his suit jacket and slowly unbuttoned his shirt, each opening exposing more of his body. I watched wide-eyed, wanting so much to see what each button's absence would reveal. Finally, he tugged the bottom of his shirt out of his pants and released the last button. Beneath were abs so defined I had to hold back from extending my hand to run my fingertips over his skin. A sexy, thin trail of dark brown hair led from his navel and disappeared behind his pants.

"Nina, tell me what you're thinking," he commanded in a deep voice dripping in sensuality.

What I was thinking? I didn't dare tell him the thoughts in my mind at that moment. That I wanted to begin kissing him at his neck and drag my lips over his body until they gave my mind proof of the reality of those abs. That the one true urge coursing through my body at the moment was to then drop to my knees and take the hard cock that had pressed against my clit into my mouth as I looked up at him to see how my worshipping him made him feel.

My mouth was dry and my breath was heavy. I whispered hoarsely, "I can't."

He slid the shirt off his shoulders to reveal a tattoo that began just above his heart and trailed all the way down his left arm to his elbow. It was stunning and accentuated the muscular ridges of his body. My eyes were riveted to the design, two black and grey copperhead snakes that formed an inverted heart shape and blended into a tribal tattoo that covered his shoulder and ran down his arm over his powerful bicep.

Stepping toward me, he brushed a wisp of hair from my face. "Where is that honesty I love, Nina?"

The honesty he loved terrified me almost as much as he did.

His hands undressed me as he tenderly peppered my neck with kisses, sending tendrils of want throughout my body. My dress slipped down over my shoulders and hips to end up in a heap on the floor, leaving me only in my drenched panties and bra, which quickly followed the rest of my clothes.

He moaned my name as he lifted me onto the bed and slid out of his pants as he climbed up to join me. I reached out to pull him to me, but he sat back on his feet and the next thing I felt was the most exquisite sensation I'd ever experienced. I pressed my head into the pillows as his tongue danced over my tender flesh, flicking and lapping so expertly that my body wanted to surrender to him long before it should.

His lips closed around my excited clit, and he sucked gently for just a moment, but it was enough. My orgasm tore through me until it reached the very ends of my body, and I arched my back to feel all of his mouth against me as I exploded into pieces. He pushed my hips down onto the bed and held me tightly as he rode my pussy with his tongue and lips. For a moment I fought against his hold, but soon gave in to his control, begging for more as my skin grew sensitive to the touch.

He groaned my name as he slid his body up mine until he covered me. His mouth pressed against my mouth, and I tasted myself on his tongue as it slipped across my lips. His hands pushed into my hair and tugged, sending a mixture of pain and pleasure skittering over my scalp. My senses threatened overload, but I would have begged for more, if need be. He was power and control, and I loved it.

A quick lean over to the nightstand and the sound of foil tearing and he was back kissing me. Spreading my thighs wider, he settled in between them with a moan and slid the full length of his cock through my wet slit. He was thick and long, nearly making me come again with one thrust over my sensitive clit. As much as that would have been pure pleasure, I wanted to hold back until he was inside me.

I slid my hands down his back and pulled him into me, desperate to have all of him. As he devoured my mouth with kisses, he pushed into my body, inch by delicious inch until every part of our bodies joined together as one.

The feeling was unlike anything else I'd ever experienced. His rhythm met mine and I clung to his shoulders as he thrust up into me, grazing some delicious spot inside me that sent strings of pleasure rippling through my body.

Tristan lifted his head from my neck and looked into my eyes. His gaze was full of need as he retreated from my body and then drove back into me with a deep groan. He was the picture of desire.

I wanted him to feel as wonderful as he made me feel. Wrapping my legs around his waist, I tilted my hips to take him deeper into me. He exhaled heavily into the pillow near my ear, moaning, "Oh, God, Nina," and buried his cock to the hilt.

My nails scratched down his back as our bodies raced toward sweet oblivion. He moved to his knees and rolled his back, his hips thrusting faster as his muscles tightened, signaling his release. In a second, my own orgasm roared through me, and I cried out in ecstasy.

Exhausted, we laid there in each other's arms silently joined together for what seemed like hours. I stroked his hair where it touched his neck, damp from our lovemaking, as his breathing returned to normal next to my ear. Even though he was much bigger than I was, the feel of him on top of me wasn't heavy or oppressive, and I would have been happy to stay like that forever.

When he finally rolled off me, he wrapped his arm around my shoulder and pulled me close. I laid my head on his chest and traced my fingers over his stomach, loving the feel of the taut muscles that rippled just beneath his skin. Beneath my head, his heart beat in my ear as he drew circles with his fingertip on my shoulder. It was sweeter and gentler than anything I'd imagined could happen with Tristan.

I had no idea where we'd go from here, but as I drifted off to sleep in his arms, I knew one thing for sure.

I wanted more.

Five

The morning sun streamed in through the bedroom window, forcing me to cover my eyes as I woke. In an instant, I realized I was alone in the bed and Tristan was gone. Running my hand over the sheet where he'd slept, I replayed in my mind our time together, loving the memory and wishing he was still next to me to make love again.

Sitting up, I looked around but saw no evidence of him anywhere. The door to the en suite bathroom was open and I listened for the sound of the shower. Nothing. Scanning the room, I saw my clothes lay neatly folded on a high backed chair near the window, and on top of them was a note.

Immediately, my stomach twisted into one huge knot. A note after a night of sex was never a good sign. A thousand scenarios raced through my mind, almost all involving him saying goodbye in his own way, probably with as few words as possible.

There was no point in putting off the inevitable. Whatever he had to say in that note, I had to deal with, so I threw off the covers and walked my naked self over to where my clothes lay. As I dressed, my knotted stomach did flips and a tiny sense of sadness made me choke up. I liked Tristan and thought we had shared something special.

The paper was folded in half, and I opened it slowly to see a much longer letter than I'd expected. Maybe that was a good sign, I thought, as I began reading.

Nina,

I've enjoyed our time together more than you can ever know. I truly do love your honesty because it makes me want to be honest with you. Toward that end, I offered you a job and it's yours, if you want it. There's only one condition: if you choose to accept the offer, you must agree to be in my employ for six months. After those six months, you may choose to end our arrangement, but you will be contractually obligated to stay for those months.

If you agree to this offer, all you must do is sign the contract I've left with Rogers. Whatever you choose, you must do so before you leave this house today and your choice will be final. To prove I'm sincere, I've also left a $20,000 advance check for you. If you prefer to have it deposited into your bank, simply tell Rogers and it will be done by end of business today.

I believe your talents are far more than ordinary, Nina, and hope you will take me up on my offer. Whatever happens, know that the night we spent together likely meant more than you can imagine.

Always,

Tristan

I stood staring at the sheet of stationary in my hand, stunned at what it said, as the dread unraveled inside me. I could have the job as assistant curator if I wanted it, but I had to agree to work for him for at least six months? What an odd length of time. Would I be sleeping with him during that time? Or was the previous night all there would be to our lovemaking? He'd said our time together had meant something to him, so maybe we would continue dating?

Questions multiplied in my mind the more I thought about his offer. Of course I wanted the job, but he hadn't even mentioned a salary. I quickly dismissed this concern as ridiculous considering how much I was getting paid by Sheila. Tristan hadn't come across as cheap, so he'd likely pay me better. If only all the other questions I had about his offer were so easily put aside.

Why hadn't he spoken to me personally instead of leaving a note and having me deal with his butler, who I knew only as a faceless voice that had interrupted a very hot moment? And why had he included the stipulation that I must sign the contract that day, which meant I wouldn't be able to have anyone else look at it before I committed to everything it entailed?

I'd been worried that a note after a night of sex with him meant goodbye. Now I was worried about what it meant if I decided to stay in his life.

Maybe Rogers had Tristan's cell number so I could talk to him before making my decision. Sure this could help me, I walked down the hall to the main part of the house to find the butler. He was standing in the foyer, almost as if he were told to wait there for me, and nodded as I approached.

Rogers looked like every butler I'd ever seen on television, and as I prepared to speak to him, I had to push down the urge to giggle at how stereotypical he appeared. He wore a dark suit, and his steel grey slicked back hair sat atop a head that showed he was at least in his sixties, I guessed. His face was long, not naturally but from what appeared to be years of frowning, if the lines around his mouth were any indication. However, he didn't look unfriendly. Just unhappy.

"Hi," I began, unsure how to approach this situation with a man who must have known I'd slept with Tristan the night before. I wasn't embarrassed, but I liked to keep my romances a bit more private.

"Miss, the master has left your contract to sign, if you so choose," he said in a deep voice as he handed me a pile of papers followed by a very expensive pen.

I looked down at the contract and pen in my hands and then back up at the butler. "Yes, about that. Would you be able to give me Tristan's cell phone number? I'd like to speak to him before I do anything."

Punctuating my request with a smile, I waited for Rogers to give me the information, only to be turned down.

"I'm sorry, miss, but I do not have that information."

"You must have his phone number. You work for him," I said in disbelief.

"No, miss," he said definitively, making it clear there was no room for discussion.

Well, if I couldn't discuss it with Tristan, I at least could discuss it with Jordan. She'd be able to help. Whipping my cell phone out, I swiped my finger across the screen and saw the No Service message staring back at me.

Terrific. I was on my own for this one.

"Is there somewhere I may sit, Rogers? I need to read the contract before I decide whether to sign it or not."

The butler extended his arm toward the living room off to the right. "Of course, miss. You may take all the time you require. The living room is at your disposal. The master has indicated, however, that whichever way you decide, you must do so before you leave."

"Got it. Thanks."

I took a seat on the very formal sofa and sat back with the contract in hand, determined to read the entire thing from the first to last word. Then I began reading it. I remembered signing the student loan papers when I was in college, and this contract made those look like crayon scribblings. Clause this and part that and on and on it went until by the end of page one I'd read enough.

By that point in the stack of papers, I knew my salary would be $60,000 for the six months and I was obligated to stay in Tristan's employment for no less than those six months. I would be given health, dental, vision, and life insurance and his company, which I found out was called Stone Worldwide, would contribute to a 401K plan, matching my contributions for as long as I was employed by the company.

I knew I should continue reading as the contract went on for six pages more, but as far as I was concerned, I had all the information I needed. I would be paid, have great benefits, and finally, for the first time since graduation, I'd be able to put some money in the bank. All of this and I'd get to work for Tristan in an art gallery. That I wasn't sure what I'd be in his personal life made me wish he and I had talked about it, but I had hope that his note had been evidence of his interest in me. With a deep breath, I prayed I wasn't making a mistake and signed my name on the last page. I looked up and Rogers seemed to have appeared out of nowhere and handed me a second letter from Tristan.

"Miss, do you prefer a check or the money deposited into your account?"

"I think the deposit would work since I assume I'm going to be paid that way. Just give me the papers to fill out," I said with a smile.

"No need, miss." And with that, Rogers turned and walked away. *No need? How was the money to be deposited if I didn't give my account number?* Before I could ask the very same question that was in my mind, the butler was gone. Unsure of what to do, I opened the note and read more from Tristan.

Dear Nina,

I'm happy you chose to accept my offer and look forward to your involvement in Stone Worldwide for the upcoming six months. You're going to need a new wardrobe for your new position, so please allow my driver to take you to Le Ciel. I have spoken to Sheila about your resignation and she's happy to hear you've found another position. I believe she's going to miss you.

Always,

Tristan

I began to think this might be all right and wandered out the front door to find Tristan's driver standing next to a Town Car. He wore a driver's uniform and appeared as stoic as the butler. I approached him and extended my hand. "Hi, I'm Nina. I guess you're supposed to take me to Le Ciel. Where is that?"

He opened the door, bowed slightly, and replied, "Yes, miss. We'll be in Midtown shortly."

An hour later, I was standing inside a Midtown Manhattan boutique and feeling like Tristan in The Last Drop. The only difference was no one at my local bar had looked at him like he was an outsider when he walked in.

Two women walked toward me as I stood in the dress I'd been wearing for far too long, and I so wished I'd changed clothes before going shopping. Feeling self conscious, I avoided meeting their gazes, instead looking out the window at the activity on the sidewalk.

"You must be Nina," the blonder one announced. "Mr. Stone told us to expect you. We have everything picked out and if you follow me, I'll take you to a dressing room."

I did as she asked and found myself in a dressing room almost as big as my entire apartment. A dozen different dresses, outfits, and business suits hung around the room. I looked at the price tag on one of the dresses and my mouth fell open.

My portion of the rent on my apartment was only slightly more. I couldn't afford these clothes.

Immediately, I opened the door and stuck my head out to find the blonde who'd escorted me to the room. She stood with her back to me hanging clothes on satin covered hangers, and I said, "Excuse me. Miss?"

She turned around and flashed me a toothy smile. "Is there something I can help you with?"

I was embarrassed to say I was too poor to afford anything in her store, so I whispered, "I think there's been a mistake. Mr. Stone didn't mention how..." I hesitated and stumbled over my words until I finally blurted out, "He never said they'd be of such high quality."

Thankfully, she seemed to understand what I had so clumsily referred to because she gave me one of her supermodel smiles and nodded. "Oh, that's been taken care of, miss. Mr. Stone will be paying for everything."

She returned to her work, leaving me alone in the dressing room that could house a small family, my head spinning from what she'd said. Not only was I now employed as an assistant curator for Tristan Stone, but now he was buying me an entire wardrobe so I could be ready for my first day at work?

It all seemed too good to be true.

I tried on one outfit and then the next, impressed that the women who worked at Le Ciel knew my size just minutes after I walked through the door. I hadn't stood there for that long, yet the clothes fit me perfectly.

As I twirled around in front of the three way mirror, swinging the black skirt that matched perfectly with the grey see-through blouse, my cell phone rang. I didn't recognize the number, but I was in such a good mood, I broke my usual rule and answered it.

"Hello?" I sang happily to whomever was on the other end.

"Good morning, Nina."

My heart began pounding wildly at the sound of his deep voice. Tristan.

"Hello."

"I'm so happy you agreed to sign the contract," he purred into my ear. "Are you happy with my choices for you?"

I looked down at the clothes I wore and then around the room at all the beautiful outfits hanging there just waiting for me to love them. "You chose these?" I asked, stunned.

"Yes."

"Oh. I don't know what to say."

I didn't. It was all at once exciting and overwhelming to know he'd taken the time to come here and pick out clothes for me.

"What are you wearing, Nina?"

"The black silk skirt and grey see-through blouse. It's very nice."

"I'm sure you look beautiful in it. I want you to take it off," he said in a distinctly commanding tone.

"Do you want me to try a different outfit on and tell you if I like it?"

"No."

Confused, I did as he ordered and stood in my bra and panties, just as I had done in front of him the previous night.

"Okay. I took it off."

"Are you wearing only your pink panties and bra I saw you in last night?"

"Yes," I said with a smile as the memory of our time together flashed through my mind.

"Good. I want you to sit on the large ottoman in the middle of the room."

I did as he desired. "I'm sitting, Tristan."

"Good. Lean back and lie down."

I did as he ordered, loving the sound of his deep voice telling me what to do. "Okay."

"I want you to close your eyes and think about how it felt with my mouth on your pussy."

An involuntary moan escaped from my throat at the sound of his words entering my ears. This was the most he'd ever spoken to me, other than telling me about his plans for his house, and I loved hearing him talk like this.

"I love the taste of your juices on my tongue, Nina. Do you want me to make you come like that again?"

"Yes," I whimpered as I remembered his mouth on my body taking me to such exquisite heights of pleasure.

"Or would you prefer me to fuck you, my cock buried deep in your cunt?"

"God, yes," I answered breathlessly.

"I wish I could be there right now, Nina. I want to fuck you until you cry out in ecstasy, loud enough for the Le Ciel women to know what I've done to you."

I wished he could too. I wanted to feel his hands on me, his lips touching mine as he brought me to the edge of everything my body wanted and held me as I tumbled over that precipice.

"Since I can't, I want you to slide your fingers inside your panties and finger that pretty cunt for me, Nina. Will you do that for me?"

"Yes," I answered quietly as my hand moved down my body and below my panties. My finger slid through my soft folds and easily found its way inside, as he'd commanded.

"Imagine my tongue gently dragging over your clit. I love the feel of it on the tip of my tongue, Nina. It's swollen and eager for me to take it into my mouth and suck on until all those tender nerve endings explode in your orgasm."

As he spoke his sensual words, my finger rubbed in tiny circles over my excited clit, creating soft waves of sensation that felt almost as good as his mouth had on me.

"But I want to feel you surrounding my cock, the soft walls of your cunt gripping me tight as I slide in and out of your willing body. You're sitting on top of me, riding my cock as you've never done with any other man."

"Yes," I whimpered as my fingers moved faster over my pussy. "Yes."

"Bend down and kiss me, Nina. Bring that beautiful mouth to mine and let me feel your kiss while I fuck you. You're getting close, aren't you?" he whispered low into my ear.

"Yes."

"Not yet, Nina. You can't come yet."

I slowed my finger's movement against my clit to stop from coming, loving the feel of holding off until he told me I could.

"I slide my hands over that pretty ass and squeeze as my cock slides into your needy cunt again. Tell me what you want, Nina. Say it."

My finger slid over my clit again, sending a spike of pleasure through my body, and I whispered, "Fuck me."

"Louder, Nina."

"Fuck me," I said in my normal voice.

"I want to hear it louder. Tell me what you want me to do to you, Nina."

In a voice no doubt loud enough for anyone outside the dressing room door to hear, I said on a near sob, "Fuck me! Tristan, I want to come. Please fuck me."

"You feel so fucking good on my cock, Nina. Time for good girls to come. Let me hear you come for me, Nina."

My finger circled tightly on my swollen and needy clit as my thighs began to tremble. I moaned softly as the first curl of pleasure came over my body, opening my legs wider as my orgasm took over.

"Oh, God! Yes, don't stop!" I cried as every inch of me shook from my powerful release.

"I love hearing you like that," he moaned as the final quakes of my orgasm waned. "Thank you, Nina."

Feeling almost boneless, I closed my eyes and took a deep breath in, loving how good he made me feel. "I've never done anything like that before," I quietly confessed as I sat up and looked around to see if anyone was standing outside the door.

"There's that honesty that I love in you. Maybe we'll do something like this again. Would you like that?"

His voice made me want to do something like that again right now. "Yes." Needing to know what this was to him, if anything, I asked, "Tristan, this isn't how you are with all your employees, is it?"

The question sounded silly as soon as I heard the words out loud, but when he chuckled on the other end, I didn't feel so stupid.

"No, I don't have phone sex with anyone else who works for me, Nina. But you're not like my ordinary employees. Now I want you to buy the clothes I picked out and whatever else you like and I'll see you back at the house later."

"I can't go back upstate, Tristan. I don't have any of my things I need if I'm going to be away for more than one night," I protested. "I need to go home to get some stuff."

The phone went silent for a long time and when he finally spoke, his tone was markedly colder than I'd ever heard from him. "Nina, you signed a contract to work for me. For the next six months, if I tell you to do something, you do it. Do you understand?"

His words stung and all the frustration I'd experienced days earlier because of his behavior bubbled up inside me. "Are you saying I have to obey you twenty-four hours a day for six whole months?"

"Nina, everything comes with a price. This was part of the deal clearly spelled out in the contract that you signed."

I sat there stunned. "What are you saying? I'm some prostitute you paid to have for half a year?" Suddenly, all the clothes hanging around the dressing room looked ugly, like everything about this made me feel ugly.

"Nina, you wanted a job where you could show off your skills and love of art. I wanted to give you that. I'm willing to make sure you have the clothes required for the position and many other things that can make you happy, and all I ask is that you agree to a few simple things to make me happy. I have a contract that stipulates you're obliged to do these things, but I'd love to think that you want to make me as happy as I want to make you."

What was I supposed to say to that? I'd been foolish in not reading the entire contract, and now I was going to be forced to pay the price. As I gathered up the clothes to take them to the register, I told myself there were worse ways to spend a few months.

At least I'd be getting paid handsomely to be someone's indentured servant.

Six

The driver carried the almost $10,000 worth of clothes Tristan had purchased for me into the house and disappeared like Rogers had hours earlier. I stood in the foyer unsure of where I was supposed to go and feeling no better after stewing over the situation all the way home.

"Nina, come. I have dinner waiting for you."

I turned to see Tristan standing in the doorway of the formal dining room. He was dressed in his suit and tie and looking like he had all the times before, except now he was my jailer or my owner. I hadn't decided which title sounded better.

He extended his hand and smiled that warm smile that had never failed to charm me. Even now, it had the desired effect and I walked toward him, almost as if my legs were controlled by him directly.

I attempted to walk past him into the dining room, but he stopped me short with his arm in front of me. Turning to look up at him, I saw a look of hurt in his eyes. As if he had something to feel hurt about!

"Did you enjoy shopping?"

I didn't know how to answer his question. I had enjoyed it and everything we'd done in that dressing room until I found out I had signed my life away, even if it was to someone as gorgeous as him.

He tilted my chin up with his index finger and stared down into my eyes. God, those brown eyes could just melt my heart sometimes. I wondered if he knew that and used them to manipulate me or if they were just the windows to a soul that was as lonely as I suspected it was.

"Nina, I want to make you happy. Will you let me?"

I closed my eyes to avoid looking into his as I spoke. "You don't want me to be happy. You want someone you bought to do as you command. There's a difference."

My eyes still closed, I felt his lips brush mine in a tender kiss. Then he spoke again, and my heart broke. "I can't be anything but what I am. I can give you everything your heart desires, but I can only do it this way."

I opened my eyes and tears slid down my cheeks. He softly swiped the pad of his thumb under my eyes to dry my tears and kissed me again. "I had the cook make a meal I hope you like. Let's eat."

We sat at the end of a long dining table with him at the head and me seated to his left next to him. In front of us were five main courses, all my favorite foods. There was shrimp scampi, roast beef, turkey with stuffing, sausage and peppers, and a cheese pizza. I scanned the heaping plates of food and looked over at Tristan.

"Did you know these are my favorite things to eat?" I asked, unsure I wanted to know the answer.

"Yes," he said in that innocent tone that seeped into his voice every so often.

"How did you know these were my favorites?"

He smiled proudly. "I asked."

For the first time, I asked the follow-up question I had never given voice to before. "Asked who?"

"Jordan. I asked her to tell me what you liked when I went to see her today."

He'd gone to my house while I was shopping? "Why?"

"Why did I ask her to tell me what you like or why did I go to see her today?" he teased.

"Please give me a straight answer, Tristan."

He knew I wasn't happy, and I saw the joy slide from his expression. "I asked her what you liked because I wanted to make sure you were happy. I visited Jordan today to give her the rest of your portion of the rent for this year. Now what would you like to eat?"

There was no point in fighting him on this. Jordan would be helped by what he'd done and I had a hard time finding fault with that. His behavior didn't seem to be intended to be manipulative, and as I accepted that, I accepted him.

"Turkey," I said with a smile.

"Excellent choice," he said as he pulled the platter toward him. He carved a slice of turkey off the breast and placed it on his plate. I waited for him to pass the plate to me, but instead he began cutting the slice into smaller pieces. He stabbed one piece with his fork and held it in front of my mouth.

"Eat, Nina."

The meat was perfectly cooked, juicy and tender with just a hint of seasoning I guessed was rosemary and thyme. He scooped up another forkful of meat and placed it on my tongue. Turkey had never tasted as good. I swallowed my food, and he wiped the corner of my mouth with the pad of his thumb.

"Do you do this all the time with women?" I asked, knowing I probably didn't want to know the answer but needing to ask anyway.

He shook his head slowly. "No."

As he readied another bite for me, I asked, "Aren't you planning to eat?"

He smiled and shook his head again. "No."

I ate another bite of turkey, and all the while he watched me as if my happiness was of the utmost concern to him. When I finished, he pushed the platter of turkey away and pulled the plate of shrimp scampi toward him. Scooping up a forkful of shrimp and rice, he turned toward me and brought another of my favorites to my mouth.

The scampi was just as delicious as the turkey, but all I could think of as I ate it was that my breath would stink of garlic. Looking around the table, I saw a pitcher of water and a bottle of wine. I reached for the water, but before I could grab the pitcher, Tristan was filling my glass.

"You don't have to do that. I mean, it's nice, but I can get it."

Handing me the glass, he said, "I don't have to do anything. I want to."

I drank all the water and placed my glass on the table. "This is very nice of you. Thank you for doing this."

"I just want you to be happy, Nina. Are you happy?"

He stared into my eyes as he waited for the answer to his question, and I didn't know what to say. No one had ever worked to find out exactly what my favorite foods were and as he'd fed me, I was sure it was the most erotic experience I'd ever had in my life. His gaze never left mine, and I felt like I was the most important person in the world—the center of his universe. With each forkful of food, I felt cared for.

"I am happy, Tristan. I guess I'm just not used to anyone being so attentive."

He turned away from me to pull what looked like a silver ice bucket toward him. Taking his spoon, he sunk it into the inside of the bucket and pulled out a spoonful of green ice cream. "Mint chocolate chip is your favorite, I believe?"

He'd even asked Jordan about my favorite ice cream. As I savored the sweet taste of it on my tongue, I couldn't help but smile. "Is there anything you don't think of?"

Shaking his head, he scooped out another helping of ice cream and slid the spoon between my lips. "Not if I can help it."

"Is it just with me that you do this, Tristan?" I asked, only half-joking.

"Is it just with me that you ask so many questions, Nina?" he asked in return, once again not giving me a straight answer.

"I liked the way you spoke to me this afternoon. Not only what you said but how much you said. One of these days, I hope you'll want to say that much to me about other things."

His expression quickly clouded over. "You may not like what you hear."

I reached out and squeezed his hand. "I've always asked lots of questions. I guess you think it's a personal flaw?"

Tristan placed the spoon in my mouth so I could have another bite. "No. It's part of your charm."

His attempt at making me feel good was sweet and I appreciated it. I don't think anyone had ever thought my questions were charming, but he did. By the time I'd finished eating, it wouldn't have mattered what he'd done. I'd have forgiven him.

Reaching out, I touched his hand. "This was wonderful. Thank you, Tristan."

"Nina, I have something to show you. I hope you're happy with it."

He led me from the dining room to a hallway on the opposite side of the house from the room we'd slept in the night before. Stopping, he gently backed me against the wall and kissed me. His lips were tender but insistent, taking from me what he desired and giving me that part of him that I so wanted.

Nervous at what it could be that he wanted to show me, I caressed his cheek with the back of my hand. "I can't wait to see your surprise."

My answer seemed to make him happy and he led me to a bedroom that looked just like his. He opened the door and proudly announced, "I had everything of yours brought here. If you need anything else, just tell me and I'll make sure you get it."

"You had everything from my home brought here?"

"Yes."

"Tristan, I need to know. Am I a prisoner here?" I asked feeling fear for the first time with him since we were racing through the city in his Jag that first night.

His expression hardened and he dropped my hand from his hold. Without a word, he turned and left me standing there feeling terrible for asking a question anyone with a brain in their head would have asked.

I checked the closet and dresser drawers, and all my clothes were in exactly the same spots and the same order as they'd been at my apartment. He'd transferred my life exactly from Sunset Park to his house upstate, the only difference in his mind that I was living with him instead of Jordan.

I couldn't decide if I should be terrified by his behavior or touched by his thoughtfulness.

Lying on the bed in my new room, my mind was a muddle of ideas, one more conflicting than the other. I had the job I'd always dreamed of, yet I seemed to have signed a deal with the devil. Tristan was everything I'd ever wanted in a man. Gorgeous, his face was pure beauty and his eyes were gentle hints at the quiet soul beneath who shone through far too infrequently. He was more successful than any man I'd ever been with and seemed intent on lavishing upon me anything I could desire, no matter the cost, yet I had to leave my home. He was attentive to my every physical need, taking my body to places of pleasure any woman would beg to experience even once, yet there was a distance he forced between us. Above all, he wanted more than anything to make me happy, but it was to be on his terms.

What had I gotten myself into?

I needed to clear my head, so I stripped down, hoping a nice hot shower would help me figure out what to do. As the water steamed up the room, I stepped in and saw every item I kept in the shower at home with Jordan was there, only replaced new. My razor. My soap. My shampoo and conditioner. Each was there brand new. Had he gone shopping too?

What kind of person did this?

Standing under the hot water as it trailed over my head and body, I wondered if I was the one who was wrong. Tristan hadn't done anything to hurt me, and even his attempts to make me feel at home I considered suspect. Why? What kind of person was I to see sinister motives behind everything?

The shower had helped me see things more clearly, so I quickly dressed in one of my new outfits and set off to find him. I wasn't sure what I'd say, but maybe if we could talk a little I'd be able to show him I knew he meant no harm.

But he was nowhere to be found. Either was Rogers or the driver, so I wandered around the house, peeking my head into every room looking for him. By the time I made it to the pool, my spirits were crushed. I'd asked the wrong question and he'd left, likely returning to his penthouse in the city, and I would be left alone here in the country. I began to wonder if I really was a prisoner.

It was a beautiful warm summer night, so I took my search outside to the grounds, knowing he was likely nowhere nearby. The fireflies were putting on their nightly show, one that I hadn't seen since moving from Pennsylvania. I sat down near the front porch and watched as they illuminated the garden, my mind traveling back to simpler times and the nights when my father would watch as I ran around our yard with a glass jar trying to catch fireflies to keep as my own.

Just thinking about his death in my senior year in college still made me cry. After my mother died when I was only five, he raised my sister and me, never having much of a life other than us. I regretted how much he gave up for me, always there to take me to art classes and dance lessons instead of finding someone to share his life with. He died alone before he got the chance to see me as an adult who so wanted him to find love again.

That was the reality of life—loneliness was often a choice. Here I was with the opportunity to have everything I'd ever wished for and all I could do was look for reasons why I shouldn't accept it. Whatever it was that I was letting hold me back—fear, mistrust—I had a chance to share my life with someone. I had a chance to not be lonely.

Now all I had to do was take it.

The sound of footsteps on the porch behind me roused me from my thoughts, and I turned my head to see Rogers. He approached me stiffly, as was his style, and descended the porch stairs to stand in front of me. The man was oddly cryptic, but he seemed to have something to say, so I waited.

"Miss, do you require anything? The master instructed me to ensure you want for nothing."

Shaking my head, I gave him a weak smile. "No, thank you, Rogers." He stood there a moment longer, so I added, "Actually, I do need something. Where is Mr. Stone?"

Whatever warmth the butler had offered disappeared at my question concerning Tristan's whereabouts. If I had ever doubted it before, I knew now that Rogers was more than just a mere butler. He was the protector of his employer's secrets.

"He is gone for the evening, miss."

I nodded, disappointed that Tristan had left me there with just this spooky shell of a human. "Oh. Tell me, Rogers. How do you stand living out here?"

For the first time, Rogers seemed like someone I might be able to relate to, but I doubted he found living in the country as boring as I already did. To my surprise, he answered, "You may avail yourself of the car if you choose, miss. I can have Jenson bring it around, if you'd like."

"Thank you, Rogers, but I have nowhere to go. I had hoped to see Tristan, I mean Mr. Stone."

The butler's expression changed back to its usual stoic look and he merely nodded before he walked back into the house, leaving me wondering where Tristan had gone.

I sat outside watching the fireflies and looking up at the stars for hours. Living in the city included many great perks, but stargazing wasn't one of them, so I found a spot on the grass and watched the night sky as it moved above my head. The night was so dark, with no moon at all, and the stars had the stage all to themselves. They winked at me as I made a wish, hoping it would come true before I grew tired and had to go inside to my lonely bed.

By midnight, my wish hadn't come true, so I laid back in the cool, damp grass, closed my eyes, and painted a picture of my perfect night sky in my mind. I'd always found solace in that ever since I was a child. Whatever was bothering me, I'd close my eyes and imagine a scene I could paint. Then I'd rearrange things exactly the way they'd look if I were painting the picture.

Finally, I gave up waiting for Tristan and walked to my room, tired and disappointed. As much as I tried to push the thought out of my mind, I was sure he was out with another woman at some event much like the one I'd first seen him at less than a week before. Jordan's comment about him sleeping with a different woman every night chased all other thoughts out of my mind until I was convinced he'd never cared anything for me and all of this was some game he played because he could.

I was still tossing and turning when there was a knock on my door at three a.m., and I braced myself for

Rogers' face on the other side of the door giving me the message that Tristan wasn't coming back. Anger at what I'd done to make that happen churned in my stomach, but there was nothing I could do now. I didn't even know where he was.

I opened the door and hoped I could at least keep my emotions together. Something told me Rogers wasn't good with tears and seeing me break down and cry would probably make the top of his head explode. But instead of the butler, there was Tristan standing in front of me dressed in a tux and looking even better than he did in a suit, if that was possible.

"Tristan!" I said with no attempt to hide my happiness at seeing him.

He was stunning in the black tux, white formal shirt, and black bow tie. The last time I'd seen a male close up in a tux was at my prom, but poor Bobby Jackson had been out of his league in that. Tristan wore it like other men wore jeans and t-shirts.

"Nina, I have something I want you to do. Come with me," he said as he held out his hand.

I looked down at my shorts and t-shirt I liked to sleep in and felt distinctly underdressed. "Should I change?"

"No. You look beautiful as you are."

Taking my hand, he led me to a sitting room similar to the one we'd sat in before, but this one had an enormous painting of an impressionist country scene on one of the inside walls. I began complimenting him on it and explaining the background of the style, but he continued walking to a door next to the painting, paying no attention to my impromptu art lecture. Opening it, he placed his hand on my lower back and escorted me into a narrow room with no lights.

"Tristan, what is this?" I asked as I turned to take hold of his of his hand and looked around in the darkness.

"Wait."

He spun me around to face the other wall, and I watched as lights began to illuminate the room. Unlike all the other rooms in the house, this one had very few furnishings and little decoration. It was painted white and had a single couch and table. Otherwise, the room was bare.

I reached my hand out to touch the wall and felt cool, smooth glass against my skin. "Are these windows?"

"Yes. I have something I want you to see," he said in a low voice in my ear.

My excitement grew with each second that passed until I saw two people enter the room, one woman and one man. Both were attractive and young, and they acted as if they were a couple.

Confused, I turned toward Tristan. "What's going on?"

"I want you to paint them."

Looking around, I saw an easel, canvas, and paint pots at the far end of the narrow room. "I don't paint portraits. I simply paint what I feel."

He caught my face in his hands. "Exactly. I want you to paint what watching them do makes you feel, Nina."

"What do you mean? Can they see us, Tristan?"

For the first time, a tiny grin formed on his lips. Shaking his head, he answered, "No, but it wouldn't matter. All I care about is what you paint."

Just in case somewhere in the back of my mind I doubted what was going to happen next, the man and woman showed me I was right in my suspicions. As I watched, they began to undress, the man slowly easing the woman's dress off her body to show her wearing nothing underneath.

"Tristan, who are these people? Why are they here?"

"They're here because they like to have people watch. We're here to watch them, and you're here to paint what it makes you feel to watch them fuck."

I wasn't sure if I was embarrassed or excited by his words. It didn't matter, though, because in seconds they were both naked and the show he'd brought home for me had begun.

I stood transfixed at the sight in front of me. The woman knelt down in front of the man and took his cock in her hands, running her tongue the full length of it. The expression on her face was one of pure joy, as if licking his cock gave her a kind of happiness that was only found in the way she made him feel.

Tristan stood next to me and whispered, "Watch her. She loves sucking cock."

His comment instantly made me wonder if he'd been with her. "How do you know?"

As he watched the woman take the man's cock deeper into her mouth, he said, "They love having people watch them. I've seen it at parties."

I liked to think I'd seen a lot, but never had I seen people perform sex at parties. That usually happened behind closed doors at the parties I attended. Jordan was right. Wealthy people were different.

His hand touched mine and I was torn from my thoughts on wealthy people and their wild parties. "You thought I'd been with her, didn't you?"

I looked at the woman sucking her boyfriend's cock and then looked at Tristan. "Yes. Since I know nothing about you before I met you, I did."

He lifted my hand to his mouth and softly kissed my palm. Looking up at me, he smiled. "She's not my type."

"Why? Because she's blonde?"

"No, because she likes to fuck in front of people so she can get off. I tend to like my women a little less attention whore."

I couldn't tell if his tone was sharp because I'd asked if he'd been with her or because he had no respect for her. Either way, I felt better knowing at least he hadn't slept with her.

Tristan pulled a chair out from the corner of the room and sat down, motioning for me to join him. "Come sit on my lap, Nina. I want you to tell me how this makes you feel."

I sat down on his lap and noticed that he wasn't aroused. He pulled my face toward his and kissed me hard, sending a rush of excitement through my body.

"Don't you like watching them?" I asked as I ran my palm over the front of his pants.

His tongue slid over his lip, and he grinned. "It does nothing for me."

"Me neither," I lied. In truth, he did it for me. I couldn't have cared less if the people doing their sex act disappeared and never came back.

Sliding his hand slowly up my leg, he gently stroked the tender skin of my inner thigh. "Nina, watch them. I want you to show me in your painting what it makes you feel."

I leaned in and whispered in his ear, "Watching them fuck doesn't make me feel anything, Tristan. You make me feel."

He closed his eyes and exhaled again. "Then paint what I make you feel, Nina."

I stood and walked to the easel to begin painting how he made me feel. I dipped my paintbrush first into red and then blue, pushing it swiftly across the canvas as I let my emotions come out for him to see. The frustration of always wanting more. The need he created in me to make him as happy as he made me. The fear that our differences were too great and would someday tear us apart. They all came out in the reds and blues that filled the picture.

His stare felt hot on my back, and I turned to see him watching me, intently interested in my work. Could he see how much he affected me and how much I wanted him? Was my painting telling him everything I so wished I could?

I looked up over my easel to see the couple had moved to full out fucking, but Tristan remained focused on me. He gave me a smile that nearly melted my insides. "Feeling the muse?"

"Yes," I answered shyly, timid he might disapprove of my work.

"Can I see?"

"Not yet."

My paintbrush continued its dance through the colors as I blurred the lines and edges to soften the ribbons of feeling he created in me. Finally, I dipped my brush into warm brown paint and began to form the abstract images of his eyes, always on me, watching me. Showing me the tenderness I believed existed deep within him.

Out of the corner of my eye, I saw him stand from his chair and walk toward me. Unsure of how he'd judge my feelings, I raised my arms to hide my work, but he moved around me and slid his arms around my waist.

In my ear, he said low and hoarse, "Tell me what you feel, Nina."

I wanted so much to tell him how he made me feel, but all I could do was let my painting speak for me. Turning my attention to the couple to avoid Tristan's critical eye, I held my breath as he studied the colors and hues of my emotions.

He pulled me to him and softly placed kisses over my neck. "The colors are beautiful, Nina. Tell me what I should see."

"The reds and blues represent my frustration and fear. I try to understand why you keep me at arm's length, but I can't. Then I fear we're too different and at the end of our time together or even before you'll cast me aside with a one-syllable word and whatever we are will be over."

He kissed my cheek and leaned his head against mine. "Why are the colors blurred?"

Shyly, I answered, "Because I can't express myself clearly when you're around."

Tristan turned me in his arms to face him. Looking deep into my eyes, he asked, "And the brown smudges?"

I let myself get lost in his gaze. "Your eyes. They can be so kind and gentle when you look at me before you kiss me or give me one of your gentle smiles. They make me believe there's more to the man who so often seems to hold me at arm's length. But they watch me always, making me ask questions that anger you and make you leave me alone."

He was silent after my confession, and my hands shook in fear that I'd said too much, revealed too much too soon and ruined everything. He cupped my cheek, and I leaned into his strong hand. "So honest all the time, my Nina."

Pulling me to him, Tristan held me close as he stroked my hair and kissed me tenderly on the lips. In the next room, the couple continued to writhe and grind against one another, but we stood silently in each other's arms and I felt more beautiful at that moment than at any other time in my life.

Seven

Tristan promised to have my painting framed and hung in his bedroom, thrilling me more than I thought was possible. I wasn't a painter, in truth, but it was a true expression of my feelings for and about him, and that he appreciated that meant the world to me.

That night, after he'd had Rogers send the couple home, he asked me to stay with him in his room and we made love again. When I finally fell asleep with my head on his chest, I was exhausted but happier than I could imagine I'd be with him.

As before, I woke up alone in his bed, already missing him. This time he'd left a note on his pillow, and I groggily focused my eyes to read what it said.

Dear Nina,

I have to go away for a few days, but I've instructed Rogers to get your painting framed so I can see it every morning when I wake. I'm sorry I had to leave before you got up, but I didn't want to disturb you since you looked so sweet all curled up next to me. While I'm gone, my car and driver are at your disposal. Feel free to use them to go wherever you like. When I return, your first official assignment as an assistant curator will begin.

Love,

Tristan

I held the paper in my trembling hands and stared at the last two words he'd written. *Love, Tristan.* Love. Not always, as before. Love.

Was this all a dream?

It had only been about a week since we'd first met. Was it possible there was such a thing as love at first sight and he'd felt that about me? I wanted to believe that more than anything, but something inside me whispered the doubt that anyone could fall in love that quickly, especially someone who could have anyone he wanted.

Times like this required a heart-to-heart girl talk with Jordan. I hurriedly ran to my room and then jumped in the shower to get ready for my trip back to Brooklyn. As I fixed my hair and makeup, I realized I hadn't thought about the trip as going home but going to Jordan's.

I, too, seemed to have become lost in my feelings.

Jenson was as accommodating as he was supposed to be, and by lunchtime I was back at our apartment and looking forward to hashing things out with Jordan. With school's ending, she was on summer vacation, so we had all the time we needed to figure out if I'd somehow won the romantic equivalent of the lottery or was just fooling myself into thinking that my situation with Tristan was good when it was anything but.

I threw my purse on the kitchen table and yelled for Jordan. Her scream from down the hall told me she was home and I found her in the bathroom cleaning smeared streaks of black from her eyelids.

"Jesus, Nina! I look like a damn raccoon now. Who walks into a person's house and screams like that?"

Three tissues later, she was back to finishing her makeup and I said in my best pouty tone, "Sorry. I thought this was still my place too."

Turning to face me, she smiled. "It is. I just got a little freaked out when you yelled. I wasn't expecting you since he came by and paid your part of the rent for the rest of the year."

The look on her face—complete with raised eyebrows of disbelief—told me she was just the person I needed to talk about things with. If there was any tough love I needed to hear, Jordan would give it to me.

"Yeah, well, that doesn't mean I would never come back. I need some friend time pronto and you're the only one I can trust."

Concern clouded her gaze. Reaching out, she squeezed my arm gently. "What happened, Nina? Are you okay?"

Nodding, I smiled. "I'm fine, but I want to stay that way. Can we talk?"

"Yeah, of course. Let's go for a walk. It's a beautiful day, so it'll feel good."

I agreed, happy I wore flats instead of the cute little pumps I had grabbed first. After listening to all the latest news about Justin, I set out with her for our walk and more importantly, our heart-to-heart.

Sunset Park in the summer was a pretty place, not like what people think big cities look like at all. The trees were all in bloom, so there was far more green than one might expect in the concrete jungle. Jordan and I walked our usual route, enjoying the weather as I told her about my new job and all its great benefits.

"So you hit the jackpot? This is great!"

I bit my lower lip. Tilting my head right and left, I said, "Yes and no. That's what I need your keen insight for."

Jordan stopped and raised one eyebrow. "I know that lip thing. Something's gnawing at you. And what's this yes and no? I've seen this man in the flesh, my friend. It's a yes. I nearly fell over dead when he showed up at the apartment. The watch that he wears alone is worth more than anything I've ever driven. And the way he says things...it's like honey dripping out of a jar."

I couldn't help but blush. Tristan was stunning, and when he stood in front of someone dressed in a suit and tie, he made quite an impression. There was no doubt about that. His physical side was a resounding "Yes!" without a doubt. It was the other parts of him that I wasn't sure about.

"He does have a way when he speaks, although I'm thinking he might have said more to you than to me by the way you're talking."

We began to walk again. "Oh, he didn't say much at all, but there's something about how the words come out. You have to tell me, Nina. Does he sound that sexy when you're...alone?"

"Since I have to assume he didn't tell you we're sleeping together, I guess it's that obvious?" I asked, wondering if I was telegraphing the fact that I was actively having sex with him.

Jordan turned her head to look at me for a second and then turned back to face forward, wrinkling her nose a bit. "Actually, it was the way he acted. No man comes to pay a woman's rent for six months and arrange to take everything she owns to his house if he isn't sleeping with her, Nina. You're obviously making him happy."

Happy. Now that was the tricky part. I sighed and blew the air out of my lungs in a heavy breath. "That's the problem I need your help with."

"You aren't going to say he's not happy with you, are you? You've been dating for less than a week and already he's taking care of you like you're a kept woman. Seems pretty happy to me."

"I'm not sure he is happy. I'm not sure about much of anything where Tristan Stone's concerned, Jordan. He had me sign a contract that I thought was for the job as an assistant curator at his hotel downtown, but I haven't done any work in that area yet. He bought me a new wardrobe for the job that literally cost nearly ten thousand dollars, Jordan, but he picked out all the clothes himself."

Pressing her hands to above her heart, she said, "I think I'm in love."

I stopped her and grabbed her arm. "I'm serious. I think I'm being paid to be his sex slave."

Jordan's laugh was so loud the children playing nearby stopped to pay attention to us. I guess it sounded funny now that I'd said it out loud.

"Sex slave? Nina, you're his girlfriend. That's how he's supposed to act. Girlfriends of wealthy men always have honorary titles and things like that. You're not expected to actually work."

I leaned in close to her and whispered, "Then what am I getting paid for?"

Jordan laughed again. "Honey, this is how wealthy men are. Think of it as an allowance. Instead of the kind you got when you were a kid, when you had to clean your room and do the dishes, this is the kind where you make him happy and he makes you happy with his money."

"But that's the problem. I don't think I'm making him happy. He goes to events and never asks me. I seem to be only the woman he keeps around his house."

"Hmmm....well, I don't think you're getting a bad deal. His driver takes you places, he does nice things for you, and you like him, don't you?"

I more than liked him. What had begun as an infatuation quickly had blossomed into something much more for me and I hoped for him too. I wanted to believe he meant what he'd written in that note, but I wasn't sure.

"Jordan, he's not like anyone else I've ever dated. Sometimes I can barely get him to answer me with more than a yes or no. Then he's affectionate sometimes only to be distant at other times. I don't know what to think."

She stopped and grabbed me by the shoulders. "That's your problem, Nina. You're overthinking this. What's wrong with a man giving you everything you want and all you have to do is be what he wants in return? Isn't that what everyone wants?"

When she explained it that way, it all sounded so perfect. He made me happy. I made him happy. Everyone was happy.

Then why were those niggling doubts in my mind still sending up red flags?

"Here's the thing," she said as she began walking back toward the apartment. "The whole relationship is brand new. Give it a while and see what happens. I think you might be pleasantly surprised. Good things do happen to good people. I think you're proof of that."

"I can't just give it a while, Jordan. I signed a contract for the next six months."

"And for that what do you get paid?"

"Sixty."

Jordan smiled. "Honey, you're getting paid sixty grand and you get to live with Tristan Stone. I think you should be more concerned about convincing him to keep you for longer than just six months."

"Maybe that's it. What happens if I fall madly in love with him and he decides to get rid of me after the time is up?"

"If you fall madly in love? I can tell by your face now, Nina, that's already happened. And I wouldn't be surprised to find out that he's crazy about you too. Just enjoy this. It's not everyday that a girl like you or me gets a guy like that. Let it ride and when the time is up, who knows what might happen."

I blushed at her ability to see through my facade, but my talk with her had helped, even if just a little. Looking at her, I saw out of the corner of my eye Jenson standing at the car waiting for me. "I guess it's time to go."

Jordan gave the man the once over and turned back to face me. "He certainly does like to know what you're up to, doesn't he? This poor guy hasn't been more than a few feet from us the whole time."

"What do you mean?" I asked as I looked over at the driver again as he patiently leaned against the car.

"Nina, he followed us the whole time. I didn't say anything because I figured you knew."

"Of course I didn't know! Who does that?"

Jordan leaned in and hugged me tightly. In my ear, she whispered, "I told you. Wealthy people are different. If he can't watch you, he'll have one of his men do it. I wouldn't worry. At least you'll never get mugged."

Her joking didn't make what I was feeling any better. "I'll call you, okay? I'm just glad you have some extra money now. Tell Justin I said hi."

"I will, honey. And I'll tell Alex you're doing fine. He's asked about you at least five times this week."

I smiled. Alex was a decent guy, so it wasn't a bad thing that he was interested. "Tell him I said hi and I'll be looking for a rematch of our pool game sometime."

Jordan's face grew serious. "Remember what I said, Nina. Good things do happen to good people. Don't forget that."

"I won't."

I returned to Tristan's house upstate hoping he'd be back, even though his note had said he'd be gone for a few days. The place was lonely without him, and I missed him already as I wandered around looking for something to occupy my time.

Rogers didn't seem to be anywhere to be found, so I explored without restraint, finding a media room and even a game room with a pool table. An hour or so of shooting pool by myself and I was even lonelier. Even the stoic butler would have been welcome company.

The house had an empty feel to it with just me in it. I'd never been to the attic, so I roamed up to the top floor and after looking around at a bunch of boxes and trunks, found one of those heavy, black old-fashioned telephones. On a whim, I picked up the receiver and heard a dial tone. There wasn't another landline in the entire house, but this one telephone sat up here all alone and worked!

Unsure if I should use it, I looked around and saw I was still alone. My cell phone got no reception out here, so I took the opportunity to dial my sister's number and heard her phone begin to ring. It was a small thing, but a rush of excitement pulsed through me. It felt like I was in one of those old mysteries and had found something no one else knew about.

"Hello?" she said loud and clear.

"Kim?" I whispered. "It's Nina."

"Nina! I tried to call you two days ago. It went directly to voicemail. Are you okay?"

Looking around, I said, "I'm fine. My phone's been acting up. How are you?"

My sister was married with two beautiful children and lived in a quiet suburban neighborhood outside of Philadelphia. I hadn't seen my two nieces for months and just hearing Kim's voice made me wish I was there to see them.

"We're all good. Jeff's doing well at the firm, and you know the girls. Growing like weeds. They've been asking about their Aunt Nina, about when she's coming to see them again."

A lump formed in my throat. "I know. I've just been really busy. I promise I won't let so much time go by between calls, Kim."

"What's wrong, Nina? Your voice sounds so sad."

Kim's voice reminded me of my father. She had a way of phrasing things that sounded just like him. Neither of them would think what I was doing with Tristan was right, and they'd let me know about it. I didn't want to hear that, but I would have given anything to talk to him again.

"I was thinking about Daddy last night when I saw some fireflies. Remember how he'd sit with me while I ran after them on summer nights?"

"Yeah, I remember. I thought you were so silly, but that was the six years between us. But where did you see fireflies? I don't know where they'd be in Brooklyn."

Damn. I wasn't very good at this lying thing. "Sure. Fireflies go everywhere," I joked in a forced voice. "We have everything in New York, Kim."

I laughed nervously, hoping she'd be satisfied by my joking, and she laughed too. "Next time you're here you can chase fireflies with the girls. They'll love that."

"Okay, it's a date. I better get going. I'll talk to you soon, Kim."

"Okay, baby. Behave yourself out there."

I smiled at the word baby. Ever since our dad died four years earlier, she'd ended every one of our conversations by calling me the name he'd used all my life. As I said goodbye and hung up, tears welled in my eyes. It would likely be a long time before I got to see her girls, unless Tristan's driver didn't mind taking a joyride to the Philly suburbs.

I scanned the attic and saw dozens of boxes and a spooky sewing mannequin standing alone in the corner. Turning to head for the stairs, I ran my left shin into a chest that sat on the floor. As I bent down to rub my leg to ease the stabbing pain, I saw that the chest's lock was open. The ache in my shin abated, and I sat down on the floor. The lid opened easily, allowing me to peer in to see what was stored inside.

Stacks of old photographs and letters tied with a red silk ribbon sat at the bottom of the chest. Leaning up against the side walls of the chest were larger pictures. I lifted one out and held it up to see a portrait of a family of four with a mother, father, and two boys possibly four years old smiling for the camera. The children were identical twins, but I recognized Tristan instantly. He and his brother shared the same features, but I could tell them apart. His eyes gave him away. There was that familiar gentleness I loved in them even when he was just a boy.

Suddenly, I felt like I was intruding on something private. He'd never talked about his family with me, not even to say he had a twin. From the moment I met him, I'd felt like he was all alone in the world, so where were this brother and his parents?

My gaze drifted up to the top of the picture to his mother and father, and I tried to find his eyes in one of them, but couldn't. Everyone else in his family had dark eyes too, but there was something different about his. He resembled his father more than his brother did, if that was possible, and as I stared at the man, I recognized a lot of him in Tristan now.

I'd heard that even identical twins could be told apart easily because of their personalities, and nothing proved that more than this picture. Beaming a smile of a gregarious child, Tristan sat next to his brother, a child who looked far more serious with his tiny downturned mouth. Each boy was positioned in front of a parent, Tristan's twin in front of the father and Tristan in front of his mother. As I stared at all of them, I imagined him being more like his mother. She was beautiful, with long brown hair, high cheekbones, and a lovely smile, the kind of woman everyone admired.

I placed the pictures back inside the chest and hurried downstairs, fearful Rogers would appear out of nowhere like he always seemed to and see me rummaging in Tristan's personal things. Another hour passed before I gave up and slipped into bed, feeling lonely and wishing Tristan was next to me.

Would I ever meet these people or did he plan to keep me a secret out here in the country, never to appear at any of the functions or events he attended or to see the people closest to him? As I tossed and turned in bed that night, I couldn't help but wish that I hadn't gone to the attic. Now I had more questions about Tristan, and he seemed content to exist only in the present with me, never mentioning anything about his past or our future.

Eight

"I missed you."

Tristan's voice stopped me dead in my tracks as I shuffled into the kitchen to look for my morning coffee. He stood leaning against the massive island in the center of the room, a sly grin on his face as he watched me gawking at him.

"You're back? I thought your note said days."

And love. I hadn't forgotten the love part. Hopefully, he hadn't either.

"I finished what I had to do early and got back a few hours ago. You must have some great boss to let you sleep in on a workday."

I liked this relaxed Tristan and smiled as he teased me. "I'll have you know that it's Friday, which is basically the weekend to many people." Walking around the island, I stopped in front of him, looking up into his beautiful face. "And my boss is the best."

He took my chin between his thumb and forefinger. "Thank you. However, your new job begins today, so you better get ready."

"My new job? The one at the hotel downtown?" I asked excitedly.

Tristan shook his head and grinned. "No."

I lowered my head in disappointment. It had been too good to be true, after all. Now he had me here for the next six months, and the best I'd likely get was the consolation prize of being Tristan's paid love interest. No matter how appealing Jordan had made that sound, it still seemed like second place.

"Don't look so unhappy. You'll love it," he whispered in my ear.

"I guess. Let me go get dressed and you can tell me all about it."

I turned to leave but he held me by the shoulders, forcing me to face him. My expression surely showed my disappointment, and I couldn't hide it. I didn't want to hide it.

"Nina, have faith in me," he said quietly, those brown eyes boring holes into my soul.

When he looked at me like that—like I meant more to him than anything else in the world—I wanted to believe he cared and wanted me to be happy like I wanted to make him happy. "I do," I said, half-believing it myself.

"Meet me in my office in ten," he ordered as he released me.

"I'm here, as commanded," I said with as much bravado as I could muster.

He sat behind his large cherry desk and crooked his finger at me. "Come. I have a surprise for you."

I walked toward the leather Queen Anne wingback chair in front of his desk, but he stopped me as I began sit down. "No, come sit with me. I want to show you what your job is going to be."

So I *was* going to be his sex slave. I knew it. There would be no art, no need for the new wardrobe, no great job. Just fucking for money. I was no better than a prostitute, no matter how he or Jordan phrased it. A whore.

"Should I just sit on your lap or would you prefer me to skip the preliminaries and just get on my knees?" I asked as I rounded the corner of his desk.

He said nothing but turned his laptop and looked up at me. "I love your idea of work, but I had something slightly different in mind."

I looked down at the laptop and there on the screen sat ten small thumbnails of artwork. My face felt red hot as I stood there staring down at the screen while my words echoed in my ears. What an ass I was!

Embarrassed, I looked down at the floor. "I'm so sorry. That was uncalled for. I didn't know."

Tristan chuckled and took my hand in his. "I love how honest you are. I've told you that. Don't ever stop being that way. There aren't enough people in this world who will truly say what they're feeling, Nina."

Biting my lip, I looked up in humiliation, his soothing words not working. "I really am sorry. I feel like such a jackass. I just assumed that...well, all I've done with you so far is..." I really wasn't explaining myself well and was probably making things worse. I definitely felt worse.

All he did was smile and stand from his chair. "Here, sit down and let me tell you what I plan to have you do. Unless you'd rather go down on me first. I'm not going to say no to that."

Oh, he wasn't going to let me live this down any time soon. I deserved it, though. As I sat down in his chair, he dragged one over next to me. "I know you want your job to involve working with art, so that's exactly what you'll be doing. Those pictures are just ideas I have for your job."

I looked at the pictures on the screen again, studying each of them and seeing no common theme or period. "What exactly is my job, Tristan?"

"I want you to choose the artwork for the penthouses and suites in my hotels. You'll have to choose pieces for each one and pitch them to me to convince me to buy them. If you succeed, then I'll buy them and put them in that suite or penthouse. If not, you'll have to choose something else and pitch that to me. I'll have the final say as to the choices, but I'm trusting that you'll show me excellent pieces."

I looked at him, instantly worried. "What happens if you don't like anything I choose?"

That gentle smile he sometimes put on spread across his lips. "Nina, I have faith in you. I'm sure I'll love what you pick out."

There was that word again. Love. Now he was going to love my choices of artwork in addition to me and my penchant for honesty.

"Tristan, this all seems odd. Don't you have curators in your hotels who do this?"

"They deal with the museums that are housed in some of the hotels. This is different. My hotels are the best in luxury resorts and the people who stay in them expect the best in their surroundings. I have people who decorate them, others who do the tile work that make some look like the finest Roman mosaics, and others who design the rooms to be one of a kind at some of my hotels. What I want you to do is choose pieces that will make all of their work come together."

Suddenly, I felt entirely inept. All those times that I'd bragged that I knew about art now seemed foolish, as did I. Tristan actually expected me to choose pieces that the wealthiest people in the world would see when they paid top dollar to stay in his hotels. What if all my big talk about art had been just that?

Just talk.

"Okay. How many will I be doing?" I asked as I folded my hands in my lap to hide their shaking.

"I haven't decided yet. Maybe a goal of one a week would be a nice place to start."

One a week. Maybe I could handle this. Okay. One was entirely doable. "I'm going to need to know everything about each suite or penthouse. Choosing pieces isn't something that can be done without seeing what the rooms look like and what style is prevalent."

"Of course. We won't be visiting every one, but I'll make sure we get to a few."

I collapsed back in his office chair, crashing against the padded leather. "We're visiting some of them? Where are they located?"

"Around the world. Why?"

"I don't have a passport, Tristan." I don't know why, but that sounded so common as the words left my mouth, like he'd see me as someone less than him because I didn't routinely leave the country.

"Then we'll have to get you one. I'll put a rush on that, but in the meantime, we'll stick with domestic properties."

Tristan began tapping away at his keyboard as I mumbled, "I guess that's that." He seemed to be happy with the way things were going, but I was still nervous and unsure of myself. While my insecurities did their best to plague my already unsettled mind, my eyes focused on him as he searched for something online and I was struck by how relaxed he was at that moment. If I didn't know how much he owned or how much money he made, he'd look like any other man working on his laptop.

I wanted to reach out and touch him to make sure he wasn't a dream. This Tristan was so unlike the man I'd seen in the newspaper and even unlike the distant one I'd begun to fall for. Even dressed for work, he looked similar to someone like me.

"How old are you?" I asked impulsively, suddenly realizing I had no idea about that or other details that would have come to light with a boyfriend by now, like where he went to school or what he'd majored in.

He stopped his typing and turned to look at me. "Twenty-nine."

"What did you go to school for?"

With a smile, he answered, "Nothing."

His answer surprised me. "What do you mean? You run an entire company. Didn't you go to school for business?"

"For a year, but it wasn't what I wanted to do. Wharton was a little stiff for me."

"Wharton, as in Penn? As in Ivy League?"

Shrugging, he went back to searching for what he was looking for. "The same."

"And that was a little stiff for you?" I found the idea that anywhere was too stiff for him amusing.

He nodded. "College wasn't what I wanted."

"What did you want?" I asked, curious about the faraway sound in his voice now that hinted at a very different Tristan.

Ignoring my question, he turned the laptop in my direction and smiled that warm smile that could make me give up almost anything. "We'll deal with my penthouse first. The poker playing dogs picture isn't working out at all, so you'll need to come up with a something else."

I couldn't help but laugh, far louder than was likely proper. Just when I thought he was stiff and distant, he made a joke like that and changed the entire way I looked at him. "You didn't take me seriously about that, did you?"

Faking sincerity, he screwed his face into a grimace. "I wasn't supposed to? Those dogs cost me a fortune."

For a second, I thought he was serious, and then he winked at me. "Let's get going. Pick out what clothes you want to take and I'll have Rogers take care of it."

"Just like that?"

He closed his laptop, sat back in his chair, and folded his arms. "Just like that. I'll give you fifteen minutes."

I began walking toward my room and turned around, feeling playful. "And if I'm not done by then?"

Without missing a beat, he answered, "Then you'll spend your time at the penthouse naked, which also works for me."

He smiled again, and I relaxed a little more. "I never know when you're kidding, Tristan."

"I'm not kidding. As far as I'm concerned, you could never wear anything again and I'd be happy."

"But what about all those clothes you bought? That's a lot of money to waste, don't you think?" I asked, enjoying our verbal sparring.

He stood from his chair and walked toward me like a wild cat stalking prey. When he was only inches away from me, he stopped and lifted my chin with his finger and stared down into my eyes. "I'd spend ten times that to make you happy, Nina. Now go get ready or you're spending our time in the city as God made you."

It was nearly impossible to think about work when he was standing there looking like that and talking about me naked at his penthouse. I hurriedly chose a few outfits and laid them out on my bed before finding him waiting at the end of the hallway that led to my room.

"Ready?"

He'd asked me that right after we'd first met and just like then, I wasn't ready. Everything was moving so quickly that I wanted to stop, ask some questions, and get my bearings. But he never let that happen. It wasn't as if he was rushing me, really. It was more that he expected things to go as he had planned and there never was a moment where I wanted to risk asking what we were doing, afraid that if I did I'd ruin everything.

What woman wouldn't want a man like him to whisk her off her feet and take care of every issue that came up in life?

Tristan's penthouse was familiar to me as I stepped out of the elevator, but this time he held my hand in his. A tiny difference, it made everything I laid my eyes on seem changed. Still appearing disinterested in his magnificent home, he led me to his bedroom and sat down on the edge of the bed across from the bare spot on the wall.

I looked at the wall and smiled. "No dogs?"

"No dogs. And if there's some picture that involves cats playing checkers or something like that, I'm going on record as saying no to that too."

"There goes my great idea. Back to the drawing board for me."

My joke got no response, and he sat silently alternating his focus from the spot on the wall to my face. It made me uncomfortable, so I turned my back to him and faced my first task as his employee.

I felt his gaze on my back, but I remained fixated on the job at hand. It was too easy to want to just turn around and climb on top of him, straddling his hips as my skirt rode up and my body slid over his. I wanted to show him that I could do this.

His home was decorated expensively in a style much like other expensive hotel rooms I'd seen in decorating magazines. I walked around looking at the furniture and coverings, but none of them seemed particularly him. They were luxurious but not unique. Certainly, whoever had chosen them knew how to spend money. From the gold and cream stripe sofas that flanked the beige marble fireplace wall in the living room to the wingback Queen Anne chairs and large mahogany coffee table that must have been five feet in diameter in the sitting room, the home had been carefully decorated to apply to no one in particular. Down the hall was a bedroom with a ceiling that showed the decorator had possessed some flair. Hand painted, the view above the bedroom Tristan didn't sleep in was a stunning design that depicted the seventeenth century Dutch settlement of New Amsterdam near the spot the hotel stood on now.

I wandered to the bathroom and stood with my mouth hanging open. The time before I hadn't gotten to see it, and as I looked around with wide eyes, I was in love. Pale shades of marble and granite covered everywhere my gaze fell, but the centerpiece of the room was a toss up. The deep soaker tub in the center of the room competed with the floor to ceiling windows that showed the splendor of the city below, leaving me unsure which was more beautiful.

Walking back to his bedroom, which while attractive was possibly the least appealing room in the entire home, I made up my mind to choose a piece of art that would reflect him, not just look good or expensive. He sat still waiting for me on the bed, looking almost uncomfortable in his own house.

"Tristan, did you have this decorated when you moved in?"

I was almost sure the answer would be no, but I had to know. I don't think I'd ever seen a home so completely unrepresentative of its owner.

Shaking his head, he said, "No. It just comes with the job."

"No wonder nothing here is like you. I mean, it's gorgeous, especially the bathroom, but nothing about this place says you live here."

"So, have you thought about what might work on this wall?"

"No, but I know I want it to be something that says 'Tristan Stone lives here' instead of something so gorgeously common and expensive that it could be in anyone's home."

"And what would this piece say about me?" he asked, his interest obviously piqued.

"The man who lives here is intelligent—a man of few words but those he does speak are meaningful."

"I knew I'd like your choices in this. I look forward to seeing what you have to offer, Nina. I'll leave you to your work and be back at five sharp. My hotel and my home are at your disposal. When you get hungry, simply call the concierge and they'll take care of you."

He stood and I moved to kiss him, as I would any other boyfriend of mine who was leaving for work, but he merely nodded and silently walked by me as I stood watching him leave. All I could guess was that I was truly on the job now.

Nine

By five o' clock, I'd narrowed the potential choices for Tristan's room to three, and I was surprisingly tired. While I hadn't done any physical work at all, my mind had been working overtime all day about what piece would be perfect for the man who lived in this expensively furnished yet characterless penthouse. I wanted it to be perfect. I wanted to show him that he hadn't made a mistake having faith in me. Most of all, I wanted to give him something that would show what he was in my eyes.

He returned right on time at five sharp looking exactly as he had when he'd left all those hours earlier. Never wrinkled or rumpled, he looked as he always did in his suit, even though that day's was black instead of the variety of shades of grey he tended to wear. The tan dress shirt was different too, but whatever he wore, he looked gorgeous.

"Did you have a good day at work?" Tristan asked in a teasing voice as he walked into the bedroom loosening his tie.

"I did, dear. And how was your day at work?" I asked as I sat on the bed watching him get more comfortable.

"You know how it is. Another day, another dollar."

Opening the closet, he removed his suit coat and tie and turned to face me once again in just pants and a shirt. "What would you like for dinner?"

"Don't you want to know about the choices I have in mind for your blank spot?" I was eager to see what he thought about my ideas.

He shook his head. "No. Once five comes, I don't want to think about work anymore. All I want to think about is you. I don't want you thinking about work anymore either."

Jesus, when he said things like that, my stomach did somersaults. He didn't want to hang out and watch TV. He didn't want to play video games. He didn't want to go to some place with his friends and never consider if I wanted to really go.

He wanted to think about me. Just me.

I was lost. And damn, I didn't want to be found.

He knelt in front of me, running his hands over my thighs and nearly driving me crazy with his touch. "So what should we have to eat? One of your favorites or something new you've never had? Feeling adventurous?"

He looked up at me, his eyes searching mine. The old me, the me before I met Tristan, would have chosen one of my favorites, but as he knelt there looking up at me, I wanted to be someone different than who I'd always been. I wanted to be worthy of feeling sexy and desirable.

"Let's try something adventurous."

"Next question—eat in or out?" he asked as he dipped his head to place a single kiss on the inside of my thigh.

My head was swimming, but I found the ability to squeak out, "In."

He nipped at my skin, sending shivers of pleasure racing up my body. Against my leg, he murmured, "In it is," before he stood and disappeared from the room. A rush of heat covered me and I crashed back onto the bed, barely able to breathe.

The way he was made me crazy. Crazy for him. Crazy because of him. Fucking crazy. He'd left this morning without a word or even a gentle brush of his hand against mine to say goodbye, and he'd returned wanting nothing but me. What was with this guy? How did he do it? I could barely keep my hands off him, and there were times he stood close enough to touch me and never did.

It was maddening. And I loved it. Without force or any restraints, he'd taken over my every thought and feeling, and I was helpless to fight against it. Hell, I didn't want to fight against it. I wanted to let my mind and body give in to everything he offered.

"I ordered seared duck," he whispered as he slid up my body until his lips met mine in a gentle kiss. "I wasn't really in the mood for too much adventure in my food tonight. Do you like duck?"

"I've never had it. What does it taste like?"

"Chicken."

I opened my eyes at his answer. "Really?"

Smiling, he licked his lips and kissed me again. Against the corner of my mouth, he whispered, "No."

"Oh. Will I like it?"

He hovered above me looking down into my eyes. "Yes, I promise you'll love it. My chef makes it with a fig sauce that tastes incredible."

"Are we going down to the restaurant to eat?" I asked, praying to God he'd say no.

He moved his body up mine until his mouth was next to my ear. "We can, if you want. Do you want to leave, Nina?" His voice was a slow whisper that made a delicious ache coil in my belly, and I would have given everything I owned to not leave that spot.

"No," I said quietly as he pushed his hips forward, sliding his hard cock against my panties. "I think here is perfect."

"Good. Have anything in mind for what we should do until dinner comes?" he murmured in my ear as he pushed his hips toward me again.

"You're such a tease."

He lifted his head and smiled that wicked smile I'd only seen once or twice. "Tease? You want me to tease you?"

"No. I hate being teased."

Tristan rolled off me and propped his head up with his hand. He looked down at me, still smiling, and ran his finger over my lips. "You're cute when you pout."

Cute. That was definitely not what I wanted to be thought of. Cute was for puppies, kittens, and little girls. Now I really pouted.

"Oh, more pouting. I must have said something wrong. Let me guess. You don't want me to call you cute."

He was teasing me, and I didn't like it. "I'm glad I'm amusing you, Tristan. Maybe I can dress up like some little girl and you can pick on me like some bully on the playground."

"Someone's touchy tonight."

That was it. I didn't like this Tristan. He reminded me too much of every other guy in the world. That bothered me. He was supposed to be more, better. Now he was nothing but a guy who seemed to have forgotten how to treat me.

I sat up and stood from the bed. "I'm going to take a bath. Let me know when the food gets here."

As I walked toward the bathroom, I felt like crying. I didn't know why either. I knew I was probably overreacting, but something in Tristan seemed less special now, and I hated that. If he was just an ordinary guy with lots of money, then somehow I felt less, like I'd let myself be fooled.

I slid into the tub and let the water run until it nearly overflowed. I wanted to get lost in that water until everything around me disappeared. Behind me through the massive windows the scenes of the city played out, but I didn't want to see them either. I just wanted to close my eyes and pretend nothing had happened.

The water soothed my body, but my head and heart still ached. I sat there with the bath water up to my chin and fought back the recriminations. My insecurities had reared their ugly heads again, and as the water cooled around me, I silently admitted that this wasn't about Tristan.

This was about me. This was about my feeling like I didn't belong here, just like I'd felt that first night when I'd flubbed Tristan's test.

I heard the door open, and he walked silently past me. I didn't want to open my eyes, hoping that if I didn't, I wouldn't have to see the look on his face.

Tristan crouched down behind me and slid his hands over my shoulders. "Nina, I'm sorry. I didn't mean anything by what I said."

That only made it worse. I had caused the problem and now he was apologizing. "Don't. It was all me."

I opened my eyes and looked down at his hands stroking my arms. This situation was desperately in need of some lightening. "This is some bathtub. I think my dorm room was this size."

He chuckled behind me and slipped his hands from my body. "And I bet you shared a room too."

Leaning back to look at him, I watched as he stepped out of his pants and boxers, leaving them in a heap on the floor. I moved forward in the tub to accommodate his body, sending water flowing over the sides, and he slid into the water behind me, taking me into his arms.

Still hoping to lighten the mood, I joked, "I don't remember being this close to my roommate in college. Maybe our dorm room was a little bigger."

Water sloshed against the sides of the tub and more spilled out onto the floor as he wrapped his legs around me. All the times we'd been together, I'd never noticed how long his legs were. They barely fit inside the tub.

"Do you know this is my first time in this bathtub?"

"That makes sense since your legs are almost too long for it."

I ran my palms over his knees and down his shins, feeling the soft hair against my skin. I'd always loved how masculine men's legs looked when there wasn't too much hair so they looked like grizzly bears or too little that I'd wonder if my legs had more when I forgot to shave for a few days. His had the perfect amount in all the right places.

"I think the designer naturally thought we'd sit the other way since the real view is out the window," he said as he moved my hair off my shoulder. "I like this way better."

"Staring at an empty shower?"

He gently pulled my head back to rest on his chest and ran his fingertips across my forehead. "With you."

Two words and he made me want to forget all my insecurities, all my worries about not being enough. He kissed the top of my head, and almost as if he could read my mind, whispered, "I like how you make me feel, Nina."

I said nothing, knowing he probably wanted to hear me say I liked how he made me feel. I wanted to say something—to tell him that I'd never felt anything like how he made me feel—but I couldn't. If he rejected me there, as I sat naked in his arms, or worse, said nothing in return, everything I feared would finally be true. I couldn't handle that.

His arm rested across my collarbone, and I bent my head to place a kiss on his wrist. I hoped he understood how much I loved hearing that I made him feel something good or special. Closing my eyes, I let myself enjoy his body pressed against mine and his strong arms around me. We sat so still the water stopped moving, as if we both wanted to stop time and just revel in this one moment. Finally, he sighed deeply and a tiny ripple slowly moved the water forward until it lapped against the front of the tub and the tops of our feet.

"I could sit here for the rest of time," he whispered in a faraway voice.

I brought his fingers to my mouth and kissed the fingertip of his forefinger, which had begun to wrinkle in the water. "I think you'd get all pruney."

He chuckled and kissed the top of my head again. "Then we'd be pruney together."

No matter how I tried to make the situation light and easy, he always brought it back right to center, right to the core of who he was. Either he said little and indicated less, or he spoke and made me want to forget everything else in the world but him.

He'd been right about the duck. It was delicious, and I did love it. I wondered if things happened the way he wanted them to simply out of his sheer desire to have them happen that way. Some people seemed to be able to manifest their desires like that. In the short time I'd known him, it had merely taken him expressing his wish for something to make it occur. Over and over, I'd seen him get what he wanted, but I couldn't say it was due to power or manipulation.

Life just seemed to give him what he desired.

And what he desired that night was me. We'd barely pushed aside the plates when his mouth was on mine, urging me to meet his passion with my own. My body was thrilled, but my mind found his changeable ways confusing. As we'd eaten, he'd said no more than five words, acting more like my boss than my lover. When I expressed how much I liked the duck, he merely smiled, saying nothing in return and continuing to eat. Then, like someone had turned on a light inside him, he looked over at me and he was that man who couldn't get enough of me again.

He led me over to stand in front of the floor to ceiling windows in the living room, and the view of the city below took my breath away. I stood just inches away from the wall of glass, my usual fear of heights pushed aside by the beauty of what lay before my eyes. High above Manhattan, the entire city seemed to be laid out in all its glory. "It's gorgeous, Tristan. It must be impossible to get to sleep knowing this is here all for you to see every night."

His arms held me tight, and he looked up from kissing my neck. "I never look at it, to be honest."

Turning in his hold, I said, "How can you not? It's so stunning."

He kissed me on the lips and pushed my hair behind my ear. "I don't have the artistic eye like you do. It just seems like a million little ants scurrying around to me."

I traced a line from his Adam's Apple to the hollow right above his sternum, drawing circles in that place where his skin was so soft. His pulse beat lightly under the skin, and I stared at the gentle throbbing against my fingertip. "Everyone has the ability to see beauty. It's just a matter of letting it in. There's beauty in everything. That's art."

"I doubt that."

I looked up, intent on proving I was right. "Do you see where my finger is? Just under the skin is evidence of your heart beating. It's just a tiny pulsation, but it's beautiful."

"And this is art?" he asked, not convinced.

"What's more beautiful than the beating of the human heart?"

He took my finger from his neck and kissed it. "I knew it from the first time I saw you. There's something special in you, something light and good that drew me to you."

His words made me blush, and I felt my cheeks warm. No one had ever spoken to me like this before, and to have someone who could have anyone in the world as he could say this to me was thrilling and overwhelming at the same time. My emotions became jumbled again, and before I knew it, words were spilling out of my mouth letting him know everything in my heart.

"When you talk like this, I think that you might truly care for me. Do you know that? Then I let myself believe it and you turn off your feelings as quickly as they came on. I'm not like that. My feelings don't turn off, even when I wish they would."

"I love that you don't try to censor how you feel, Nina. It's one of the things that makes you so incredible."

His compliment was genuine, but it didn't help.

"I want to be able to censor them, though. I want to be able to do what you do. I want to be able to stand next to you and not want to touch you, like you can do with me."

A tiny look of sadness crossed his face for just a moment and then it was gone.

"You wouldn't be who you are if you repressed your feelings."

"How do you do it, Tristan? How do you control what your emotions do to you?"

He leaned down and kissed me softly on the lips. "I told you. This is how I must be. It's who I am. Can you live with that?"

"Can you promise me I'll always know what's in your heart, no matter what?" I asked, laying bare my fears for the first time.

Cradling my face in his hands, he pressed his forehead to mine and whispered, "No matter what you see on the outside, no matter what I say, what's in my heart will always be just what's there at this moment. You."

He took me there, in front of those windows—in front of the entire city—my body pressed up against the glass as he thrust into me again and again. I clung to him, first to calm my fears that I'd fall through the glass and plummet to the street below and then for the very happiness only he could give me. His hands held me to him, protecting me as he invaded my body with his cock and my heart with his words so passionate I would have believed them even if they were blatant lies.

We laid on the floor near where we'd made love, his hands worshipping my body as I tried to force my heart to harden over for the next time he shut off his feelings. I'd accepted who he was. Now I needed to accept who I'd have to become to love him.

Ten

I was sorry to see our time at Tristan's penthouse end. We hadn't done much except make love and eat, and I couldn't remember a weekend I'd enjoyed more. We'd talked about so many things, yet I didn't believe I knew him any better after all those words between us. In truth, he'd gotten me to speak more than he had, but as he'd hung on every word, I felt safe and opened up about my past. My tales of life in a small Pennsylvania town seemed to enchant him, so I'd told him likely more than anyone would like to know about growing up as the younger daughter of a father who was a writer. By Sunday night we were back in the country, me in my part of the house and him in his until night when I once again slept next to him. As always, he was gone when I awoke the next morning, and there was a note waiting for me.

Dear Nina,

Tonight when I return, we'll discuss the piece you've chosen for my bedroom in the penthouse. I look forward to seeing what you believe represents the man I am and have faith that your artistic heart lets you see what no one else can.

Love,

Tristan

I'd made my final decision before even returning to the house, so my day was spent in searching for it. After hours of looking through gallery and art retailer sites, I found exactly what I was looking for. It wasn't priceless or even expensive, but I was sure it was right for him. My heart soared at my success. If I could choose a piece so perfect as to show the man he was, I could do the job he was paying me for and do it well.

Tristan returned shortly before five and found me waiting for him in his office. Like any other employee, I was dressed and ready to impress my boss, sure my first assignment would end in a great success.

Dressed in a pale grey suit and sapphire blue shirt, he sat down behind his desk and straightened his tie. I waited for him to begin, barely able to contain my excitement at my finding. As I watched him attend to paperwork, the thought of how his other female employees saw him crept into my mind. A tiny flicker of jealousy sparked at the idea of someone like me sitting across from him studying his dress and mannerisms like

I did. Did she love to watch his mouth as he spoke, wishing to feel his lips on her skin? Did she notice his hands, the long fingers and strong grip of the pen as he wrote a note to himself? Did she find how incredible he looked in his clothes as fascinating as I did, desperately wanting to loosen his tie as she ran her lips over his strong neck?

"I'm eager to see what you've chosen, Nina."

"I'm excited to show you. I think it's you to a T, and it fits with the decor of your bedroom there. Would you like to see the picture of it? I have it ready on my laptop."

He nodded and I made my way around his desk to show him. A few clicks and the image of my choice was sitting on the screen.

He studied it for what seemed like hours and then turned to look up at me. I couldn't tell anything by his placid expression, so I waited for him to say something to let me know what he thought. But he wasn't going to make it that easy for me.

"Tell me why you think this is what I should have taking up that blank spot on my wall in my bedroom. This will be the first thing I see in the morning and the last thing I see at night before I fall asleep, so convince me this is what I should have on my mind at such important times."

I looked down at the picture I'd stared at for an hour before he came home and began. "The frame is a dark wood, but in truth, it could be any frame you prefer and work with what the decor is there. It's the print inside the frame that's perfect. A masculine design with Greek inspired scrollwork, the words 'No legacy is so rich as honesty' speak to everything you've told me about yourself from the first night I met you. You have all the money and wealth you desire, which I'm sure includes the luxuries of fame, others desiring you, and any material possession you could want. Yet you've told me over and over in the short time I've known you that you value my honesty. I have to believe that for all your wealth you don't have people in your life who will give you this one thing you desire."

He waited a long time before he finally spoke. With a smile, he finally said, "Very impressive, Nina. Your talents were sorely underutilized at the Anderson Gallery. That's more than clear. Do you have anything else you'd like to present in your proposal?"

I knew he was trying to unnerve me, but I wasn't going to be shaken. I believed in my choice and stood by it. Shaking my head, I tilted my chin upward slightly. "No. That's all."

That sexy, slow grin I loved spread across his lips. "It's perfect. I knew you'd be wonderful at this. Give Rogers the details tomorrow and he'll see that it finds its way to that blank spot on the wall."

I couldn't help but beam my satisfaction. My first assignment was a smashing success, and even more, I'd shown him that I understood the kind of man he was. In some ways, that meant more to me than his approval of my choice.

"Are you hungry?" he asked as he stood from behind his desk. "I've got a craving for pizza."

"I'm always in the mood for pizza! Is there a good place around here?"

"There is. It looks like it's straight out of a movie with checkered tablecloths and placemats with pictures of the map of Italy on them, but the people who own it know how to make good pizza."

This felt like a real date! Excited, I said, "I can be ready in minutes, if you can."

Before he answered, I was off like a shot to grab my bag and make sure I looked presentable. A few minutes later I returned to find him standing there in his suit and tie looking particularly unready for slices at a little pizza place. Likely, dressed like that, he'd stick out as badly as he did at The Last Drop. Stepping toward him, I ran my finger down his tie and smiled up at him. "Maybe you could loosen this tie and look like it's not your first time eating pizza."

Tristan arched one dark eyebrow. "Are you insinuating that I look uptight?"

"You've gone to this place before, right? I'm going to guess that nobody spoke a word to you the whole time you were there."

I saw by the slight downturn of his mouth that I was right. They'd probably thought he was some FBI agent coming to town to track down some serial killer. He had that icy, government official vibe sometimes.

As I slid the tie from around his collar, I explained, "They probably got the wrong idea about you. Small town pizza places don't likely get too many customers who look like you do."

"You make it seem like I'm some sultan. It's a suit and tie, Nina."

I stepped back and looked him up and down. "It's a suit that costs more than many people make in a month and a tie that likely cost more than most teenagers pay for a pair of sneakers, Tristan. Ordinary people don't wear that to get a slice of pizza."

He took the tie out of my hands and brought my fingers to his lips for a kiss. Settling his gaze on me, he said quietly, "Neither of us are ordinary, no matter how much you want to be."

His stubborn belief that I was anything but the regular person I'd always been made me smile. "Well, we don't have to flaunt our extraordinariness all the time. Sometimes it's just nice to appear like ordinary people, so off with the tie and jacket."

Tristan narrowed his eyes slightly for a moment, surprised by my order, but the jacket followed the tie and he was ready to go. "Better?"

"The top button can be undone too, if you really want to look relaxed," I teased.

He opened his collar and motioned toward the door. "I hope the car is going to be okay," he said in a mocking tone. "Or do we have to walk or buy some used car?"

As I headed for the front door, I said, "Now you're not taking this seriously at all, are you?"

"On the contrary. I'm up for buying another car. Or maybe a horse and buggy would help with toning down the...what did you call it?"

I turned around at the car and laughed. "Extraordinariness. It's a word."

"It's a mouthful," he joked and lifted my chin to kiss me. "Now get in the car. Pizza's waiting."

He hadn't exaggerated in his description of Tony's Pizza Heaven. Red and white checkered tablecloths covered the old square Formica tables and at each place setting were paper placemats with red, white, and green maps of Italy and cartoon drawings of major tourist attractions, like the Leaning Tower of Pisa and the Coliseum, on them. The wooden chairs were old and hard, but the place was warm and comfortable.

I skimmed over the laminated menu while Tristan seemed to study it, but when the waitress came over to take our order he was quick to tell her we wanted a large pizza and a pitcher of soda. I sat staring at him thinking how surreal this scene was.

He noticed my confused expression. "Something wrong?"

I wasn't sure if something was wrong. Maybe it was how comfortable he seemed at a place I'd been so sure he wouldn't fit in. Shaking my head, I answered, "No. You seem quite at home here."

"Surprised? You think you know me, but you don't know everything about me, Nina."

"I guess I don't. That's okay. You don't know everything about me either."

Smiling, he remained quiet, making me feel like he knew more than I suspected. The silence between us made me feel uneasy, and I shifted in my chair and looked past him at the pictures on the far wall. Black and white photographs of Italian architecture were scattered along the walls of the restaurant and set me at ease. Very much like art, they were beautiful to look at, even in their cheap faux wood frames.

As the silence between us continued, I wanted to ask if he'd been to this place with his family. The images of their faces stayed in my mind, making me wish I could learn more about them. The idea of an exact duplicate of Tristan out there somewhere in the world intrigued me, and the fact that he never mentioned anything about him or his parents made me want to know about them even more.

But if I'd learned anything in the time I'd known Tristan Stone, it was that he spoke only when he wanted to and only about things he wanted to let the world know.

True to his claim, the pizza was terrific and after he'd gotten a slice into him, he became even more relaxed and began talking. This was the man I loved being around, and there he was sitting in that tiny pizza place in the middle of nowhere, of all the unlikely places.

"I think you'll be tackling Dallas next," he said with a wink.

"Talking about work after five? Doesn't that break your rule?"

"Isn't that what rules are for?"

Who was this man? "Are you saying you like to break the rules? Mr. Suit-And-Tie wants to flout convention?"

"Let's take it easy on the flouting," he said with a chuckle. "As for Dallas, let's plan on Wednesday."

"Well, since you want to talk about work, what can you tell me about Dallas?"

There was that devilish grin again. "Let's just say it's going to be a golden opportunity for you to stretch your imagination."

"Sounds pretty cryptic. Care to offer any more details?" I asked as I leaned over toward his side of the table.

He leaned in toward me and smiled. "Just remember I have faith in you."

I waited for him to continue, but he just sat there staring and smiling at me. Finally, I said, "I think you're making me nervous. Are you just trying to psyche me out?"

"Me? Never."

"Well, that's good because I'm a woman on a mission. You'll see. Expect to be impressed."

His mouth grazed mine, and he licked his lips. "I already am."

When we got back to the house, I expected us to get into bed as we had most nights since I began living there, but he disappeared almost as soon as we walked in the door. I waited for him to come to my room, but an hour later he still hadn't and I made up my mind to find him.

I was surprised to see him coming out of his room dressed in a tux. He was leaving again to attend some affair and not taking me. Instantly, it felt like someone had stabbed me in the chest. I was good enough to sleep with or hang out with at some out of the way restaurant, but I wasn't good enough to show off to his fancy friends.

"Nina, I'll be back later if you want to talk."

Choking back tears, I angrily blurted out, "Talk about what? How unworthy I am to be taken anywhere anyone might see you with me?"

"You're being silly," he said as he tried to push past me.

I pushed against him, refusing to let him leave. "Don't treat me like I'm merely your goddamn employee."

"You are my employee, Nina, even if we are more than just that to each other."

His voice was flat and so much colder than it had been just a short time earlier as we ate pizza together. Why did he have to be like this? Was I really that embarrassing to be seen with at his parties?

"If we're more, then why don't you ever ask me to go wherever you go when you're all dressed up like this?" I asked, hating the needy sound of the words coming from my mouth.

"You wouldn't like these kinds of events."

"Don't dismiss me like this. I don't deserve it."

He pushed past me and walked toward the front door. I caught up with him just as he opened the door to leave, and he turned to face me. "I never said you did. I can't take you to many of the places I have to go, but that doesn't mean I don't want you by my side. It just can't be. That's the way it is."

"Why? I'm good enough for you to basically beg me to work for you and good enough to fuck, but I'm not good enough to be seen with you in public? Is that it?"

He stood silently staring at me for a long time before he finally said, "No. That's not it."

"More evasive answers that say nothing! That's what I get after everything we've done together?" I screamed as tears began streaming down over my cheeks.

My outburst made him cringe, and I saw in his eyes my words had affected him. In a low, almost sad voice, he said, "I told you, Nina. I can give you everything your heart desires, but I can only do it this way."

I watched him walk away and knew I had no answer for that. I'd thought that we were getting closer and he'd begun to open up, but all that was just my imagination. We were the same as we'd been since that first night he showed up in my life.

Tristan Stone and Nina Edwards. Two souls worlds apart, no matter if we lived in the same house or not.

Eleven

I marched up the stairs to the attic, needing to speak to someone from the life I'd left behind. The black phone sat on a wooden box hidden away in the corner, right where I'd left it, just waiting for me to reach out and touch someone. I slowly dialed Jordan's number and put the receiver up to my ear. It rang four times and then I heard her say, "Hey, this is Jordan. Leave me a message and I'll get back to you A.S.A.P."

My disappointment kept me silent for a few seconds and then I mumbled, "Hey, it's me. Nina. I'd say call me back, but I don't know the number and I don't even know if I should be using this phone. I'm still out at Tristan's house and just wanted to talk to someone. I hope everything's okay."

I put the phone down and slumped on the floor, pressing my back up against the wood slat wall. Sadness settled into me as I replayed the conversation Tristan and I had, and I wanted to cry but there weren't any tears. All I felt was a heaviness in my chest, like someone was pressing down on me trying to crush me.

What was I to him? That was what was crushing me. He treated me like a girlfriend, yet I was never to be seen. But I was his employee too, a fact that he seemed to impress upon me always at times when it hurt the most. I existed in some limbo between being someone he was willing to show off to the world and someone who was merely there to do his bidding.

As I sat there with the hard wall pushing against my back and my hurt feelings pressing down on my heart, a sense of regret slowly spread over me. I'd been such a fool! No matter what Jordan believed, good things didn't always happen to good people. That was even assuming I was good. I'd accepted Tristan's offer hoping for more than a job, but that's all the contract had promised. What did that make me? He'd never promised anything in that contract other than all that he'd already given me. I was being paid to do a job. The hope of something more was never part of the deal.

But hadn't he promised in every kiss and every time he'd made love to me that something more was what he wanted too?

Never before had a man tangled my emotions in such knots. When he touched me with those hands so strong yet so tender, he made me feel like I was the most important thing in the world to him. When he was inside me, moaning my name as he clung to me and his body shook from the feelings I created in him, his every word and movement said he cared.

Fuck! How had I let this happen to me? I wasn't some pathetic little schoolgirl who had no idea how things worked. I knew how men were and what they wanted. I may not be supermodel gorgeous, but I'd been with other men and knew the ways of the world. How had I fallen so quickly for Tristan and not seen what was really happening?

The problem was I didn't know what was really happening. To me, not showing me off as his girlfriend was a huge sign he didn't care, but in every other part of our relationship it was clear he felt something for me. What that was I didn't know, but I wasn't sure what I felt either, so I couldn't fault him for that. We'd moved fast since the beginning, so being unsure was fine.

Being ashamed of being seen with me at his parties and events wasn't fine.

The phone ringing jolted me out of my thoughts, and I scrambled to answer it before anyone heard the noise downstairs. Pressing the heavy receiver to my ear, I whispered, "Hello?" and held my breath as the line stayed silent.

"Hello? Is anyone there?"

"Nina? Are you okay? It's Jordan."

I sighed my relief and my heart began its normal beating again. "Jordan, how did you get this number?"

"It came up on my phone. Are you okay? You sounded like something was wrong on the message. What's going on out there?"

"I don't know. I think I made a mistake."

"Why? Did something happen?" she asked, her voice full of concern.

"For the second time since I've been here, he's gone off to some event he needed to wear a tux to and didn't invite me to go. I don't know what I'm doing here or why he's ashamed to be seen with me."

"Oh, sweetie. I'm sure he's not ashamed of you. Look at you. You're beautiful and smart and he's crazy about you."

Sniffling back the first of my tears, I sobbed, "He's not crazy about me. I'll bet anything he's at whatever affair he had to go to with one of those women he takes to things like that. Tomorrow he'll be in the paper standing next to some gorgeous, rail thin supermodel."

"Honey, don't cry. I'm sure there's a reasonable explanation why he doesn't take you to these things. Maybe they're boring and he doesn't want you to think he's boring."

"Jordan, I saw the picture in the paper. Did those people look like they thought that party was boring?"

She was silent for a few moments and then said, "He didn't look like he was having a good time. I remember you saying he didn't look like that with you. Oh, Nina, don't cry. It's going to be okay."

"How? How is it going to be okay? I'm contractually obligated to be around him for the next six months and even though we're sleeping together and he treats me like his girlfriend in private, he never takes me to places where other people like him will be. How is it okay that I'm basically some concubine?"

Jordan said nothing as I sobbed into the phone. What could she say? I was crying over something I couldn't have and she couldn't give it to me or help me get it.

"I feel so stupid, Jordan. I know it's only been a short time, but I can't help the way I feel. Why is this happening to me?"

Quietly, she said what I already knew. "Because you're trusting and good, Nina, and you think other people are the same. It's that small town upbringing in you."

"So I'm destined to be a fool for the rest of my life."

"Honey, I don't think you're foolish for caring for someone. And I'm not sure he doesn't care for you either. I don't know why he doesn't take you around those upper crusts he hangs out with, but I want to give him the benefit of the doubt. Not every guy makes a point to find a girl's best friend and ask her about your favorite foods. I bet he picked one of those and had that for you that first night, didn't he?"

I wiped my tears and hung my head. "He had all of them made for me," I admitted.

"See? I know it hurts now, but give him time. Maybe there's something you don't know about and he's not trying to be hurtful or cruel."

"Some best friend you are. I think you're supposed to tell me to dump his ass and that I can do better," I joked.

"You want that? I'm on it. You know I think you're one of the best people I've ever known, so if this is something you can't handle, you need to end this thing now."

That was easier said than done. "I have a contract, Jordan. I can't end it."

"You have a contract to work for him. That's it. If you don't want to be anything more than an employee, then I say you stick to your guns and be just that. An employee."

Jordan always knew what to say to make me feel better. Sitting up straight, I took a deep breath in. I could do that. There was nothing in the contract that said I had to sleep with him. Well, at least I hoped there wasn't.

"I could do that, couldn't I?"

"You could. But be careful, Nina. You may just get what you wish for and there will be nothing between you and Tristan but work. Is that what you really want?"

That feeling of something heavy pressing on my chest came back with a vengeance at the thought of Tristan being nothing but my boss. I didn't want that, really, but I didn't want to feel like I was something to be ashamed of anymore either.

"I don't know what I want, but I do know I hate feeling like this. If he can't be proud of being with me among people he socializes with, then we shouldn't be together. Maybe if I stop being his whatever I am, he'll see that."

"I don't know, Nina. I think you need to be very careful. I think there's something you don't know and if you do this, you could lose him."

"I'm not sure I have anything to lose, Jordan."

We sat silently for a long moment before she said, "Just take care of yourself, okay? And call me whenever you need me."

"Okay. I will. Oh, and don't call this number again, though. I'm not sure I'll be around to hear it."

"I won't. Just be careful and don't do anything without thinking it through first. Promise me you'll at least do that."

"I promise. I'll talk to you soon."

I hung up the phone and closed my eyes to calm the nervous energy that was already taking over my emotions. The mere thought of ending things with Tristan made my body shake, but I had to take a stand. I couldn't live like this, hoping that what he felt in private would someday be how he'd act in public.

Armed with a plan, I left the attic without looking for more details about Tristan and his family. My mind was intent on keeping strong and focused on what I could do about this. I may not have been able to control what he did, but I was able to control how I reacted.

I awoke from a good night's sleep ready to tackle my problems and the world. Stretching my arms above my head, I focused my eyes and there on the table near the window stood the biggest bouquet of roses I'd ever seen in my life. There had to be fifty long stem roses in the tall glass vase if there was one. Deep red, they looked like they were made of velvet, and their sweet fragrance filled the room.

They were beautiful and screamed of guilt. A tiny flicker of satisfaction ignited inside me at the thought that Tristan had felt bad about not taking me with him. Smiling to myself, I saw a note tacked to the large red bow around the roses. As always, he'd chosen to say what he needed to in a letter. It was very Tristan.

Rolling out of bed, I padded over to the gorgeous gift he'd left me—with a tiny nagging question in my mind of when he'd put them there—and buried my nose in the flowers. They smelled heavenly. I gently touched one of those blood red petals and felt its silky smoothness between my thumb and forefinger. As with everything else Tristan did, they were extraordinary.

The note was folded and in an envelope. I pulled it out and held it up to see a short message that left me speechless.

Dear Nina,

A great job deserves a great reward. Keep up the terrific work!

Love,
Tristan

I felt like a balloon whose knot had been untied. All the good feelings I'd had about the roses and how things stood with Tristan left my body in a huge whoosh until I felt totally empty. This gift was merely an attaboy, a pat on the back for a job well done.

Disgusted, I wrapped my hand around the thick bunch of stems and yanked the entire bouquet out of the vase, spraying everything including myself with water. Thorns stuck into my palm, making the whole thing even worse. There was no garbage can in my room, so I marched the dripping flowers down the hall to the kitchen and threw them away, feeling as if I had struck some kind of blow for women everywhere.

And then as I rejoiced in my newfound strength I turned around and saw Tristan standing there looking hurt, of all things. Those deep brown eyes stared past me at the garbage can with all those flowers sticking out and then at me. I wanted to say something, but no words came to my brain. What had seemed such a triumph now turned into a weird sense of guilt that poked at my gut.

He said nothing as we both stood there staring at one another, and the need to flee suddenly came over me. With all the bravado I could muster, I stomped past him through the doorway and bolted down the hall, sure that if I didn't go as fast as my legs would take me that they'd begin shaking uncontrollably and give out from underneath me. By the time I reached my room, I was out of breath and so confused I didn't know whether to congratulate myself or feel bad for hurting his feelings.

As I stood there, my back pressed against the closed door, I told myself I was doing the right thing. *Don't forget how you felt when he walked out that door last night.*

And then an idea hit me. If I could just remember that feeling for another twenty-two weeks, everything would be fine. That was easier said than done, though.

I took my time getting dressed, part of me dreading the fact that I had to face him at some point and he might have that wounded puppy look in his eyes. Another part of me worried that I wouldn't be able to keep up my strength when he touched me or did any of the dozens of things that made me crazy about him.

Jesus, if he got close enough for me to smell his delicious cologne, I knew I'd likely be lost. And if he gave me one of his sweet smiles, I didn't know if I'd be able to remember anything, much less how I felt the night before.

It was going to be a long six months.

"Nina, we'll be leaving early tomorrow morning and we'll be gone for two days and nights, so feel free to take today to get anything you need done."

His tone was decidedly cool, which in a strange way made me feel better. Now he got to feel how I did. Plus, if he stayed upset with me, it could make staying away from him much easier. Things were looking up.

How I was going to handle the sleeping arrangements in Dallas was beyond me, but I'd cross that bridge when I came to it.

"Fine. I have some laundry to do. If that's all, I'll see you tomorrow."

I waited for him to say something, but he just stared vacantly at me and proceeded to begin typing on his laptop. If he had any thoughts on what had happened to the flowers, he wasn't saying and I wasn't asking.

Rebuffing Rogers' offer to wash my clothes, I loaded up the machine and returned to my room. While my laundry did its thing in the washer, I checked my email and found a message from Jordan. All she'd typed was a link so I clicked it, looking forward to some cute pictures of kittens or even some lame chain letter. Anything to take my mind off Tristan.

As the page opened, I sat stunned at what appeared on my laptop's screen. There he stood in his tux looking like he was some marble statue of himself, a blonde on his arm, and other beautiful people around him at some event. I read the caption, needing to know what he'd done the night before.

"Stone Worldwide Charity Benefit at the Fairview Grand Hotel"

My heart sank at the sight of him holding the woman's arm. Some gorgeous blond woman's arm. I couldn't take my eyes off the screen, first analyzing every last inch of his date and then fixating on him. Her hair was the pale color blonde that appeared naturally on Scandinavian women and for a price on anyone who could afford a Fifth Avenue salon. I couldn't tell what color her eyes were, but I was sure any description of them would include the word sparkling. Perfect, brilliant white teeth sat in a mouth with bee stung lips that made me think of those bright red wax lips I used to buy at the candy store as a child. Worst of all, she looked genuinely happy and at home on his arm as they posed for the camera.

He looked less comfortable, which at least was one saving grace. In fact, he looked just as he had in the last picture Jordan had shown me of him on the gossip page and the ones I'd seen of him online back at the apartment. His eyes were cold, and that smile that never failed to melt my heart was nowhere to be found. He was just as gorgeous as always, but he seemed like a shell of the person I'd grown to know.

I so wanted that to make me feel better, but it was fleeting and it didn't take long before that horrible feeling like someone had carved out my insides was back. He'd left me behind to go to some charity event with some blonde bombshell, and there was no denying that. The proof was sitting on my laptop screen staring at me, mocking me.

Closing the tab, I hung my head and willed the tears to come. At least if I cried there was a chance I'd feel better eventually. Crying was useful for that. But nothing came. My emotions were telling my eyes that it was time to do the crying thing, but they didn't seem to get the message. They simply continued to stare at the screen, as if something was going to pop up to make all the emptiness I felt go away.

It was no use. I officially felt like shit and had the photographic evidence to prove that the man who I'd thought was my boyfriend was actually someone who didn't care for me enough to take me to his fancy society function so he'd found a gorgeous woman to go in my place.

And it wasn't even noon yet.

I checked my email once more with the hope that maybe Alex had sent me a message. At moments when a girl felt like nobody loved her, it was always nice to hear from a guy who liked her, even if she wasn't crazy about him. I didn't dislike Alex, but I wasn't really interested in him either. For what it was worth, he was beginning to look like a very good prospect after the whole Tristan thing, though. There was something to be said for a man who was straightforward.

Alex hadn't sent anything, but just as I went to close my laptop, I saw an email come in from Tristan with the subject "Hi." Unsure I wanted to know what it said but unable to stop myself, I opened it and began to read.

Dear Nina,

I'm looking forward to our trip to Dallas tomorrow. If you'd like to talk about it, I'll be back at five. Rogers hung your picture up this morning. It's perfect and exactly what I want to see when I open my eyes.

Love,

Tristan

Love, Tristan. It should have read as a command, Love Tristan, since that was what it seemed like. I closed my laptop and decided then and there I wouldn't be available to talk at five or any other time that day.

I'd made the decision to go down this path and I was damned if I was going to be swayed from it by his soulful eyes, sweet words, and every other weapon in his arsenal of seduction. If I wasn't good enough to be seen with in public, then he wasn't going to see much of me in private either.

Twelve

It's amazing how being stubborn always made situations so much worse. I quickly found that I was playing in a much bigger league with Tristan than I was used to. After avoiding him all the previous day, if I was thinking that a new day would make everything better, I was sadly mistaken. It seemed that Tristan Stone could be very much the personification of his last name at times and quite able to deal out the silent treatment as well as he took it.

Unfortunately for me, I was more big talk than anything else and the plane ride in his private jet nearly broke my resolve. I'd only been on a plane twice before and never anyone's private jet, so my excitement made the words want to come bubbling up out of my mouth. What stopped them was Tristan's icy demeanor as he sat across from me, only rarely acknowledging my presence with a knowing look and never saying a thing to me the entire three and a half hours it took to get from New York to Dallas.

If I hated the feeling I'd had that night when he'd left to go to the charity benefit, I hated this more. It was like torture to be so close to him and know that he could basically ignore me even as I sat less than three feet away.

He even did the silent treatment well. I sat there across from him admiring how good he looked and wondered if there anything this guy wasn't incredible at.

By the time we arrived at the hotel, I was chomping at the bit to say something, anything, but his hard expression made it clear he didn't feel the same urge. So I remained silent.

The Richmont Dallas was every bit as luxurious as Tristan's New York hotel, even if it had a more distinctly western feel to it. I had no idea what suite I'd be working in and followed his lead as we made our way to the rooms on the ninth floor. When he finally stopped at a door at the end of the hallway, I hoped that now I could at least get lost in work.

Two steps in and I understood his joke from the restaurant. Whoever had designed the Presidential Suite at the Richmont Dallas had been in love with the color gold and all its varied golden hues. From the draperies to the upholstery to the carpet, the color gold was everywhere.

"Golden opportunity," I mumbled accidentally. "Funny guy."

I realized I'd broken my silence and turned to see him smiling at me. There was that warm smile that had a way of breaking down the walls I'd tried so hard to build around my heart. It went all the way up to his eyes, making the skin around them crinkle slightly at the corners.

"I have faith in you, Nina. All you have to do is find art that will make this room appear less gold."

Looking around, I wondered if he'd given me an impossible task. "Wouldn't it just be easier to redecorate?"

His smile grew wider. "Probably, but then I wouldn't have had any reason to bring you here to Dallas."

And with that he rendered me speechless again. I didn't want to be a slave to his charms. I just didn't have a choice.

Swallowing hard, I tried to keep myself all business. "Must I keep to any particular style or period?"

He shook his head. "No. Make your choices based on what you believe will complete this suite and take the attention away from all this gold."

"How many pieces can I choose? This suite is four rooms."

Tristan scanned the rooms in front of us. "As many as you like. My faith is entirely in you."

"Will we be staying here? There are two bedrooms, I see."

He moved around me and walked over to the bar. Pouring himself a drink, he lifted his glass in the direction of the two bedrooms. "So we're to continue our living arrangements from the house?"

His voice had an edge to it. He was unhappy about my insistence on making him understand how much he'd hurt me. I imagined he didn't have many people in his life who dared to do that. I also sensed he wasn't a man who liked being made to do anything.

"I better get going. I've got my work cut out for me," I said with a forced smile.

Tristan took a sip of his scotch. "Dinner is at six, Nina. I hope I'll see you there."

Nothing in the way he said that told me he hoped anything. It was a clear command that I join him for dinner. What wasn't clear was if I'd obey.

Just a few hours later, I'd found some great pieces and was hungry, despite my wishing I wasn't. Tristan hadn't bothered me while I'd worked, but now as six o'clock loomed, I heard him in the outside room pouring himself another drink. The aroma of the dinner he'd ordered in wafted through to where I stood looking at myself in the mirror.

I would have known that delicious smell anywhere. He'd ordered roast beef.

A peace offering?

I stared into the mirror at the face that looked back at me and asked her, "What do I do? Do I let him back in?"

My reflection didn't have the answer either, and I walked out to find Tristan standing in the middle of the main room in a tux. My heart sank. He was going to do it again. I'd sit there alone in that room eating my roast beef he'd so graciously given me while he spent the night out on the town in Dallas with another gorgeous blonde or brunette.

Before I could say all the terrible things that were begging to be let out of my mouth, he took my hand and kissed the back of it. "I seem to be a little overdressed. Perhaps you should change so I'm not all alone in this getup."

"Why? So you can go meet up with your blond girlfriend and I can sit here like some teenage girl stood up for the prom?" I snapped.

"Blonde?" he asked, looking genuinely confused as to how I knew who he'd spent his time with the night before.

"I saw your girlfriend. Nice lips. Does she mind that you look like a statue when you're with her? I think I have it all figured out, Tristan. You want someone who looks like her for in public, but you want someone who makes you smile like I do in private. Well, sorry. Maybe you should figure out how you can make her do the things that make you happy because I won't be some in-house concubine you keep hidden from everyone but your fucking butler and other household help."

My outburst surprised him for a moment, but then he just smiled. "Oh, you mean Janelle. You misunderstand. She's not my girlfriend. She's paid to be with me at those affairs."

"Paid? You pay a hooker to go with you instead of taking me? And this is supposed to make me feel better?"

A look of distaste crossed his features. "No. She's not a hooker. She's a..."

Waving my hand, I cut him off. "Fine. You're too wealthy for a hooker. What do they call them for someone like you? Call girls? Escorts? Either way, it's still you paying someone to be there instead of being seen with me."

"Nina, you've got it all wrong. She's not there to have sex with or even to date. She's there to act."

"Act? What do you mean, act?" I asked, completed baffled.

"Janelle is an actress who's an employee of mine. My company compensates her to appear at functions like the charity event and act like my girlfriend. There are about half a dozen who I pay very well to pretend I'm with them. Their entire job is to be at my beck and call so I don't have to attend those things alone. I can't imagine it's that bad a job, especially since I pay them handsomely."

I sat down on the chair nearby and struggled to process what he was saying. Who hired people to act like their dates? Jordan was right. Wealthy people did hire people to do their work for them.

"Why not just have a real girlfriend and take her? Is it because I'm not stunning like them?" I hadn't meant to sound so pathetic, but the words had come out far sadder than intended.

He knelt down in front of me and took my hands in his. "I don't take real girlfriends to those things because the press is always there and I learned my lesson a long time ago. It doesn't take long before having to be in front of cameras all the time takes its toll on a relationship. The board of directors likes me to present a successful image, and to them that means having a woman on my arm at all official events."

"Oh. So they aren't even ex-girlfriends?"

Smiling, he said, "No. Just actresses who agree to act like my girlfriends for a lot of money." He leaned forward and kissed me softly on the lips before he whispered, "You are stunning, Nina. And unlike those women, I want to be with you."

I couldn't stop the smile that broke out on my face. His words made me want to beam with happiness. "I don't know if you know this, but it's pretty obvious you don't want to be with them in all the pictures. You look like a really miserable boyfriend to those women. I'm not sure anyone's believing that you really like them."

"Maybe I should look happier? I could pretend better, I guess," he said with fake sincerity.

"No, no. You're doing a great job. Leave the acting up to the professionals," I joked.

He kissed me again, making my stomach do flips as his tongue slid across my lower lip. "I couldn't pretend to like them more than I do anyway."

"I think I feel bad for them now, Tristan. I know what it's like to work for you. To not even get a smile would make the job awful."

Looking up at me with his soulful eyes, he said, "I save my smiles for you. I hope what I've ordered for dinner means you'll give me one. It's roast beef, one of your favorites, if I'm not mistaken."

"It is, but you know that."

"Of course. Let's eat and then see what Dallas has to offer," he said as he stood and we walked toward the table.

"I've never been here, so I'm a newbie in the Lone Star state," I joked, trying to sound clever.

"Hmm, a virgin. I promise I'll go easy."

I sat down across from him and giggled. "Was that a joke?"

He leveled his gaze on me, looking sexier than a man ever should. "It happens sometimes."

As I reached for a piece of roast beef, I said, "I like it."

Tristan licked his lips and grinned at me. "I'll keep that in mind."

We visited Fountain Place, a beautiful park with lit fountains and pathways where we walked and talked about the gold rooms and what I thought might work to take the focus off the overwhelming use of the color. Tristan listened to each idea as if he were truly interested, but I had the sense that I could have been talking about any topic and he'd have been happy. Just as when we'd gone for the ride in his car that first night, I had the feeling he simply wanted company.

He stopped and sat on one of the benches near one of the streams, holding his hand out for me to join him. As we watched the water slowly move by and the fountains leap in the air, he put his arm around me and I leaned against him. It was a very common gesture but strangely unique between us. For as long as we sat there,

I felt like we were moving toward something familiar I could relate to.

When we returned from our walk, he left to attend to some business calls that had come in while we were enjoying our time together. I sat on the sofa in the living room and stared at the gold all around me, mulling over my ideas for how to fix his art problem. Slowly, my mind drifted to the sleeping arrangements and the two bedrooms in the suite.

Should I go back to the way it had been before, now that I knew he wasn't spending his time with other women at those events? Maybe it was better if we kept sex out of our relationship for a while since it only seemed to muddy the waters between us.

I closed my eyes and thought about Tristan in his tux kneeling in front of me. Who was I kidding? My physical attraction to him had been so intertwined with what I felt for him from the moment I'd first seen him that the mere thought of denying how he affected me was laughable.

The man himself came back and interrupted my deep thoughts about not having sex with him, and I quickly knew it was not going to happen. He sat down next to me and leaned back against the sofa. Loosening his bow tie, he let the two ends hang around his neck and undid his top button.

Closing his eyes, he whispered, "Is it ever possible to atone for the sins of the past?"

I watched his mouth turn down in a scowl that marred his handsome face and wondered what his statement referred to. It sounded far too serious to be about the misunderstanding between the two of us, but I didn't feel comfortable asking any questions.

Reaching out, I lightly ran my fingertips over his closely cut brown hair, loving its softness against my skin. Seeing him like this bothered me, made me want to fix whatever was wrong, but he kept it inside him, locked away from where I could reach it.

His eyes still closed, he pulled me onto his lap and held me close. We sat together, our bodies pressed against one another, without saying a thing. It wasn't sexual but simple closeness. It was sweet solitude, and I wanted to believe for those moments I was able to give him some respite from what troubled him. When he finally spoke again, any trace of what had bothered him was gone, and he was the Tristan who could seduce me with just a few words or a glance from those beautiful eyes.

Cradling my face in his hands, he said in a voice full of emotion, "Nina, I want you in my bed tonight and every night. I don't know if things should be moving so fast or where we'll be in the future, but I don't want to spend another night without you."

I stared into his eyes and saw that flicker of apprehension I'd seen before. Did he actually fear that I'd deny him what I so desperately wanted myself?

I kissed his lips tenderly and sensed his desire grow inside him as he responded to my unspoken answer to be his with a kiss so passionate it nearly took my breath away. Pulling my body to his, he moaned into my mouth a sound so full of need that it sent an ache to the deepest part of me. I wanted to be the one to fulfill that need.

I tilted my hips into his body, and I was sure he knew how excited he got me, but I didn't care. This was who I was and I wanted him to accept me like I'd accepted him. He slid his finger under the cotton fabric and through my drenched slit, making my breath hitch.

"You're so wet," he groaned next to my ear. "I love how fucking wet you get when I touch you."

I tried to ignore his use of the word love again in relation to yet another thing I did, but I couldn't. I hung on every syllable he uttered, thrilled by the words he strung together as he stroked my tender flesh. The deep sound of them as he told me that he loved something about me only excited me more.

His mouth plundered mine, his tongue snaking in and out as he flicked the tip against my lips. I clung to him, my fingernails scraping across his neck as he inched me toward that feeling my body begged for. He knew what he did to me, and I loved it. He was power and control and expertly used them both to make me want him more than I'd ever wanted anyone else.

Sliding one finger and then another into me, he rubbed his fingertips over that one spot deep inside that sent my body into overdrive. I rocked back and forth on his hand, riding it as I desperately searched for relief from the need he created in me.

A vibrating sound jarred me from my ecstasy, and he pulled his phone out of his jacket pocket, never stopping his fingers' movement inside me. A quick look and then he set the phone on the table beside him, still focused on me.

"Do you need to get that?" I half-heartedly asked as I continued to ride those incredible fingers.

His dark gaze fixed on me and he shook his head. "That can wait. I want to see you get off first. Let yourself go, Nina."

I loved when he talked like that, his voice deep and husky telling me he wanted to give me pleasure. Spreading my legs wider, I rubbed my pussy against the heel of his hand, sending waves of bliss rocketing through me. He thrust hard into me, inching me closer and closer to orgasm, and I moaned at the feel of the first delicious contraction of my body around his fingers.

Tristan cradled the back of my head with his other hand, forcing me to meet his stare as I began to come. I wanted to close my eyes, afraid of what I looked like as he took me over that edge, but he sternly ordered me to keep them open.

"Look at me, Nina. I want to watch you come from just my fingers inside you. Don't look away, baby."

My orgasm roared through me and I stared into those gorgeous eyes completely focused on me and my happiness. He watched my every movement, whispering sexy little things as my release rolled on and on.

When my body finally finished and only tiny quakes continued to flutter through me, I collapsed on top of him, panting and weak. In my ear, he whispered, "I love watching you come. I want to see that again when my cock is deep inside you. Choose one of the bedrooms and wait for me. I'll be right back."

Pouting at his leaving, I moaned, "Don't go. Whatever it is, it can't be that important at this time of night."

"I promise I won't be long. And when I get back, I want to see that sexy look in your eyes again."

I slid off his lap onto the sofa and watched as he took his phone and left the suite. Frustrated, I trudged off to the closest bedroom and flopped down on the bed. I'd barely slipped out of my dress and he was back standing in the doorway grinning at me as I lay there in just my panties and bra.

"That was fast," I said with a smile, thankful that he'd gotten rid of whoever had called him so quickly.

He slipped out of his jacket and slowly unbuttoned his shirt as he circled the bed like an animal stalking his prey. "I had to take that. Some things can't be handled by anyone else." He shrugged his shirt off his shoulders and leaned down to kiss my lips. "Like what I'm about to do."

"More work?" I asked with a smile.

He climbed onto the bed and pulled me to him. "No more work. Just pleasure."

"Mmmm, I like that," I cooed as he kissed my neck, his tongue gliding gently over my skin and sending shivers over my body as we began to make love.

We laid there in each other's arms, and I looked up at him to see him staring vacantly off in the distance. "Hey, you look like you're a million miles away."

"Not that far. You're there too," he said quietly, but his eyes still looked so far away from our bed.

Running my finger over his tattoo, I traced the intricate design across his chest and over his shoulder, feeling a raised scar just above his heart. I'd never seen it before, but now it was as obvious as the tattoo.

"What's this from, Tristan?"

He looked down at where my finger touched and frowned. "That's where a piece of metal went through me."

"That close to your heart? What happened?" I asked, horrified at the thought that anything had come so close to killing him.

"I was in a plane crash with my brother and parents. I was impaled by a metal rod which pinned me to the seat. The doctors said it missed my heart and everything else by millimeters."

His voice was full of sadness, and I squeezed him tightly to me. I was afraid to hear any more, but he continued. "I sat in that seat, unable to move, as my family died around me. My twin brother was sitting behind me and was stabbed by the metal rod, but it hit him right in the heart."

"Oh, Tristan. I'm so sorry."

My words felt so inadequate, but he wasn't listening to them. He continued to talk, his voice low and sad. "My mother died instantly, thank God, but I watched as my father lingered in agony, crying out for someone to help us. I couldn't speak, couldn't let him know that I was still there right behind him so he wasn't alone. I don't know how long he lived, but by the time the crews arrived, he was gone too. I didn't know about Taylor until they finally got me out and days later told me the metal rod that had somehow missed my heart had found his."

"When was this?" I asked, thinking about that portrait of a happy family sitting in a dark trunk in the attic.

"It will be four years this December. That's how I ended up as the CEO of Stone Worldwide. I never wanted to be that. That was Taylor's dream. He wanted to take over when my father retired. He'd groomed him since high school. Remember when I told you I attended Wharton? So did my brother, except he graduated. He'd just finished his MBA when the accident happened."

His story broke my heart. I understood all too well what it felt like to lose someone you loved. My mother had died when I was just a little girl, and my father had been murdered just around the time Tristan's family had died. To watch them in agony and not be able to do anything to save them was more than I'd be able to stand.

Tears filled my eyes at the thought of him sitting there, helpless to save the people he loved, injured, and not knowing if he too was going to die. Gently stroking his cheek, I kissed him, wanting to take away the pain he held inside. "I had no idea, Tristan. I'm sorry."

He shrugged and pressed a smile onto his lips. "So I'm all alone, I guess."

I cradled his face in my hands, looking into his sad eyes. "You're never alone. I'm here, and the ones we love never really leave us. As long as they stay in our hearts, they're with us."

His smile softened. "That sounds like something my mother would say. My father and brother would never think that way."

"Are you more like your mother?" I asked, curious about the beautiful woman with the hint of sadness in her face I'd seen in that portrait.

He closed his eyes. "I don't know. I never felt like I was like my father or brother, so if I was like anyone it was my mother."

"I never really got to know my mother. She died when I was five, and from then on, it was just my father, my sister, and me."

Tristan's opened his eyes and turned to me, pushing my hair off my face to kiss my cheek. "I'm sorry about your mother. I guess I was lucky to have twenty-five years with mine."

"I lost my father right around the time you lost yours. Someone gunned him down one night while he was working on his latest exposé of some industrial problem or something. I don't remember. All I know is that one night he was gone, and I felt like I was alone. But then I remembered that he told me when my mother died that the people we love never leave us as long as we keep loving them. It's hard, but I think he was right. It's four years next month, but he's still with me."

Pulling me closer to him, Tristan's body tensed. "I'm sorry, Nina. I guess we've both seen a lot."

Thirteen

"So what do you think?" I asked nervously as Tristan stood next to me, his arms folded.

His face was expressionless, something I suspected was intentional, even though the twinkle in his eye made me believe he liked my choices for the Presidential Suite. The series of prints showing hand painted blue and white vases was simple, but just the thumbnails on my laptop screen gave the overly golden room an entirely different and more pleasant feeling.

I knew I was feeling pleased with my choices. Now it was just up to Tristan to give them his seal of approval.

His silence was unnerving, though. While I didn't mind standing there staring at him, I could think of better things to do that involved the two of us together.

"Well?" I asked again, hoping to egg him on.

Tristan turned toward me and smiled. "I don't think so. I'm not in favor of these."

Everything in my body sagged for a moment before my brain clicked into defensive mode. What did he mean he wasn't in favor of them? "What's wrong with them?"

He tilted his head as he looked at the pictures again. "They don't work for the feeling of the place."

"You mean the gold feeling?" I asked sarcastically.

A slow smile spread on his lips as he straightened his head and looked over at me. "I like the colors, but the images aren't right. You'll have to try again."

"Hmmmph."

"What was that you said?" he asked, obviously teasing me.

I stuck my tongue out and pouted. "Nothing. I have work to do. Art doesn't just happen you know, Mr. Stone. When I'm ready, I'll request your approval again."

He flashed me that warm and sexy smile that made me think about him on top of me in bed. "Thank you, Ms. Edwards. When you need me, I'll be in the other room. Dinner is at five."

Grabbing my laptop off the desk, I turned and walked toward the end of the suite as I yelled back, "I'll be hungry by then, so I can see me showing up, Mr. Stone."

I didn't look back to see his expression at my comment because it was too hard to keep my hands off him when he looked so good. How anyone could make a pair of black pants, brown dress shirt and a tie look so incredible was beyond me. Suddenly, an idea jumped into my mind. Who picked them out?

My curiosity quickly took up every inch of my mind, and I returned to the outer room to find him standing and reading the newspaper. "Tristan, do you buy your own clothes?"

He looked up from the Wall Street Journal and raised his eyebrows. "No."

"Oh." That wasn't the answer I wanted to hear. Now I had a vision of one of his actresses trolling upscale men's stores picking out his wardrobe with loving care. Or worse, one of them picking out his clothes and then calling him like Tristan had called me in the dressing room. I was nothing if not ordinary when it came to the green-eyed monster.

"I have a personal shopper handle that. His name is Angelo. Is there something you want me to tell him for the next time he does my shopping?"

For the moment, my ugly jealousy crawled back into the dark recesses of my mind and I rejoiced at the idea that Angelo was the one with the incredible taste. "No. He's doing a great job."

Tristan put the newspaper on the coffee table and came to stand in front of me. Looking down, he ran his finger along my jaw line. "I'm sure Angelo will be happy to know my girlfriend approves of his choices."

Girlfriend. I was his girlfriend.

"Well, at least *he* is successful with his choices," I joked as I turned to go back to my work, pleased with that one word he'd said with such ease.

"Okay, this time you're going to be blown away by my choices. I see what the problem was with the first group, but this will get the Tristan Stone seal of approval. I know it."

To be honest, much of what I'd said was bluster, but I did want him to approve of my art choices. As much as I truly wished to succeed at my job, I wanted more to make Tristan as happy as he made me.

I held my arm out like a hostess on a game show and introduced him to the thumbnails of a series of five watercolors of blue and white Mexican owls. Charming yet sophisticated, they were more in line with a southwestern motif and still helped to diminish the effect of the overwhelming gold found everywhere around me. Now all I had to do was convince Tristan they were as perfect as I thought they were.

"Let me introduce you to the Mexican owls."

He leaned down and rested his palms on the table as he studied the pictures of those sweet birds. I saw his eyes move slowly from left to right across the screen before he turned his head to look at me. "Okay. Tell me why these are perfect."

"These are pictures of owl pottery from Mexico. Containing a number of different shades of blue from navy to royal blue along with pure white, they're examples of Mexican folk art, as can be seen in the floral motif painted on the part of the bird's body below his head. As we're in Texas, which has been heavily influenced by Mexican culture, the pictures of these pieces work with the area, and the blue and white colors are perfect to alleviate the overpowering gold your decorator seemed to fall in love with courtesy of your checkbook."

His gaze never wavered from mine as I spoke, and when I was done, he looked back at the pictures and stood to his full height. "Very nice, Nina. Very nice. Thank you."

As we were in work mode, I suspected that was all I was going to get. Perhaps I'd receive a bouquet of flowers tomorrow, though. That might be nice again, and this time I wouldn't throw them in the trash.

"Thank you, sir," I said playfully. "I'm pleased you like my choices for your suite."

"Sir?" he asked in a stern voice.

My face warmed at his question, which told me I might have taken my teasing too far. "I was just playing around. You know. Lightening the mood a little."

He looked down at the watch on his right wrist for the time and lifted his eyes to me. "It's five, so we're not working anymore. Are you hungry?"

"Not really."

"Good. I've decided we're flying back to New York early, so we'll take off in about an hour. My staff will make sure our bags are taken to the plane, so we best be on our way."

"Tristan, I haven't packed anything. All of my things are all over the bathroom," I said in protest, uncomfortable with the idea of one of his people touching things like my razor and moisturizer.

"I'll buy you replacements when we get back then."

I wrinkled my nose at the thought of wasting money like that. "That's ridiculous. Why can't I just pack my things myself? Why would you spend money when you don't have to?"

He lifted my chin with his fingertip and smiled at me. "I'd spend all I have if it made you happy, Nina."

Wrapping my hand around his finger, I brought it to my mouth in a kiss. "You don't have to spend money on me like that. I mean, I love the clothes, and it was very sweet of you to buy me all that new shampoo and conditioner when I moved in, but you don't have to. I thought that wealthy people had money because they didn't spend it."

"Wealthy people have money because they spend it wisely. I think buying things to make you happy is very wise."

There was no point in fighting him on this. He had decided the issue, and I was expected to be content with it. In truth, I knew there were far worse things than a man buying me whatever made me happy whenever I wanted it.

But the stubborn part of me still thought it foolish.

"I'd be happy if you never bought me a thing again just knowing you love me."

And as soon as the L word left my mouth, I felt like crawling into a hole. He'd never said he loved me—just written it—and the look on his face screamed that he hadn't meant what I'd hoped when he used it in his notes.

That same look of fear I'd seen in his eyes a few times before returned, and he quickly looked away toward the bedroom. "Well, you better get your things packed so the bags can be ready. We're going to be late if we don't get moving."

I'd done it. Ruined everything by using the L word too soon, and now I felt like a fool. I hurried into the bedroom to escape the look of discomfort in his eyes. He was probably thinking of how he could let me down easy. He could be sweet like that. Maybe he'd disappear back to the city, leaving me out in the country. Or maybe he'd suddenly have a lot of work functions to attend with the actresses, again leaving me alone out in the country.

Whatever he would do, I cringed at what I'd done. I knew better than to introduce that word into a relationship so early. Nothing worked better to send a man running for the hills than to start talking about love this soon, and I'd gone and done it. What an ass I was!

I quickly packed my things and returned to the living room. Tristan stood waiting, and as we left, I had the feeling whatever progress we'd made while we'd been in Dallas was gone, blacked out by my silly slip of the tongue.

Men were funny when it came to expressing what they felt, but a woman knew the truth about the man she was with if she cared to pay attention. Tristan was very much the same man he'd been with me all along as we rode on the plane and the drive back to the house. He laughed at my forced jokes, which was nice since I felt like I was walking on eggshells, and even held my hand as we rode from JFK to his house upstate.

But there was something different about him. It was subtle, but it was there.

By the time we got back to the house, all I wanted to do was skulk into my bedroom with my tail between my legs and hope that a little time apart would repair any damage I'd done. I wouldn't have blamed him if he wanted to escape to the city. He seemed as interested as I was in going off on his own and made some excuse about having work to do as we walked through the front door.

A quick shower and I was ready to crawl under the covers. I changed into my t-shirt and shorts and flopped down on the bed, physically and emotionally exhausted. How he travelled like he did baffled me. Just the trip to his penthouse and then to Dallas had worn me out, but I knew what I was feeling was more in my heart than in my bones.

Regret was exhausting. And for two days and two nights it nearly wore me out. I busied myself with researching possible art groupings for future suites and penthouses, just trying to keep my mind off what had happened. Noticeably absent were any flowers in my room when I woke up either morning.

On the third day, I checked my email and saw that Jordan had sent me a message. I stared at my laptop's screen in terror, praying to God that she hadn't sent me anymore links to pictures of Tristan and stunning women. Finally, after a long tug of war between wanting to know what she'd sent and pure, unadulterated dread at the thought of him with someone else, I clicked on the little envelope icon and breathed a tremendous sigh of relief. No Tristan and hot women, thankfully. Just an email to tell me I needed to pay my cell phone bill. Seems I'd forgotten to pay it and the fine people at the phone company had been good enough to send me a reminder that had ended up in her mailbox that morning.

I tapped out a quick thank you email, making sure I let her know that everything was so much better now between Tristan and me. Lying to my best friend made me feel worse, but I didn't know how to explain that I'd actually succeeded in finding out he wasn't with other women only to ruin everything with a rookie dating mistake.

Despite not having even a bar of service out there, I had to keep my cell. I may have been out in the country, but I wasn't back in time. A few clicks and I was at my bank's online site with the hope that I had enough in my account to pay my bill. Poor and I were long time friends since college, but if Tristan had deposited the $20,000 advance in my account, I'd be in better shape than ever before.

I logged in and for the first time in my life, a number took my breath away. My eyes were glued to the page for so long they began to dry out. I rubbed them and opened them again to see my bank account had a balance of $25,085.47.

There must have been some mistake. Over and over I told myself those exact words as I clicked to check the source of the deposits. One for $20,000 had been made the day I'd signed my contract and one the day after we returned from Dallas for $5000. But what was that for? I wasn't due to be paid for my first month for weeks.

A knock on my door that night shook me out of feeling sorry for myself and my lovelife woes, and I opened it to see Tristan standing there in just the silk pajama bottoms I'd seen draped over a chair in his room.

"I'd hoped you'd be in my room," he said with that innocence that sometimes seeped into his voice.

I looked away and bit my lip nervously. "I just figured you'd want to be alone. I mean...well, I thought maybe you'd be back at the penthouse instead of staying here."

"Why?"

His question made me turn to look at him, and he seemed genuinely confused by what I thought. There was a gentleness in his eyes that made me want to say what was on my mind, so I came clean.

"I'm so sorry I said that back in Dallas, Tristan. I didn't mean to put words in your mouth. It's only been a short time that we've known each other. I mean, it feels much longer since we've spent so much time together, but..." I let my sentence trail off and finally said, "I didn't mean that I actually thought you felt that way."

He extended his hand and held it out for me to take it. "Come with me."

I took a deep breath and slowly lifted my hand to place it in his. He closed his fingers around mine and began leading me to his bedroom. We said nothing as we walked, until finally he closed the door behind me and whispered, "You belong here with me. And you don't have to be sorry for anything you said."

For the moment, remaining silent seemed like the best idea. What could I say? That I wished he really felt that way about me so I wouldn't feel ridiculous for falling in love with someone after only two weeks? I knew how that would sound. I mean, I'd been the person who'd told friends time and again that it took months or even years to truly fall in love with someone and here I was full on, head over heels in love with Tristan Stone, no less.

He sat on the edge of the bed and looked over at me like he wondered what I was doing all the way over near the door. The chair near the window was empty, so I sat there, so not wanting to talk about this anymore.

"I think we should talk."

Ugh. There it was. The international signal for what's about to come next is going to rock your world. I said nothing while my stomach dropped and I swallowed hard. I had no idea what he'd say, but as the seconds ticked by and he still hadn't said a word, the room began to feel like it was shrinking around me. The fun house feeling was anything but fun.

"This has been moving pretty fast, Nina. I didn't intend on things getting to where they are so quickly."

It was so much worse than anything I'd imagined. He was dancing around the elephant in the room, but it was no use. He was breaking up with me. This explained the extra five grand. That was my parting gift, like the losers got on game shows.

I wanted to run away and hide. Standing up, I tried to steady my legs and get the hell out of there, but I didn't take three steps toward the door before they gave out and I was in a heap on the floor. All I could think was that was the perfect moment to be struck by lightning and disintegrated into dust.

"Nina, open your eyes. Talk to me."

Tristan's voice was laced with concern, and I opened my eyes to see a matching look on his face. Or maybe it was pity. Either way, I was still there in one piece and he was leaning over me.

I propped myself up on my elbows and plastered a smile on my face. "I'm fine. Just slipped. No big deal."

Scooping me up from the floor, he lifted me in his arms and onto the bed. He was so gentle, but I was even more convinced that he was breaking up with me. Now he probably just felt bad.

"Are you okay?"

Silently, I nodded. I was fine. The same old Nina I'd always been and always would be. It had been fun and the thought of being Tristan Stone's girlfriend had been very seductive, but it was over now.

"Tristan, I think I should go back to my room now. I don't feel so well."

"You should stay here where I can be sure you're okay," he said so sweetly with that tender smile that melted my heart.

I looked up at him and suddenly everything came flowing out of me. "Why? I know what you're going to do. My falling shouldn't stop you. I understand. Guys like you don't need or want just one woman. You can have anyone in the world, so why stick with just one?"

His eyebrows lifted as I spoke and he grimaced. I guess the truth hurt. Well, I understood that.

"What are you talking about?"

"Don't play dumb with me. You're breaking up with me. Don't worry. I'll be fine. It's not like we were together for years. I won't make any trouble for you either."

"Oh. Well, that's good. I wouldn't want to have to sic my lawyers on you."

Before I could tell him that I thought he was acting really shitty, he smiled and smoothed my hair from my face. "I wasn't breaking up with you. I just wanted to talk after the awkward business the other day."

I sat up and stared at him, confused. He wasn't breaking up with me? "What do you mean? I thought I scared you off with the L word."

He sat down next to me and hung his head. "I have to admit I did freak out a little when you said it. Sorry about that."

"I just said it because you kept writing it in your notes. It wasn't like it was a big deal."

Tristan turned to face me. "It is a big deal. I don't say I love you to every woman I date."

"That's good to hear," I mumbled.

"I don't think one word is a reason for two people to stop spending time together, Nina."

"I guess not." Sitting up, I blew the air out of my cheeks. "So what do we do now?"

"We could forget anything like this ever happened and continue like we were," he said in a hopeful voice.

"What were we doing, Tristan? You meet me one night, convince me to work for you, make me move in here, all the while sleeping with me. I haven't dated thousands of men, but I can safely assume most people don't call that dating."

"I'm not most people, Nina." He leaned toward me and pressed his forehead to mine. "I need you to trust me. This is the only way I can do this. Can you trust me?"

I closed my eyes and imagined not having Tristan Stone in my life. Suddenly, my chest felt hollow, like my heart had been drained of every drop of blood and all that was left was an empty, useless part of me. I didn't want to lose Tristan. I wasn't sure what this was we had together, but being with him was so much better than not.

"Yeah. I can."

He kissed me long and deep, making my legs go weak all over again, but for a good reason this time. We may not have been at the place where we said we loved each other, but it felt like it.

And I loved that.

Fourteen

The summer went by and every day Tristan and I grew closer and closer. By the time we'd known each other for four months, I could honestly say I loved him. I loved the way he left flowers in my room some mornings and surprised me with jewelry other days. I loved how he slowly withdrew from attending events with the actresses to spend time watching movies with me.

I loved how attentive he was, even if I didn't understand it sometimes. Like why after he shot down one of my choices for a penthouse or suite he always deposited more money in my bank account. Or why he made sure Jenson watched over me when I went back to Brooklyn to see Jordan. I'd asked him about these things once or twice, but he always just smiled and said something about how much he enjoyed taking care of me.

It was a comfortable existence, even if it wasn't the type of life many women would like. I understood not to ask questions about certain things, and I didn't. It was a trade off I was willing to make.

The summer night air grew chillier, signaling autumn's coming in upstate New York. It had been a long, hot summer and I welcomed the change fall would bring. As the leaves began to slowly turn the vibrant golds and reds so typical of the trees in the Northeast, Tristan announced at dinner one evening that we would be leaving to see another suite. It had been over a month since he and I had traveled to San Francisco on what had ended up feeling like the trip of a lifetime, so I couldn't imagine what could top that.

"We'll be gone for at least a week, so be sure to tell Jordan," he said casually as he poured himself a drink.

I couldn't help but smile. "I think it's really great that you don't want me to forget about her."

"Why would I? She's your friend. Plus, I owe her. If it wasn't for her information, I wouldn't have been able to surprise you that night."

How long ago that night seemed now. Then we'd been basically strangers, learning those first things about one another. Now, just months later, we were like an old married couple eating dinner each night at five, laying in bed late on Sunday mornings, and bickering about which movie to watch on Saturday nights.

I stood behind him and wrapped my arms around his waist, pressing my cheek to his back. "Where are we going?"

Covering my hands with his, he turned his head to face me. "Venice."

I moved around him and stood looking up in amazement. "Venice? As in canals, gondola rides, and the Doge's Palace?"

"Yes, yes, and I have no idea."

"I can't believe it. And how can you have no idea what the Doge's Palace is?"

"Just wait until you see it, Nina. The hotel is on the Grand Canal, and although I can't say most of my hotels do much for me, the one in Venice is an exception."

"What am I going to be able to add to one of your suites in Venice?" I asked, feeling immediately incapable to do anything to improve anything in that great city.

He lifted my chin to make me face him. "Don't doubt yourself. I believe in you."

That was easy for him to say. He didn't have to pick art to improve on one of the most artistically beautiful cities in the world. "Is this some sort of final exam or something? My six months are almost up, so is this the big test to see if I can keep my job?"

Tristan winced ever so slightly at the mention of my contract. "No. Think of this as merely a vacation."

"A working vacation," I corrected him. "Will we be able to visit some of the museums?"

"Of course."

Just as I began to chatter on about all the great museums in Venice, his cell phone vibrated in his pants pocket, and as he seemed to do more and more, he apologized for having to take the call and left the dining room. Of all the changes that had occurred over the past months, this one I disliked. Ever since that night in Dallas, it seemed like his phone was always interrupting our time together. It rang almost constantly, and at least once a day, he left to speak to someone, even though with me he claimed that after five was a time he wanted nothing to do with work. I didn't know if he answered only one person's call or if he allowed himself one call each night, but whether it was during dinner, as we relaxed, or just as we fell asleep, he took that one call, always leaving before he answered it.

At first I'd been suspicious and worried that it was another woman, but each night he returned to the house and me and rarely left. Even when he went out to attend some work function, he told me where the event was to be held and which actress he was escorting that night, even joking about his stiffness and being a bad fake boyfriend. And every morning after, I saw him and the girl du jour on Page Six, with Tristan as uncomfortable and rigid as always at just the place he'd said he'd be.

I'd considered asking him about the calls, but something told me I shouldn't. Maybe it was the stressed look on his face every time the phone vibrated, but I didn't want to know what made him unhappy. And I didn't believe he wanted me to know.

When he didn't return for nearly thirty minutes, I began to get worried. Had he left on some emergency he couldn't tell me about? After roaming around the house for ten minutes more, I finally found him down near the indoor pool just sitting on one of the chaise lounges. Leaning back with his eyes closed and a slight frown, he looked very much like he always did after his daily phone call.

"I think people generally take off their shirt and pants in this room," I joked, hoping to cheer him up.

He said nothing, but the tiny beginnings of a smile formed on his lips. They never really got to a full grin, but for a moment he seemed happier.

"Is everything okay, Tristan?"

Opening his eyes, he sighed and sat up. "I need a drink." Before I could say anything in reply, he was up and gone from the pool leaving me standing there alone. When I caught up to him, he'd poured himself another double scotch and was doing his best to get the alcohol into his system as quickly as possible.

I stood in the doorway of the living room and saw the sadness in him. It hit me in the middle of my chest and made me want to take him in my arms and never let him go. His posture screamed that he was dealing with something that weighed on his mind. He sat in a chair in the corner of the room, his shoulders drooped and his head tilted back. He watched me approach him, but I had the sense he was far away and looking right through me.

"You can talk to me, Tristan. I'm more than just your in-house art expert," I said sweetly as I ran my fingertip over his closely cut hair. "I hate to see you so unhappy."

Those deep brown eyes looked up at me and he said, "It's nothing I can't handle, Nina. Don't worry about me."

I was worried, though. The drinking, the frown, the phone calls that seemed to affect him more and more.

Bending down, I kissed the top of his head, loving the feel of his soft hair against my lips. "I don't like seeing you like this, Tristan," I whispered.

He caressed my arm and gave me a forced smile. "It'll be fine. Once we're in Venice, everything will be better."

I hoped what he said was true, but I feared there was something slowly coming between us—something that he wanted to keep hidden but was gradually separating him from me. Later that night as he held me in his arms after we'd made love, nearly all traces of whatever was troubling him were gone and he was the sexy and charming man I'd fallen in love with. He played with my hair as he always did when I laid my head on his chest, wrapping it around his finger and then releasing it again and again, while he told me about his first time visiting Venice years ago as a teenage boy, long before he was the owner of Richmont hotels.

"You sound like you had a great time."

"I did. It was one of the best times I had with my father. It was just the two of us that time. Taylor and my mother stayed behind because he got sick at the last minute, so for one of the few times in my life, it was just me and my father."

There was something unsettling, something darker in his voice as he talked about how his father had spent the entire week in meetings as he'd wandered around the city alone. His words were all about how much he enjoyed Venice and the freedom to explore it at the age of sixteen, but beneath them was an emotion I didn't think even he knew was there. I listened as he recounted stories of late nights on the Piazza San Marco with girls he barely knew and his first night of drinking while he laughed at his youthful foolishness, yet all the time his left hand rested on the bed balled into a tight fist.

I kissed over the ridges of his stomach, loving the feel of his body against my lips. "Am I going to have to worry about you and Venetian girls on this trip, Casanova?"

"No, I promise to behave this time," he joked.

Sliding up his body, I kissed him on the lips. "I love it when you smile like that. I like to think that it's a smile you save only for me."

"You've seen pictures of me, haven't you? I don't ever smile for them."

I placed a tiny kiss on the tip of his nose. "Good. I like that."

Tristan cradled my face in his hands. "You're the only person in the world who's allowed to know that I'm nice. Everyone else thinks I'm that cold man who shows up at work and those charity things I have to attend."

"So if I told your other employees how you are with me they'd be surprised?"

"I don't usually talk to the people who work for me. I have managers and assistants for that. In fact, you're the only person who works for me that I speak to."

I wrinkled my nose at his distinctly elitist comment. "I guess little ole' me should feel blessed."

He either didn't pick up on my sarcasm or didn't care to pay attention to it. "I don't know about blessed, but you certainly can consider yourself special."

"Oh, can I?"

Sliding his hands down to cup my ass, he pulled me into him. "Yes. You are the only person I smile for and the only one I sleep with. I think those are two very good reasons to think you're special."

I wanted to say "I love you" at that moment as he smiled up at me and held me close, but I didn't. It wasn't fear of rejection now, but I didn't want to ruin things between us. He probably knew how I felt even though I hadn't said it, and in my heart, I believed he loved me. That we hadn't said it didn't mean a thing. They were just words. We told each other every day with our actions that we loved each other, and I was content with that.

"We should get some sleep. Venice waits for us tomorrow," I whispered as I rolled off him onto the bed.

In my ear, he whispered, "Good night, Nina," as he wrapped his arm around me, pulling me to him.

I brought his hand to my lips and kissed it gently. "Good night, Tristan."

I love you.

I twirled around the living room in our suite at Tristan's hotel in Venice, my eyes straining to open as wide as possible to take everything in. Nearly nine hours on the plane and even though I hadn't slept the whole time, I was keyed up and eager to see as much of Venice as I could that day.

"It's gorgeous! I can't believe I'm here in Venice and this incredible hotel is yours," I gushed. "No wonder you love this place!"

Every wall I set my gaze on was more beautiful than the last. Frescoes and reliefs adorned the walls, evidence of the expert artistic hands of Venetian craftsmen from long ago.

Tristan stopped my turning and stood behind me with his arms around my waist. "I'm glad you like it. It really is nice, isn't it?"

Turning in his hold, I looked up at him and couldn't believe how understated he was about all of the beauty around us. "Nice doesn't do it justice. It's the most beautiful place I've ever seen. I can't believe this is yours."

"Aw, shucks," he teased. "It's nothing."

"Don't get all humble on me now. This is extraordinary. I don't think I have the words to describe how extraordinary this is."

He leaned down and whispered in my ear, "Then get ready to be speechless when I show you the balcony."

I followed him out the enormous glass doors to a balcony that overlooked the Grand Canal of Venice. Gondoliers steered their boats through the water past hundreds year old pink and gold colored gothic buildings. These were the places I'd spent hours fantasizing about as an undergrad art student, and here I was staring across the water at them from my very own balcony.

"Oh my God, Tristan...it's the most incredible view I've ever seen. Thank you."

He said nothing and after a few minutes of staring at the beauty in front of me, I turned to see him watching me. "What? Am I gushing too much?"

Shaking his head, he smiled. "No. I'm happy you love this like you do. And I'm happy I'm the one who could give you this."

He kissed me so tenderly I thought I might cry. There I was standing in a scene straight out of a picture with a man unlike anyone I'd ever met and he was saying he was happy because he'd made me happy. If there was a luckier woman than me, I couldn't imagine how.

"I thought we'd visit the museums tomorrow. Would you like that?" he asked as he nuzzled my neck. "I figure it's about time I see some art in this city."

"I'd love that! Is it too late to go today?"

Tristan lifted his head from kissing my shoulder and cocked one eyebrow. "Aren't you tired from the flight?"

"No way. I'm in Venice, baby. I could probably stay up the whole time we're here."

"Well, I'm exhausted. Plane rides do that to me. I thought we could stay in tonight and have dinner before we spend some more time out here on the balcony."

I knew the flight had been stressful for him. Each time we flew anywhere, he grew quiet. More than once on the flight there, I'd noticed his knuckles were nearly white as his hands tightly gripped the armrests on his seat. It wasn't surprising after what he'd been through.

Standing on my toes, I stretched to kiss him on the cheek. "I think that sounds perfect."

That smile I loved came out and he hugged me tightly. "Good. I'm going to speak to the concierge, but I'll be back in a few minutes. You stay and enjoy the view."

"Yes, sir. I can do that, sir," I joked.

"Sir? Be careful. I hear your boss is a real bastard. Seems he's miserable to his employees. Never smiles, I hear."

"Oh no. He's nothing like that. They just don't know the real man. I'm not worried. He's pretty fantastic, actually."

Tristan turned to leave and stopped as he opened the suite door. "Just pretty fantastic?"

"Okay, he's extraordinary, but he doesn't flaunt his extraordinariness all the time," I said with a wink.

After he left, I turned back to look at the view from our balcony. That's how I thought of things. Our balcony. It had a romantic ring to it. Leaning against the wrought iron railing, I scanned the canal below and saw couples in love on their gondola rides enjoying the beautiful Venice evening. It was the most enchanting thing I'd ever seen in person, and I felt like I needed to pinch myself to be sure I wasn't dreaming.

I didn't know how long I stood there, but when I finally looked up from the romantic scene below, the sky was dark and the stars that twinkled overhead made it look like the perfect painting. The sound of the suite door closing signaled Tristan's return, and I turned around to see not only him but three uniformed waiters with trays full of food.

He opened his arms wide as the men set the table across the room. "A feast fit for a queen, my lady."

I was embarrassed for a moment, but the waiters didn't seem to care who was in the room, so I took

Tristan's outstretched hand and let him kiss me in front of them. "It's so much food."

"Enough for my queen." Tristan looked past me. "Thank you, gentlemen."

Turning, I saw the three men bow and leave us with a table full of food. Fruits, vegetables, meats, breads, and desserts covered the five foot round table, leaving no room for either of us to place a plate down to eat. Looking at Tristan, I asked, "Where are we eating? You've gotten enough food for a queen and her entire court."

"I like the idea of dinner in bed. Breakfast shouldn't have all the fun."

At times like this when he was utterly charming and funny, I couldn't help but smile. He really was adorable. "Dinner in bed it is then. What does one wear to such an event?"

Taking my hand, he led me to the bedroom and turned me around so I faced away from him. His fingers tugged the zipper down on the back of my dress, and he whispered in my ear, "Nothing. Dinner in bed is definitely a no-dress affair."

My dress fell to the floor and I turned around to face him to slide his suit coat off his shoulders. "I like how this dinner is shaping up already." A few gentle pulls on his perfect Windsor knotted tie and I tossed it on the bed nearby. As I unbuttoned his black dress shirt to reveal his solid chest and stunning abs, I couldn't help but lick my lips. He was like a Greek god standing there in front of me.

He looked down at me with eyes full of desire as I slid my fingers beneath the waist of his pants. In a needy voice, he groaned, "Maybe we'll have dessert first."

Fifteen

My fingers grazed the head of his already excited cock, and I heard him take a sharp breath in above me. As I stroked his silky skin, I looked up to watch him close his eyes and tilt his head back. I loved seeing him like this. He was sex incarnate, and I wanted to feel every inch of him on me.

He moaned softly when I unzipped his pants and took his cock in my hand. He'd gone commando, so I slid his pants over his hips and they fell quickly around his ankles. This was what had been in my mind that first night when he'd asked me what I was thinking, and now I wanted to show him exactly what he made me want.

Dropping to my knees, I ran my hand from the base of his cock to the head and back again as I watched his face relax in pleasure. I slid the mushroom-shaped head into my mouth and sucked gently as I eased my lips down over his cock until they touched my hand gripping the base. He tasted incredible on my tongue, like a slightly salty treat I'd waited too long to enjoy.

He buried his hands in my hair and began to move my head at a rhythm both of us liked. Humming against his skin as my mouth slid down over him again, I sent vibrations up and down his cock, making him moan a noise like I'd never heard from him.

"Oh, God, Nina...don't stop. Just like that."

His voice was hoarse and strained from desire, and I loved the sound of it. I made him sound like that. Me. I wanted to hear him tell me how much he loved it again and again. It made me wet just listening to the need in every word. The need for me to give him what he so desperately wanted.

I looked up to watch him as I took him into me, loving the expression on his face as he watched me. Leaning my head back, I slid him out of my mouth, my hand still stroking his hard, silken shaft. He was thick and long, and I licked my lips at the feel of him so heavy in my palm.

"Fuck, don't stop," he moaned. There was almost a painful sound to his voice now.

My tongue slid over the head and I licked around him like a lollypop as my hand cupped his balls. His eyes grew wide with desire before he closed them and a strained look crossed his face. "Baby, you're killing me."

"Time for good boyfriends to get what they want then."

I drew him into my mouth slowly, my tongue darting over the area just below the tip of his cock. His breath left his lips in a hiss, and he whispered deeply, "Faster."

Humming against his skin again, I took as much of him as I could into my mouth and sucked gently as I moved up and down his cock. His grip on my hair tightened as he worked to direct my efforts to exactly where he wanted them, sending a delicious mixture of pleasure and pain shooting across my scalp and down my neck.

His movements grew to short, stabbing motions into me, and I knew he was getting close. My hand slid faster around the base, giving every inch of his cock pleasure. I wanted to feel him lose control, to feel him experience that release that came from letting go.

He sounded like he was on the verge of losing his voice as he whispered in a deep, hoarse rasp, "Nina, much more and I won't be able to hold back anymore."

I stared into his eyes so wild now and prayed he understood how much I wanted him. All of him. *Don't hold back, baby.*

His cock twitched and grew larger, telling me it was time. I relaxed my body to take as much as he offered. He pulled my head down onto him, exciting me more than I'd ever thought possible, and my throat accepted everything he gave as he exploded into me.

When he finally pulled out of my mouth, my legs were weak and shaking and I sat back on my heels to catch my breath. Closing my eyes, I got my bearings as he removed the last of his clothes. His lips brushed mine and I opened my eyes to see him kneeling in front of me.

"See what you do to me? You bring me to my knees."

I smiled at his confession. "Are you happy?"

"Happy isn't the word I'd use," he said as he slipped my bra strap off my right shoulder and then my left. "More like ecstatic."

I looked down as he slid his hands behind me to unhook my bra. "Good."

"And now I plan to do the same for you, so get those panties off before I tear them off with my teeth."

Lying back on the floor, I slithered out of my panties as Tristan moved forward to catch me with his hands, pressing my hips to the floor. I let my legs fall open, and he moaned, sending a shiver of desire straight through me. I wanted his mouth on me, devouring my pussy as that gorgeous tongue of his lapped my tender and needy clit.

He flicked his tongue and grinned a sexy smile. "Don't close your eyes. I want you to watch me, Nina. Watch me give you what you gave me."

Lowering his head between my thighs, he kept his gaze focused on my eyes as he ran his tongue up my dripping wet slit. Those brown eyes looked so sexy staring up at me, nearly making me come at the first touch of his mouth on me. He sucked my delicate skin into his mouth, sending waves of pleasure washing over me.

I squirmed as he moved up to gently suck my clit into his mouth, and he moaned against me, "No fidgeting. Don't make me hold you down."

His command resonated deep inside my excited pussy, thrilling me, and he placed his hands on my hips. "Just in case there's any more wriggling. I want to see you fucking come apart because of my tongue."

I looked at his large hands on my stomach, so powerful as they rested on my tender skin, and I loved it. I squirmed again just to have him take total control, and his reaction was swift. He pressed hard against my hips, pinning me to the floor.

"I told you. No more wriggling."

His tongue plunged into me, making me desperate to buck against him, but I was trapped. Fucking me with his tongue, he stabbed into me as his thumb drew tiny circles on my clit. The sensations were exquisite and better than anything else I'd experienced before. I wanted to lay there open for him to do what he wanted forever.

My orgasm began to uncoil inside me, and my eyelids lowered as my eyes rolled back in my head. Just as they closed, I heard his deep voice order, "Look at me, Nina. I want to see you looking at me when you come."

I did as he commanded and watched as he sucked my clit into his mouth one last time, sending me crashing over that sweet edge. My release roared through me, and I cried out his name while he rode me until the last tiny quake finally subsided. When he sat back from me to place a tiny kiss on my quivering inner thigh, he whispered, "Feel good?"

"Mmmm...ecstatic."

He nipped at my skin and stood up. I took his hand when he held it out, ready for whatever was waiting for me, but I was surprised when he said, "I think it's time for dinner now that we had dessert first."

My expression must have signaled my disappointment because he quickly added, "Don't worry. We'll get back to that after dinner. I need to make sure you're fed so you have enough energy for later."

I stood up and walked with him toward the table full of food. "Enough energy? Whatever could you mean?" I said with a giggle.

He turned around and leveled his gaze at me. "You know what I mean."

I did and I loved how he thought. We loaded up our plates and walked back to the bedroom to have our dinner in bed. As I crawled into the king size bed, Tristan popped a strawberry from his plate into my mouth and followed it with a kiss.

"I guess I should have asked if you liked strawberries."

I put the plate down on the bed and grabbed at my throat. Making my voice hoarse, I croaked out, "Actually, I'm allergic to strawberries. I only have ten minutes before..." I fell to the bed and closed my eyes, doing my best to playact an allergic reaction.

"Jesus, Nina! I didn't know. We'll get you to a hospital!" I peeked out from behind my lashes to see him jump out of bed, knocking over his plate onto the floor. He raced around grabbing his pants and shirt, hobbling on one foot as he struggled to get dressed. "Baby, I'm sorry. Don't worry. Don't worry."

I opened my eyes as he rushed over to my side of the bed. Dropping to his knees, he leaned over and said in a tortured voice that made me feel instantly guilty, "Baby, don't leave me. Talk to me, Nina. Please say something."

His face was the picture of fear, making me feel even worse. "I'm sorry. I was just kidding, Tristan. I'm not allergic. I was just joking around. I didn't think you'd take me seriously. I'm sorry."

He sighed heavily and his shoulders sagged, as if just hearing me say that made every ounce of stress leave his body. Taking me in his arms, he squeezed me tightly to him. "Don't ever do that again. I thought I'd lose you."

"I'm sorry. I didn't mean to ruin everything," I said quietly as he continued to hold me.

When he finally released me, I saw how much my joke had affected him. Those soulful brown eyes were full of sadness and his mouth was turned down in a soft frown even as he told me how happy he was that I was okay. My heart broke at what I'd done—at what my callousness had done to him.

Caressing his cheek, I kissed him softly on the lips. "I'm sorry, Tristan. I didn't mean to be so thoughtless. I didn't think before I did it."

"I'm just happy you're okay."

I felt like shit that I'd ruined everything so wonderful that he'd tried to do. He'd brought me to Venice and his stunning hotel, worshipped me like no man had ever done, and I hadn't even been good enough to consider the idea that maybe someone who'd lost his entire family wouldn't find it funny that he'd mistakenly fed his girlfriend a food poisonous to her.

"Tell me I haven't wrecked our entire trip. Please don't let this spoil our good time."

"You haven't spoiled anything, Nina. Let's have a drink and eat something."

He stood and walked out to the suite's living room to pour himself a scotch while I cursed my stupidity and cleaned up the mess he'd made when he jumped out of bed. Sometimes I could be such a jackass, but rarely had I felt so awful about being one.

I found him sitting naked on the couch with a nearly empty glass in his hand. His face was drawn, and he looked tired as he swallowed the last gulp of alcohol. He stood to pour himself another drink, a sign that no matter what he said things weren't okay.

This was my doing, so I had to fix it. I knelt in front of him as he sat back down and leaned my head on his leg. "Did you eat anything? Do you want me to get you a plate?"

He shook his head. "No. I'm fine with just a drink. You eat, though. The food is impeccable."

I didn't want to eat. My appetite was gone. All I wanted was to fix what I'd done, but I didn't know how. There was something sad between us now. It was nothing obvious, but I felt it as I sat so close to him. Looking up at him, I wished more than anything that I knew the right words to say.

"I'm looking forward to visiting the museums tomorrow," I said quietly. "Are you?"

He smiled sweetly. "Only because you're going to be there."

"We're going to see some great works of art. I think you'll like it."

"I know I will because you like it."

"Love it, actually. Ever since I was a little girl, I've loved art."

He placed his hand on the back of my head and stroked my hair. "Love then."

We sat there saying nothing for a long time until he finally cupped my chin in his hand and said, "Let's go back to bed."

Taking my hand, he led me to the second bedroom past the one we'd been in earlier. He closed the door behind us and leaned down to press a passionate kiss onto my lips. His tongue slipped into my mouth to mingle with mine, making moisture rush to between my legs. I ran my hands over the soft skin of his back and moaned into his mouth.

As I was beginning to think we'd moved past the problem of earlier, he pulled back and stared down at me. My blood ran cold that he was angry or upset, but when he spoke, his words were full of tenderness that touched my heart and brought tears to my eyes.

"Your happiness and safety is all I care about. The thought of losing you terrified me."

"I know. I'm so sorry. I just didn't think," I said, wanting so much to make him feel better.

He kissed me to stop me from talking and shook his head. "Don't apologize. It made me realize I should have said this a long time ago. I love you, Nina, and I don't want to lose you."

Tears streamed down my cheeks at his words. He loved me like I loved him. Smiling through my tears, I sobbed, "I love you, Tristan. I'm the luckiest woman in the world because of you. You've given me everything a girl could dream of."

"I haven't given you anything you don't deserve. Don't ever forget that."

Within just a few minutes, the melancholy that had covered him lifted and he was the Tristan I loved to be around. We made love sweetly and tenderly, and as we lay there in each other's arms, I tried to forgive myself for what I'd done.

The truth was that I sometimes didn't know how to act around him. He was so hard to gauge at times, which made me feel like being myself was inappropriate. In the beginning, I had thought it was the money—the way he spent money on me unnerved me, making me feel as if he believed I was someone I wasn't. I'd never pretended to be anyone but myself, but I found it hard to believe that a man would simply give gifts just because he could. It was never him but me who had the problem. Just because I'd never been fortunate enough to meet someone like him didn't mean I didn't deserve him.

I didn't know if he knew how troubled my mind was over things like that. If he did, he never spoke a word about it. But that was his way. He wasn't a man who spent hours talking about what was on his mind. He decided on matters and they happened.

It was one of the many things about him that I admired.

I absentmindedly ran my hand over his ribs, loving the feel of his body under my touch. Even now after a wonderful lovemaking session, I could spend hours worshipping his body again. He had that effect on me, unlike any other man I'd ever met had.

"Tristan, are you asleep?" He twirled my hair around his finger, a sign that he was still awake. "I'm really looking forward to seeing the museums tomorrow."

"Good. It will be educational for me since I know little about art."

I lifted my head from his chest and looked up at him, confused. "I've seen your house and penthouse. I think you know a great deal about art."

He smiled and pursed his lips. "I know a great deal about hiring people to decorate the places I live in."

I didn't know why, but his remark stung my feelings. The truth was that I was an employee of his, no matter how intimate we were after work hours. But something in his tone signaled a disdain for the people he'd hired to decorate his homes, and I suddenly felt like I was grouped in with them.

Rolling over, I turned my back to him and worked to push these thoughts out of my mind. I was sleeping next to him in our hotel room in Venice where he'd brought me for no other reason than to enjoy a city renowned for something I loved. Whatever slight I'd felt was silly.

His arm snaked around my waist, and he pressed his body against mine. "What happened there? Suddenly tired?"

"It's been a long day," I said as I stared at the wall.

He kissed my neck, nuzzling the space between my shoulder and my ear. "I love you. Get some sleep and we'll head out bright and early so you can teach me all the things I should know about art so I'm not a philistine anymore."

His self-effacing way made me smile, and I turned my body to face him. Kissing him, I said, "You're no philistine, even when it comes to art."

"Well, I'm a cultured philistine then," he joked.

Wrinkling my nose, I said, "I don't think such a thing exists."

He leaned forward and kissed me. "Then maybe I just want to impress the woman I love."

And with just those words, any slight I'd felt melted away. "I can report that the woman you love is already impressed."

Pulling me close, he held me and kissed the top of my head. "She loves me and is impressed. I must be doing something right."

"Definitely."

He fell silent for a long time, never releasing his hold on me. Finally, just as I was about to fall asleep, I heard him say quietly above me, "She loves me."

I did. More than I could ever explain to him.

Sixteen

Sunrise in Venice was just as incredible as the sunset the night before had been, and after a light breakfast, I was ready to show Tristan some of the greatest artwork in the world. The idea that I could be better than him at something thrilled me, and I wanted to impress him as much as he wanted to impress me.

Dressed comfortably in a light yellow cotton dress and flats so we could visit as many museums as time allowed, I walked out of our bedroom to see Tristan ending a phone call. His grimace was profound, marring that beautiful face.

"I'm going to have to miss our tour of the museums today, Nina. Something's come up that I need to deal with."

His body language was stiff, telling me he was unhappy about whatever the problem was. I wanted to cry my disappointment was so great. All my fantasies about showing him my knowledge of the art world disappeared in a heartbeat, wrecked by another of his phone calls.

I tried not to pout, but my efforts weren't very successful and I lowered my gaze to look at my shoes so perfect for walking around Venice. He walked toward me and lifted my chin with his forefinger. Looking down into my face, he wore an expression of disappointment mixed with something else. I just couldn't put my finger on what that something else was.

Anger? Disgust?

"I'm sorry. I wanted to go with you, but it's important I take care of this."

I bit my lip and tried to control my tongue so I didn't make his situation even worse. "I know. I just so wanted to show you..." I let my sentence trail off. My desire to impress him sounded silly now.

"I want you to still go. One of my men will escort you, so go wherever you want."

"I don't need an escort. You roamed around Venice all by yourself when you were sixteen. I'm sure I can handle myself."

He shook his head definitively. "No. One of my men will be with you, if you choose to go."

There was no arguing the point, so I didn't. I wouldn't have Tristan, but I'd have a shadow. "I guess one of your guys will be okay," I mumbled.

Placing a kiss on my forehead, he whispered, "I promise I'll make it up to you."

"You better. I'm thinking The Louvre might be the only thing that could make this better."

"It's a date," he said and flashed me a smile that made it next to impossible to be angry with him.

Whatever the problem was, it required him to leave immediately, but within ten minutes my escort arrived. Nearly as tall as Tristan, Jared was much bigger, like bouncer-at-a-club bigger. I guessed he had little appreciation for art. After trying twice to strike up a conversation as we stood there in the living room of the suite, I surmised he had little appreciation for talking too.

"Well, Jared, it's nice to meet you. My name is Nina. I guess you're going with me to visit some museums today."

My giant shadow nodded once and said, "As you wish, ma'am."

Ma'am. Oh, I was sure I wasn't going to enjoy my time with him.

After visiting two museums, I had all but forgotten about Jared and immersed myself in the works of art at the Ca'Rezzonico museum. The landscape painting exhibition on the first floor took my breath away. I stood staring at paintings showing eighteenth century Venice as it truly had been back then, mesmerized at how similar so many things in the city still were. Yet the paintings showed a different Venice in many ways, and I was taken back to those days I'd studied about in school, finally feeling like I was experiencing them for myself as I studied those pictures that hung on the walls.

I moved through the floor wishing Tristan was at my side so I could tell him about all the wonderful history of landscape painting in Venice. A touch of sadness came over me, but I pushed it out of my mind, reminding myself that while Tristan had given me time off from my job for this trip, no one had given him any.

Lost in thought about landscape painting, I didn't see the man next to me until he spoke. Surprised, I jumped and turned to look at the stranger. "Excuse me? I didn't hear what you said."

"I said it's beautiful, isn't it?"

"It is." I continued to look at the man, surprised by his American accent. "You're an American?"

He nodded. "Yes, I am. It's nice to meet another person from back home."

I studied his face as I tried to determine his age. The corners of his eyes were wrinkled slightly, but his face was tanned, giving him a glow that made me think he might be in his thirties. His hair had streaks of grey at the temples, leading me to believe he might be older, though.

"Where are you from?" I asked, thinking I picked up a Midwest accent.

"Minnesota. Land of ten thousand lakes."

"That's a lot of lakes," I joked.

"Beautiful country there. Where are you from?" he asked as he studied my face, likely to ascertain the answers I'd sought a minute earlier.

"Pennsylvania. We don't have that many lakes."

The man extended his hand and introduced himself as Derek. I smiled and said, "It's nice to meet you, Derek. I'm Nina."

"I used to know someone from Pennsylvania with a daughter named Nina. His name was Joseph. I met him on assignment years ago."

"Assignment? What did he do?"

"He was an investigative journalist."

"Do you remember his last name?" I asked excitedly, amazed at the idea that I might be talking to someone who'd known my father.

"Edwards. His name was Joseph Edwards."

"Oh, my God! That was my father!"

"He was a good man. Great writer," Derek said in a solemn voice, using the past tense, which told me he knew about my father's death.

"It's so wonderful to hear that. He loved what he did."

"He did. I remember him talking about you too. You were the apple of his eye. His little artist is what he called you, if I remember correctly."

I beamed at Derek's memory, loving that my father had spoken about me like that. "I haven't heard that in so long. I miss hearing him call me that."

Derek's eyes narrowed. "I think it's a shame they never charged the people responsible."

My heart slammed against my chest at Derek's implication. The police had repeatedly told my sister and me that all the leads had gone cold, but it sounded like he was saying someone knew who'd murdered my father. "Do you know anything about that?"

"Ma'am, it's time we got going."

I turned to see Jared ready to do his best escort impression. "I'll be ready in a minute. I'm talking right now."

My shadow looked around and then back at me. "Ma'am, I think he left."

Jared was right. Derek was nowhere in sight. I took off to find him, but it was like he'd vanished. I searched all four floors, but I never found him. As Jared escorted me back to the hotel, the man's claim echoed in my head.

Someone knew who had murdered my father.

I left Jared behind in the lobby and raced up to the room to get my head together. I needed a cool drink and some time to think about what Derek had said. The idea that the people responsible for my father's death still roamed free while he lay cold in the ground tore at me. I'd never believed what the police told us, but without any proof, all I had was my gut feeling that what they knew about the case was only the tip of the iceberg.

Throwing my purse on one of the chairs in the suite's living room, I stripped nude and ran myself a bath in the soaker tub. I poured myself a glass of red wine and slid into the water, wanting so desperately to calm the craziness that was racing around my brain. The wine quickly dulled my senses, as alcohol always did, and I closed my eyes to silence my thoughts.

At last, my brain calmed and all that was left was the feeling of loss that I'd had since the moment I learned that my father had died of a gunshot wound in an abandoned warehouse in Newark. My father and mother for so many years was gone, taken from me in a moment of hate or passion. I didn't know which. As I sat in the warm water there in the hotel suite I shared with Tristan, all I really knew was that my father was murdered and gone forever.

I'd cried so many tears since that night that I hadn't thought there weren't any left in me. My emotions had traveled from sadness to rage to nothingness. I'd felt so much that where it concerned my father's death, my heart was numb. But Derek's words had pricked at that numbness like a needle in a dead limb and I'd felt it.

"How were the museums?"

I opened my eyes and saw Tristan standing in the bathroom doorway. He smiled, but his expression did a poor job of hiding the fact that whatever the problem was that he had been dealing with all day was still plaguing his thoughts.

"I missed having you there. It was nice, but it would have been better with you by my side."

His smile widened into a warm grin, and he walked over to crouch next to the tub. "I know. I'm sorry. The Louvre, right?"

Chuckling at his recollection of my words from that morning, I flicked a few drops of water at him. "You better believe it. I'm holding you to that, you know."

"I'm counting on it."

He leaned forward and kissed me gently on the forehead, making me feel loved and cared for. Closing my eyes, I sighed. "Thank you."

"For what?"

I looked up into his curious eyes. "For making me feel so loved."

Pushing my hair behind my ear, he whispered, "Always."

His touch was so comforting, and I leaned into his palm to rest my head. "Do you ever find yourself thinking back to before your parents and brother were taken from you? I can't get my father off my mind tonight."

Tristan said nothing for a long time. I worried that I'd said something wrong by asking about his family, but finally he quietly said, "Sometimes it's all I can think of. There are things that happened when they were alive that still haunt me today."

Something in his voice told me he understood what I was feeling. The loss. The regret that not having the chance to say goodbye brought with it.

He kissed my head and leaned his against mine. "Did something happen today?"

I wanted to tell him about Derek, but what did I have to go on? The word of some guy from Minnesota who'd made some vague claim? I didn't want to ruin our vacation, and I could tell him everything when I found out some actual facts.

"No. I just had a lot of time alone today and visiting art galleries reminds me of when I was a little girl and my father would take me to the Philadelphia Museum of Art. It was there that I first fell in love with art."

None of that was a lie. I just hadn't told Tristan about Derek.

"He sounds like a great father, Nina. You were lucky."

Things were getting too serious, so I slid up against the back of the tub and took a drink of wine. Forcing a smile, I said, "I was. So what's on the schedule for tonight? A little dinner in and some TV with the ball and chain?"

He raised his eyebrows in surprise. "I had something a little different in mind, but if you'd rather watch TV..."

"No, no. I can watch TV any night. It's not every night I'm in Venice. What do you have in mind?"

His face turned sheepish. "I know it's pretty clichéd, but I thought we'd take a gondola ride."

I couldn't help but smile. He really was so cute when he was romantic. "That's so cool! Give me a few minutes and I'll get ready. A gondola ride! I get to cross off another thing on my list of things to do before I die."

Nearly leaping out of the tub, I raced to get ready, eager to experience what I'd only seen in movies and paintings. It may have been clichéd, but I didn't care. There was no way I was visiting Venice and not taking a gondola ride, and that I'd be taking it with the man I loved was better than anything.

"Isn't this romantic?" I cooed as the gondolier guided the boat past those great Gothic buildings that lined the Grand Canal, the ones I'd looked out at from our balcony the night before.

Tristan slipped his arm around my shoulders and pulled me close. "It's actually really nice. I'd heard horrible things about the canal water, but this isn't bad."

I rolled my eyes at his understatement. "Nice? Isn't bad? You really know how to seduce a girl."

Nuzzling my neck, he whispered, "You want seduction? I'll give you seduction."

I turned my head to catch his mouth in a kiss. He tasted like scotch, and I liked my lips as I pulled away. "Promises, promises."

Our gondolier eased his craft around another stopped gondola as Tristan whispered, "Did you know that all gondoliers must wear black pants and a striped shirt?"

I looked our guide up and down and saw he was wearing that exact uniform. "I'm impressed."

"Good. But I feel compelled to tell you that the concierge at the hotel gave me that tidbit of information," he admitted in a low, husky voice that hit me deep inside, oddly enough considering what he was saying.

I ran my hand up his thigh and licked my lips. "I love honestly in a man. Now I'm even more impressed."

As the gondola drifted to a stop, Tristan winked at me. "Time for that seduction."

We walked into the Piazza San Marco as the first drops of rain began to fall. Tourists and locals headed for cover in the restaurants and hotels nearby, leaving just a few of us alone in the enormous square. Puddles quickly formed on the stone patio, forcing us to zigzag toward the Moorish style arches that lined the piazza as the skies opened up above us.

Thunder boomed overhead, chasing nearly everyone from the square. Soaked to the bone, we ran for shelter behind the colonnade. My hair was drenched and plastered to my head, and I slicked it off my face just so I could see. I looked up at Tristan, who was scrubbing his face dry with his hands. He looked as incredible as always. Dipping my head, I wiped under my eyes to get rid of any smeared mascara and mumbled, "I must look like a nightmare."

He lifted my chin to force me to look at him and shook his head. "You look beautiful. Come here."

Pulling me close, he kissed me deeply, sending a rush of arousal through my body. His hands fisted my hair as he slid his tongue over mine seductively. His hips pushed forward, brushing his hardening cock between my legs and making me tilt my hips to eagerly meet his thrusts.

"You wanted seduction, didn't you, Nina?" he asked in that deep voice that made me want him more than anything at that moment.

"Yes," I answered breathlessly as he gently pinned me against a column.

"Yes," he repeated as he slid his hand under my dress all the way up to my panties. "Yes." He moaned softly in my ear, "Right here, Nina. Right here."

Were there people nearby? I didn't know and I didn't care. I wanted him inside me now. His mouth plundered mine and mine plundered his in return as I fumbled with his belt, finally pulling it loose. My hand reached into his pants and tugged on his boxer briefs, yanking them down below his balls so his stiff cock sprang out at attention while the other hand yanked his shirt out of the way, sending buttons flying in all directions. I slid my hand over his smooth cock and drew a sharp breath in as he tore my panties from my body.

He was like a man possessed, his hands grasping at my face and neck as he kissed me. Lifting me onto him, he slid his cock inside me and wrapped my hands around his neck. Those dark eyes stared into mine, wild and full of desire, and he began pumping into my body raggedly. His grunts filled my ears as with each thrust he pushed me back against the marble column, but I was oblivious to pain or anything other than Tristan.

He was everywhere around me—his mouth, his hands, his cock becoming essential to the happiness every part of my body cried out for. I clawed at his scalp, looking for some leverage as he fucked me wildly there behind a column for anyone to see. My legs ached from their hold around his waist, and with each plunge of his cock inside my wet pussy, I pushed my heels against his back, praying this time he'd finally bury himself deep inside me.

"Faster, Tristan. I'm almost there," I cried as the first twinge of my orgasm began. "Harder."

My pleas were met with exactly what I wanted—he pounded into me like a madman, his hands gripping my ass tightly and roughly pulling me into him. His moans and grunts surrounded me, edging me closer to coming as his cock moved like a piston in and out of me.

I cried out, "Yes!" and squeezed his neck as I began to come. Every part of me felt release as my orgasm shuddered through me, and I pushed down to take every inch of his thick cock as my legs quivered against him. He buried his face in my neck and grunted one last time as I felt him explode into me, bathing my insides with his own release.

His legs shook as he moaned my name over and over until there was nothing left for either of us to take from the other's body. I was his completely, and he was mine. Tristan lifted his head and pressed it against mine, his forehead drenched with perspiration.

"God, I love you," he groaned. "I can't fucking live without you, Nina. Promise me no matter what you won't make me. I can't do it."

I caressed his face and kissed his lips as the last word left his mouth. There was nothing in the world that could tear me from him. He was everything to me, as essential as the air I breathed or the food I ate.

"Never. I'm yours like you're mine. Forever."

Seventeen

Venice had been the turning point I'd hoped and prayed for with Tristan. With every word and every action, he proved he was as devoted to me as I was to him. We'd even made it through a whole night without any phone calls souring his mood. When we fell asleep in each other's arms that night, I was happier than I ever thought a person could be.

My happiness was shattered within minutes of waking up the next morning, however.

Once again, I woke up and Tristan was nowhere to be found. I'd half expected to find a note sitting on his pillow, but reaching out to run my hands over the fine Egyptian cotton pillowcase, there was nothing.

I didn't have to wait long to find out what had taken him from our bed so early. His footsteps pounding against the floor in the next room told me something was wrong, and I slipped into the white dress shirt he'd left slung over a chair the night before and made my way out to see him.

He stood near the glass doors to the balcony with his arms folded across his chest. His profile showed a grimace as I walked toward him. I gently touched his sleeve, saddened when I saw his expression as he turned toward me.

"Hey, what's wrong?"

Tristan leaned down and kissed me softly on the lips. "Work. I'm sorry, but we're going to have to cut our trip short. I wish I didn't have to get back, but you know how it is."

I couldn't hide my disappointment and turned away to look out through the doors at the Grand Canal. "Oh. Okay."

"I'm sorry, Nina. I promise to make it up to you."

Nodding, I looked up at him and forced a smile onto my face. "I know. Such is the life of a bigwig."

My joke made him laugh, and at least for a moment he appeared happy, even if there was a hint of sadness in his words. "Bigwig, huh? Well, this bigwig would take a smaller wig and being able to stay here with you."

I stood on my toes and wrapped my arms around his neck. Those deep brown eyes stared down into mine, almost as if he were begging forgiveness.

"You do know women often don't like men with smaller...wigs," I teased with a giggle.

His smile in return was genuine and warmed my heart. "Well, thank God I've been blessed in the wig department."

Sliding my hand down his torso, I ran my palm over the front of his pants before I turned to head into the bath. "Blessed indeed."

I didn't get far before he pulled me back against him and said in a deep voice, "I won't be able to get any work done if you keep making me think about last night."

His reference to what we'd done behind that pillar in the Piazza San Marco made an ache form between my legs. Finally, I'd seen the man behind the expensive suits and hardly any words—that passionate heart that no one but me saw. I would have given anything for the world to go away and have him all to myself for the rest of time.

Blushing at the memory of the rawest, most erotic moment of my life, I covered his hands with mine and leaned my head back against his shoulder. "You're going to make me so completely crazy about you that I become your love slave, Tristan Stone."

He nuzzled my neck, sending chills down my spine. In a husky voice, he whispered, "You've figured out my diabolical plan."

Turning in his arms, I smiled up at him. "I knew you had an ulterior motive."

"I have to get some work done before we leave, Nina. We need to be ready in little more than an hour."

Even the mere mention of work changed his mood from playful to serious, almost worried. His beautiful face became marred by a deep frown. I wanted to ask what the problem was, but I let it be. For all I knew, it could be the flight we had to take. So I toddled off to take a nice hot bath before having to spend eight hours on a plane, satisfied that even with the abbreviated holiday, it still had been the most incredible few days of my life.

Tristan vanished almost the minute we arrived home, so I headed straight to my room, ready to throw myself into my next assignment with the Miami Richmont hotel. I opened the door to the room that had become my home and instantly knew something had changed. Nothing I'd left on the desk while we were in Venice was there, including my laptop. Frantic, I ran down the hall yelling Tristan's name. Didn't he have security that handled things like this?

Rogers heard my screams and in his usual fashion seemed to appear out of nowhere as I reached the kitchen. Fully convinced my belongings had been stolen, I blurted out, "We've been robbed! My laptop and a bunch of other stuff is gone, Rogers! Did you see anyone?"

"Miss, we haven't been robbed. I think you'll find all your personal belongings have been moved to the master's room, as per his orders. If you'd like, I can escort you there where your things are safe and sound."

I stood stunned at the butler's words. Unsure of what to say, I mumbled a quick thank you and quickly made my way to Tristan's side of the house to find everything as Rogers had claimed. My laptop sat in the exact same position on his desk as it had in my room. Every stitch of clothing I owned, even down to my underwear, had been moved and placed in the enormous walk-in closet just beside his clothes. My hand instinctively reached out to touch his suits and dress shirts hanging perfectly on their hangers, loving the feel of their crisp softness against my fingertips as I ran my hand all the way toward the furthest point of the closet. I checked the bathroom and there were brand new, unopened bottles of everything I used—shampoo, conditioner, facial scrub, moisturizer, and even a tube of my favorite toothpaste.

Tristan had arranged for all of this, but when?

I walked out of the bathroom impressed with his attention to every detail, even the tiniest one. Other women may have loved his money or stunning looks, but for me, his way of noticing what other men didn't was one of the best parts of him.

Grabbing my laptop, I plopped myself down on the bed and opened it to begin searching for information on the Miami hotel. There on the keyboard was an envelope. I opened it and found another of Tristan's letters I'd grown to love.

Dear Nina,

It's only right that the woman I love be in her rightful place next to me. When I get home I'll be eager to see your ideas for Miami. I'll be spending my day fixing problems, but you can be sure that our time in Venice is on my mind.

Love always,

Tristan

I beamed as I reread his letter, loving the sweetness of him writing one at all. I stared at the note, running my finger over the handwritten words. God, I loved him! Folding the heavy stationary back into the envelope, I pressed it to my heart before I slipped the letter into my purse to join the others.

As much as I wanted to lounge around and think about Tristan, I had work to do. Just because he was as crazy about me as I was about him didn't mean I wanted to slack off at my job. In fact, it made me want to be even better at it. Doing a great job would help him in some small way, and that made me feel like I deserved that rightful place next to him.

Before I began searching for the perfect artwork for the Miami Presidential suite, my email lured me in like a siren's song. Jordan had sent me a message just a few hours earlier. Clicking on it, I read her email to find that I had some kind of letter waiting for me. She didn't say much about it, other than that it looked official, which piqued my curiosity, but that would have to wait. She and Justin seemed to be fine and moving toward bigger and better things, and our neighbor Mrs. Phillips on the first floor was just as crazy as she'd always been, but now that madness included a long-lost grandson who Jordan hated because he was one of those people who kept eye contact for too long.

I had to laugh at Jordan's rundown of life back in Brooklyn. She was happy, and things were just as she'd always said they'd be. Good people were having good things happen for them, and this time, we were those people too.

I tapped out a quick email to tell her I'd be dropping by the apartment the next day, and then I was a woman on a mission with her nose to the art world grindstone. The suite in Miami had recently been redecorated to reflect the varied cultures and artistic styles found in that city. The pictures of the suite were breathtaking and intimidating. Tristan's decorators had spared no cost in creating a wonderful suite of rooms showcasing the fusion of Latin American flavors and Caribbean influences so key to Miami. The vibrant blues, yellows, and reds made the suite look like the perfect getaway spot, and I wished we'd visit there just to experience it.

That I now had to find that one perfect piece of art to bring the rooms together felt like a Herculean challenge. Of all the assignments he'd given me, this one threatened to show that I wasn't as good at this as I wanted to be.

I rubbed my temples and rolled my shoulders. *You can do this, Nina. You can do this.*

My pep talk worked a small wonder on my psyche, and I set myself to the task of finding that one piece I had to believe existed. Thankfully, the designer hadn't gone with the obvious choice of art deco for the Miami suite. I could appreciate that. Her choices had made the Richmont unique in a sea of luxury hotels in South Beach.

Rubbing my hands together, ideas began popping in my mind and I had a brainstorm. My fingers set off clicking away on the keyboard, but two hours later, I still hadn't found what I was searching for. What had seemed like such a great idea didn't seem to actually exist. The thought occurred to me that I could create something on my own, but my skill as a painter wasn't great enough to have one of my pieces hang in the Presidential suite.

By late afternoon, I hadn't found anything and Tristan was set to be home any time. I had to find something to show him. Even if he vetoed my idea, it was better than letting him down completely. Another quick inspirational talk with myself and I was determined to find something to show for my day's work.

After another exhaustive search, a purple and gold circle print by a Miami artist that would work perfectly was what I finally came up with. To be honest, I was pretty sure Tristan would give it a thumbs down, but at least it was something.

Satisfied, I bookmarked the page at the gallery and closed my laptop just in time to see him enter the bedroom. Whatever he'd been dealing with had taken a toll on him as I'd never seen his face look so drawn and tired.

"Hey! Somebody stole all my things and then left them in here, oddly enough," I joked as he sat down in the high backed chair near the window.

Tristan loosened his tie and smiled. "That's what I love most about you, you know that? When nothing or no one can make me smile, you can." He leaned his head back against the chair and closed his eyes as he let out heavy sigh.

"Tough day?"

"Too tough."

Walking over to behind him, I leaned forward and slid my hands over his shoulders. They were tight and knotted and almost up near his ears. Slowly, I began kneading his stressed muscles, whispering in his ear, "I thought men like you didn't have to deal with the everyday hassles we ordinary people do."

He groaned low and deep. "No, we have to deal with bigger hassles."

"Want to talk about it?"

Tristan shook his head. "Nope. Tell me about your day." He arched back to look at me. "You liked my surprise?"

I leaned down to kiss his forehead. "Very much. And your note. Would you like to see what I came up with for Miami."

"Later." He held my hands on his shoulders. "Tell me what you did other than work and don't stop the massage. That feels good."

"Jordan emailed me. I'm going to stop over to see her tomorrow. She says someone sent me an official looking envelope."

I felt his shoulders tighten under my hands, even as he sat with his eyes closed. "Are you expecting something official?"

Chuckling, I pressed into his muscles, kneading even more deeply. "No. I can't imagine who would send me anything official. The last time I got anything from the government or a lawyer was years ago after my father's death."

"Maybe the IRS has a bone to pick with you," he joked.

"Don't say that. I've heard horror stories about being audited."

He laughed at me. "Nina, I don't think the IRS is auditing you, but if they are, just let me know and I'll have someone take care of it. It's not something to worry about."

This was that attention to detail thing I loved. An IRS audit would make me shake in my shoes and stress out for weeks, but he just took it all in stride and made me feel like if it happened, he'd handle it. I could get used to that.

I pressed my lips to his ear and kissed him, nuzzling his neck. "I love how you do that."

"Do what?"

"Just take care of things. I do love a man who takes care of business."

He tilted his head to look up at me. "What kind of men have you been dating?"

I returned to massaging his tired muscles and sheepishly admitted the truth. "The wrong kind, obviously."

He groaned softly as I hit a tender spot where his shoulders met his neck. "I'm glad I took care of that then."

"I'm going to see her after school tomorrow. I should be home by the time you get home for dinner."

He sat quietly as I attempted to ease the stress from his body. I loved these moments when it was so clear I made him as happy as he made me. After a few minutes, he spoke up, as if he'd been thinking about my last words. "We can meet at the penthouse so you wouldn't have to take that ride in and out of the city."

I kissed him on the cheek. "No, I'd rather come back here, if it's all the same."

Tristan turned his head to look at me, his eyebrows raised. "You mean you'd rather come back to this out of the way house in the middle of nowhere?"

Leveling my gaze at him, I stopped my hands' work and grinned. Rogers had obviously mentioned my comment from that night we'd chatted outside. "Yes. If you must know, I've grown to appreciate this house, even though it's a bit secluded. I like to think of it as our home."

He took my hands from his shoulders and brought them to his lips for a kiss. "I can't tell you how happy that makes me, Nina."

The unspoken reality that my six-month contract was almost up hung in the air like a heaviness that pressed down on us. I hadn't mentioned it because I feared what he might say. Even now, after all we'd shared together, he was still a mystery to me in many ways. I'd expected him to say something about it ending soon, but as each day passed, he was silent on the matter, as if he'd forgotten.

I'd just as soon have had him forget, to be honest. What if he was able to let me go as easily as firing any other employee? In my heart, I knew he loved me and no longer thought of me as merely someone who worked for him, but in the past few weeks I'd sensed something between us holding him back from me. I wanted to believe it was whatever he was dealing with at work, but a tiny fear sat in the back of my mind whispering that no matter what we'd been to one another, when the six months was up, so was our time together.

Pushing that out of my head, I said, "So it's settled. I'll visit Jordan and then be back so we can have dinner. Maybe tomorrow night can be pizza night?"

"Tony's?" he asked with a smile in his voice.

I stroked the hair near his nape, loving its softness. Bowing my head, I ran my lips over it and whispered, "I like that."

"Okay. Tony's at six. It's a date."

"A date," I said as I kissed along his neck to just below his left ear. "I'll be there."

Eighteen

The next day went by quickly as I proudly showed off my choices for the Miami hotel, which Tristan vetoed as I suspected he would, saying he liked the artist but not that particular circle piece. So I continued my search. It was more difficult than I'd anticipated, but when I contacted the artist's representative and told her I was looking to purchase one of Delgado's purple and gold series for the Richmont hotel in Miami, she was far nicer than I'd expected, even offering to have him sign the piece we chose.

The old saying really was true. Money did talk.

By mid-afternoon, I was feeling triumphant about my new acquisition and couldn't wait to tell Tristan about it at dinner, even if it meant breaking the "no work after five" rule. It was a breezy early October afternoon, so I dressed in a dark red dress that fell to right above my knees and black pumps, a celebration outfit of sorts and one I was sure Tristan would love for our date. As I looked at myself in the mirror in our bedroom, a decadent idea popped into my mind. Sexy stockings and a garter belt would be even better.

I slipped them on and attached them to the garter, loving the feel of their silkiness against my skin. I'd love it more when they drove him mad with desire as he tried to concentrate on the road in just a few hours.

Pleased with how I looked, I hurriedly checked my bank account to pay my cell phone bill and saw once again that I had more money than I'd anticipated. Despite working for the stated salary of $60,000, after five months I had over four times that amount in my checking account. Even after all this time, I still marveled at the numbers as they sat there on the screen. For the first time in my life, money wasn't a concern.

It also added to my fear that Tristan was going to simply let me go when my six months were up. Why would he make sure I had so much money if he was going to want me to stay? I wanted to believe that this was just one of his ways of showing me how much he loved me, but every time I checked my balance, an emptiness formed in the pit of my stomach.

Jordan's famous words echoed in my head—*Good things happen to good people, Nina.* I wanted to believe that more than anything. Closing my laptop, I hoped she was right.

I stepped out of the black Town Car in front of the apartment and a brisk wind blew my dress up nearly around my waist, a la Marilyn Monroe on the subway grate. A group of men across the street whistled, making me feel right at home back in Brooklyn. I bounded up the steps, dying to see my best friend, as the men yelled my name and compliments on my red dress.

As I reached the door, I turned around and waved, yelling, "Thanks!" Jordan waited in the apartment doorway at the top of the stairs with a huge grin on her face.

"Look at you! I love it! This new life of yours looks good on you."

I reached her and took her in my arms for a big hug. "It looks good?" I asked as she held me out at arm's length to check out my outfit again.

"Oh, honey. You look incredible. Same old Nina in a wonderful new package."

I beamed at her compliment. I felt wonderful and wanted the whole world to know it.

"Well, come in. Tell me everything. I need to know the details," Jordan ordered as she pulled me into the apartment.

Everything looked the same as it had when I'd left months earlier, except now there were some pictures on the living room walls. Turning toward Jordan, I pointed at them. "I leave and now there's artwork on the walls?"

She sat down in her chair across from my seat on the couch and chuckled. "I wouldn't call it artwork. Just some pictures. I had a little more money since your boyfriend paid your portion of the rent and more that day."

"More? How much more?" I asked, suddenly worried he was trying to buy me.

"About two grand. I told him I didn't feel right taking it, but he insisted. I assumed you knew because you asked him to."

I shook my head and frowned. "No. He never told me. And as much as you know I'd give you my last dime, I didn't ask."

"Why the frown? It's okay that you didn't ask."

"It's not that, Jordan. I just worry that he's trying to buy things he shouldn't."

"Like your love?"

"Yeah," I answered quietly.

"Honey, if he was trying to buy your love, wouldn't he have told you he did this?"

"I guess. It's just..." I didn't know how to complain about all the money in my bank account and not sound like a spoiled child. "He's done the same thing with me. Instead of paying me the amount I'm supposed to get, he's paid me nearly five times more."

"And the problem with that is?"

Jordan's expression told me she still thought I was acting silly all these months later. "I know what you're going to say. I should just enjoy this, right? It's just that my six months are almost up. What if he is giving me all this money because he doesn't plan to stay with me and wants to make himself feel good about it?"

"Still overthinking this, I see."

"But what if it's true?"

"Have you asked him?"

Looking down at my hands as they sat folded in my lap, I shook my head. "No. I'm too afraid of what he'd say."

"How much longer is there on your contract?"

"A few weeks."

"And has he been acting weird, like a boyfriend getting ready to break up with you? You know. Not answering calls or texts. Not showing up for dates. Has the sex fallen off?"

As I listened to her laundry list of signs, I couldn't say yes to one. He always answered my texts, never failed to be where he said he would be at exactly the time he said he would, and the sex had continued to be mind blowing.

"No to all," I admitted with a shrug. "He's wonderful, even though things at work seem to be constantly on his mind."

"So, let me get this straight. Your gorgeous, billionaire boyfriend treats you like a queen and makes sure you have piles of money to spend on yourself, and you're worried he's going to leave you? You're a bright girl, Nina. Figure it out."

"I know it sounds stupid, but I can't help it. I'm dreading the day that contract ends."

That was the cold, hard truth. I was sick to death over a date on the calendar. It never left my mind, no matter how much money he put in my account, no matter how many times he told me he loved me.

Jordan leaned forward and touched me on the knee, jarring me out of my thoughts about that day just weeks away. "Enough of this crazy talk. Tell me how he is in bed. And don't leave out the details. I'll know if you do."

A blush spread from the top of my head all the way to the tip of my toes. Even before I said a word, she clapped her hands together and exclaimed, "I knew it! No man who sounds so incredibly sexy when he speaks about something as boring as paying someone's rent could be bad in bed."

"Stop it! You're embarrassing me!" I cried, half joking. "I'm not telling you a thing."

"You don't have to say a word. It's written all over your face. I bet he's hung like a horse, isn't he?"

"Jordan!" The blush intensified at her words, confirming that she'd hit the nail on the head.

"I swear there's not a thing wrong with this man, Nina. If you say you're worried about anything with him one more time, I'm going to kick you out of this apartment and never speak to you again."

"That's harsh."

"I'm not kidding, Nina. I could understand if he lacked in one or two areas, but he's perfect."

"He's not perfect. I think many women wouldn't like how he's so possessive."

She laughed out loud. "The only time any woman dislikes a possessive man is if he keeps her from doing things she likes. Tristan doesn't do that, so I doubt there'd be many women in this world who wouldn't be madly in love with him just as he is."

I must have had a worried look on my face because she added, "And don't start thinking he's cheating on you or you have to be concerned about other women. That's not what I'm saying."

Putting my hands up in surrender, I smiled. "I know. I'm being stupid. You don't have to say it again."

"Good. I don't like telling people I love that they're being stupid, but I will when I have to. Tough love."

"Enough about me. Tell me about Justin, school, everything," I said, giving the subject a much needed change.

Jordan gave chapter and verse about how things had progressed with Justin, how she thought they were moving toward possibly moving in together, her class of third graders and how cute they were, and all the news of the neighborhood, including what she thought of the new weird guy on the first floor.

"Do you think Mrs. Phillips will be okay?" I asked, growing concerned about the elderly lady.

"I hope so. I haven't seen her in a few days, but you know how she is. If she doesn't come out for grocery day on Friday, then I'll be worried."

"I'd hate to see something happen to her, Jordan. She's always so nice when she invites us to her apartment for cookies and that crazy spiked egg nog at Christmastime. I'm going to stop in just to see if everything's okay."

"Well, now you've guilted me, so I'll go with you. I just hope I don't have to see that guy."

As we left, I grabbed the letter I'd come for and stuffed it into my purse to read later. We walked down to the first floor as Jordan explained how creepy Mrs. Phillips' grandson was. Even without seeing him, I was repulsed. Greasy blond hair and crooked, yellow teeth were never a good combination.

The elderly woman's door was open just a crack, but I had a bad vibe about going in. Tugging Jordan back as she pushed the door open, I whispered, "No way. If that creepy guy is there, who knows what he'll do. This has the beginning of every Law and Order episode written all over it."

Nodding, she agreed. "Yeah, let's get the hell out of here. I'll check on her later with Justin."

The two of us hurried out of the building to grab a bite to eat and ran straight into Mrs. Phillips' grandson as he hit the top of the front steps. I scanned his face and saw he was more than just ugly. He was definitely high on something. Gripping Jordan's arm tightly, I whispered, "We need to go. He's not okay."

His bloodshot eyes stared into mine, and I knew he'd heard what I said. Before we could get away, he lunged at us and yanked on the straps of my bag. I tried to pull away from him, but whatever he was on made him superhero strong and he wrenched the bag down my arm to the crook of my elbow, pulling me down with it. Jordan screamed, scaring him, and he gave one last violent tug. The bag ripped down my forearm, and as he grabbed it, his elbow slammed into my head. Pain spiked out across the top of my skull, radiating all the way to my ear, and I fell back into Jordan in agony.

"Nina! Are you okay?" she asked as she cradled me in her arms.

I heard Jenson's voice barking some order at Jordan as I closed my eyes in agony from the pain. A headache instantly tore through my head, making me cry. I don't know how long I laid there with Jordan, but at some point Jenson lifted me from the concrete porch and carried me to the car.

The leather seat felt so cool against my skin as I lay there in the back of the Town Car while Jordan smoothed my hair from my face. Jenson returned a minute later and took off, driving quickly through the streets of Sunset Park.

"Honey, how's your head?" Jordan asked quietly. "Let me see."

I leaned forward, making me feel like my head was swimming, and Jordan lightly rubbed her hand over the back of my hair. "It hurts, Jordan. Am I bleeding?"

Lifting my head, I saw a tiny red splotch on her palm. "I don't know, honey. It doesn't seem like you're bleeding a lot, but you're starting to swell up." She turned around to speak to Jenson. "Hey, are you taking her to the hospital? She might need a doctor."

"Miss, Mr. Stone has been contacted and he wants her back at the house."

Jordan wanted to say something more to the driver, but I grabbed her arm and shook my head slowly. "It's okay. I'm sure if I need something, Tristan will take care of it. But you get to see the house," I said with a smile, but even that made my head hurt even more.

"How long will it take?" she asked as we raced toward the Taconic.

"At the rate he's going, no time. Don't worry. Everything will be fine," I joked, trying to hide how terrified I was as my head began to throb all the way down to the base of my skull.

Jenson held his hand back toward Jordan. "I found this on the steps."

She took what sat in his palm and held it up to show me. "He got your phone, at least."

I laughed a little. Leave it to Jordan. "Yeah. At least he knows what's important. Did he get my bag?"

Leaning forward toward Jenson, she asked, "Did you get Nina's bag?"

"Yes, miss." He held out his hand and passed my purse back to Jordan. "I'm afraid there's nothing left in it, though."

She looked inside and saw Jenson had told the truth. Shrugging, she said, "At least he didn't get the bag. It's a gorgeous bag."

I moaned in a mixture of pain and amusement. "Yeah. But my letter is gone. Now I'll never know if the IRS was going to audit me."

"What?" she asked, confused by my inside joke.

"Never mind. I think I'm just going to close my eyes and relax until we get there."

I felt the car stop and then the door flew open and hands reached in and scooped me up from the seat. They were strong and I knew they were Tristan's. Opening my eyes, I saw his face and those brown eyes so full of concern staring down at me. I was in bad shape if his expression was any indication.

"Tristan..."

"Shhh. Don't talk. I want you to lay down while we wait for the doctor."

I rested my head against his shoulder and closed my eyes again. Just knowing he was taking care of everything put me at ease, and I couldn't imagine feeling safer than in his arms. He placed me gently into our bed and sat beside me, still wearing a look of worry.

"I'll be right back. I need to deal with Jenson," he said sternly.

Reaching out, I grabbed his shirt sleeve as he stood. "Jenson didn't do anything wrong. Please don't do anything to him. If it wasn't for him, I don't know what would have happened to me or Jordan."

Tristan studied me for a moment and then nodded his head. "He's supposed to make sure this doesn't happen, Nina."

"Please. He's not to blame. It all happened so fast. He got to me as soon as he could," I pleaded.

He leaned down and kissed me softly on the lips. "I'll send Jordan in until I get back."

Nineteen

Jordan sat with me and tried to make me feel better as Tristan reprimanded the driver right outside the door. I couldn't hear everything he said, but as Jordan raved about how beautifully the house was decorated, I heard Tristan say, "I want him taken care of. Now. Do I make myself clear?"

I truly hoped he wasn't talking to Rogers about firing Jenson. It wasn't his fault Mrs. Phillps' crazy grandson was some kind of addict and probably stole my bag for money to buy his drugs. I tuned out much of what Jordan said as I strained to hear more of what Tristan was saying, but his voice was so low I couldn't make anything more out.

When he returned, his expression was softer and he smiled when his gaze met mine. As he sat down next to me, he squeezed my hand. "How are you feeling? The doctor should be here any minute."

"How did you get here before us?" I asked, realizing he couldn't have left the city before Jenson left Sunset Park.

"I drive faster than Jenson," he said with a laugh. "Remember how fast my car is?"

"Yeah." The memory of that first night and us racing up the highway toward this house flashed through my mind, and then I heard Jordan speak.

"I think I need to go home, Nina. You look like you're in good hands here."

All I could think about was her going back to where that asshole was. Who knew what might happen if he caught her alone? I looked over at Tristan and squeezed his hand. "Jordan can't go back there. That guy might be there, Tristan."

"Honey, I have work. I have to go back to the city," Jordan protested.

I silently pleaded with Tristan, hoping he understood the look in my eyes. When he spoke, I fell in love with him all over again.

"Jordan, Nina's right. You can spend a week or two at my hotel downtown while my people find the man who did this."

"Are you sure? That's really nice of you."

I brought Tristan's hand to my mouth and kissed it, mouthing "Thank you."

He looked deep into my eyes as he said to Jordan, "It's my pleasure. I think you'll enjoy one of the suites, and the menu for room service is second to none." Breaking his stare, he turned to face her. "I'll be sure to check in on you to make sure you're comfortable. Jenson will escort you back to Brooklyn and wait until you get your things."

Jordan leaned over the bed and hugged me tightly against her. In my ear, she whispered, "Feel better, sweetie. And if you let this man get away, I'll never let you live it down."

Rogers appeared as he always did, just at the right time, and took Jordan to the car. Alone again with Tristan, I pulled on his tie to bring his mouth to mine. Never before had I wanted to show someone how much I loved them as I wanted to at that moment. He kissed me like he'd missed me for ages, covering my mouth seductively as he caressed the inside of my mouth with his tongue. The feeling was sensual and caring at the same time.

I pulled away and ran my hand over his cheek. "Thank you for what you did for Jordan. I can't tell you how much it means to me."

"I would do anything to make you happy, Nina. I'll find the man who did this and he'll understand what happens when he hurts someone I love."

Something in his eyes told me Mrs. Phillips' grandson was in danger, but before I could ask him what he planned to do about him, Rogers knocked on the bedroom door to announce the doctor had arrived.

"Good. Show him in, Rogers," Tristan said in the butler's direction.

The doctor examined me and pronounced me healthy, other than a tennis ball size goose egg on the back of my head. He assured me there wouldn't be any permanent damage and that I'd be fine. It took all of ten minutes for him to complete the entire examination and prescribe a pain killer, and Tristan thanked him and led him out to meet Rogers, returning to my side not a minute later.

He looked at me oddly, and I realized I still wore my red dress and stockings. I didn't know where my shoes were, though. "I wanted to surprise you for our date. Do you like it?"

He removed his black suit coat and tie and laid down next to me. Taking me in his arms, he slid his hands up and down my leg, feeling the stockings. His touch excited me as the pain killer began to dull my pain.

"I do. Did you wear this just for me?" he asked in a voice heavy with sex.

I ran my hand over his shirt and unbuttoned two buttons so I could touch his skin. It felt cool against my fingers. Lowering my mouth to his neck, I licked just below his earlobe. "I did. I thought it would be sexy."

Tristan groaned and ran his hand further up my thigh to where the garter belt connected to the stockings and then between my legs, where my sensitive skin lay bare. "You went into the city like this?"

His voice had a strange edge to it, and I lifted my head to see his expression had changed from just a minute earlier. His eyes had narrowed into angry slits.

"It's okay. I just went to see Jordan, and you know what happened after that. Nobody else saw me." I didn't mention the guys across the street from the apartment or that the wind had blown my dress so high it was likely that at least a few of them had seen a bit more than I'd wanted to show.

He slid his hand between my legs and stroked his fingers slowly over my tender folds. "I don't want you leaving the house like this without me."

The odd mix of gentleness in his touch and the harsh tone of his voice confused me. "Okay. It's no big deal, though."

One finger slid over my clit and sent a jolt of excitement through me. He stared down at me as my face showed the effect of what his fingers were doing to me. "It is a big deal. You're with me, Nina. No one else sees that part of you."

The possessiveness he was showing me was new between us. Until that moment, I'd never gotten the sense that he was jealous or overprotective when it came to me. There hadn't been a moment since I'd met him when he didn't act as if he were the only man in my life. This change in him baffled me even while it excited me. I liked the idea that he was protective about the woman he loved, although I knew there was no reason for him to be jealous.

I loved him so completely I couldn't imagine even thinking of another man touching me the way he did. Looking up into his eyes so intense, I smiled. "I don't want anyone else but you, Tristan."

He drew circles with his fingertip over my excited clit and kissed me deeply before he pulled away and I watched him slide down my body and settle in between my legs. Lifting my dress around my waist, he lowered his head and whispered against my skin, "No other man, Nina."

The feel of his mouth and tongue on me was exquisite. He slid up and down my moist folds, teasing me with the tip of his tongue when he reached my now swollen clit. His fingers thrust inside me, pushing against the tender spot inside that sent ribbons of pleasure racing through me.

His mouth inched me toward my orgasm, taking me to the edge of oblivion just to ease me back again each time as if he knew the very moment my body would give in to his expert touch. Just as I felt the first tiny tug of my release, he pulled away and stood up from the bed.

"Wha...What's wrong?" I asked trying to catch my breath.

He slowly unbuttoned his shirt and slid out of his pants and boxer briefs, revealing his cock pressed against his belly. I wanted to feel him inside me and held my hand out for his. He sat down next to me and without a word, pulled me onto his lap. I straddled my legs over his hips as he held me above him by the waist.

"Tristan, don't make me wait," I pleaded as I pushed against his hold.

Pushing the thick head of his cock through my wet pussy, he teased me to the point that I could barely hold back, and then stopped, leaving me tense and needy. His gaze fixed on me, watching my reaction, as if all this was a game.

"Don't tease," I cooed as I tried to lean forward to kiss him, stopped abruptly as he pushed me down on his legs. Confused, I attempted to feel some closeness from him, but his hands held me tight in place away from him.

He stared into my eyes until I couldn't stand it anymore. "What's wrong? Why won't you even kiss me?"

"I need to know you're mine, Nina. I've given you everything your heart desires, including enough money to ensure you can have anything I may not have considered. When I see something like this, I get concerned."

His words stunned me. "Why are you saying things like this? I wore the stockings and the garter belt for you—to go to dinner with you."

Tristan's gaze never wavered, telling me he was serious. He thought I'd done something. My mouth dropped open in amazement, and then a rush of defensiveness came over me. "As if I'd be able to do anything with your man hovering over me wherever I go. It's not like I'm ever alone, Tristan. You haven't trusted me from the very beginning of us."

He said nothing for so long I worried he might never speak to me again, but finally, he said in a low, solemn voice, "Jenson is there to protect you. Your safety means everything to me."

"Safety from what? I lived in Brooklyn long before I met you. I can handle myself."

And with that, his part of the conversation was over. He placed me on the bed next to him and left to walk to the bathroom, closing the door behind him. Closing me out.

Leaning back onto the bed, I covered my head with a pillow, angrier than I'd been in ages. I'd gotten all dressed up for him and then that fucked up asshole had mugged me, and all Tristan could think of was that I must be sneaking around behind his back? Hadn't I shown him every day and every night how much in love with him I was?

When he didn't come out after five minutes, something inside me snapped. I loved him, but this jealous bullshit based on nothing wasn't going to work. If we were going to stay together after my contract was up, he had to know that.

I marched to the bathroom, threw open the door, and stormed in to find him in the shower. I was all upset, and he was enjoying a nice shower at the end of the day! I stood there staring through the glass shower doors watching him until I became too impatient to wait any longer for him to notice me.

"So that's what you think of me? That I would take your money and everything else and go with someone else?"

He didn't even turn to face me at the sound of my voice, but I wasn't ready to let this go. Not yet. Opening the shower door, I walked in still fully dressed and stood in front of him, my arms crossed as the water hit me. "What? Now you're just going to ignore me? You basically accuse me of cheating on you and now I don't get to answer those charges?"

"Don't, Nina. I'm not in the mood for this with you."

I poked my finger into his chest. "Then you shouldn't have started it."

He looked down at me, those dark eyes barely hiding his anger, as the water rolled down over the beautiful features of his face, making me want to reach out to touch him. I extended my hand to caress his cheek, but he caught me by the wrist and held my hand away from him. Stunned, I tried to pull away, but he wouldn't allow that either.

"Nina, be careful with what you do now."

Yanking my arm from his grip, I snapped, "How about I do nothing with you now?" I spun on the wet tile and moved to take a step, but his arm shot out and wrapped around my waist before my foot could hit the floor. In a flash, I was up against the wall with him staring wildly down at me.

The man in front of me was different now—more powerful than I'd ever seen him. I knew I should have been frightened, but he looked so sexy, so commanding that I was more turned on than I thought I could be. His dark hair glistened with moisture, and I slid my hand over his head to feel its silky wetness. My touch made something break in him.

"Nina..." he moaned deeply as he lifted me onto his hard cock, pushing into me with one fast thrust.

I wrapped my arms around his neck and laced my fingers tightly as he kissed me hard, his mouth and tongue demanding mine respond with the same level of urgency, nearly taking my breath away. His cock pounded into my body, hard and fast like a piston as it stroked in and out of me, and he moaned and grunted into my mouth the sounds of a man driven by need. Our bodies bounced and slammed against the marble tile—

my back, his legs—each in turn smashing against the hard surface, but neither of us cared.

It was like all the frustration he'd endured in the past weeks exploded out of him and now he sought someone to share his pain. I knew he may never tell me what had been on his mind, but as we clung to one another's wet bodies and raced toward our release, I felt him reach out for me like he never had before.

Our sex was primal in a way that both thrilled and frightened me, but at that moment as he filled me and my body reacted as only he could make it, I felt closer to him than any other soul on Earth. His hands left the back of my head and skidded down the wet tiles behind me, making him sag against my body. I held his head to my heart, listening as he panted softly against me and murmured my name.

He silently lowered me to the floor without saying another word. I stood looking up at his face that now wore a tortured expression. He gently wiped the pad of his thumb over my lips and leaned forward to press his forehead against mine.

"Tristan, what's wrong?" I whispered.

"Nothing," he answered quietly and walked out of the shower. His tone told me that was his only word on the subject, so I let it go, hoping that when he needed to tell me, he would.

After I'd washed up, I found him sitting in bed, just staring toward the wall at the picture I'd painted for him. He seemed to be looking right through it.

I crawled into bed and lay there wondering what to say. Instead of speaking, I let my actions say what was in my heart and curled up next to him. Drawing little circles on the hard ridges of muscle just above his hip, I waited to hear any words come out of his mouth, but as the minutes ticked by, there was nothing. Finally, I closed my eyes, content and safe in his strong embrace but so wishing to know what he was thinking.

His words came out like a whoosh of air from his lungs. "Don't leave me like everyone else has. I'll do whatever it takes, but don't leave me, even if I screw this up."

I knew as soon as the first word left his lips that this had been what was on his mind. Work had been bad recently, but this was what had been plaguing his thoughts. That I'd leave him.

Lifting my head from his chest, I looked up and saw the torment in his face, just as I'd heard it in his voice. At that moment, all I wanted to do was make him happy.

"I'm not leaving you. Is that what that back there was all about? Me leaving?"

"Yes." His voice was a mixture of fear and shame.

"Why would I leave someone who adores me?" I asked, hoping to calm his fears. "I've never even thought of going anywhere. If anyone should be afraid, it's me. You made me sign a contract, which is up in just a few weeks, and you seem to have given me enough money to ensure when you break up with me that I'll be fine."

"I gave you that money to show you how much more you're worth than the salary I offered. I'd hoped you'd see that."

"All I saw was that you were throwing a lot of money at me and never mentioning anything about what was going to happen when the six months was up."

"So you think I'm going to leave you then?" he asked wide-eyed.

As I laid there listening to him, my fears sounded foolish. "I guess that sounds silly, but I did. Jordan tried to convince me that I was all wrong, but you've been so distant sometimes recently that I didn't know." I stopped talking and looked down, sheepishly adding, "And all that money."

Tristan pushed the hair out of my eyes. "I wasn't throwing anything at you. I have enough money to last for five lifetimes. What good is it if I can't share it with someone I love?"

I heard the loneliness in his words. Without his brother and parents, there was no one to share his money with, except me. But what about the contract?

"I notice you're not saying anything about what happens after the contract."

"What do you want to happen?"

I knew what I wanted. I wanted him to tell me he loved me without any need of some paper that said I was obligated to be with him. I wanted him to show me that his feelings had nothing to do with a contract or money.

"Tell me, Nina. What do you want?"

"It's not fair answering a question with a question," I said, sidestepping the issue.

"You didn't ask a question, so my question doesn't answer anything."

No kidding.

My potential answers receded into the corners of my mind, each one afraid to step forward and show itself. How was I supposed to tell him that even though he hadn't really told me what he wanted after our contract ended, I wanted what every woman in love wanted?

A husband who loved me. A beautiful life. Maybe kids down the road.

"You know I hate when you do that."

"Do what?" he said with a hint of a smile.

"Whatever this is. I always feel like I'm being talked into a corner."

"All you have to do is answer the question, Nina. What do you want?"

All my answers found great hiding places, except for the smart ass ones, which raced toward my mouth. "You know. What everyone wants. World peace. Cheaper prices at the pump."

He cocked an eyebrow at me and grinned. "Funny."

Climbing up his body, I kissed the tip of his nose. "Well, you put me on the spot. Maybe if you gave me some time, I could come up with something better."

He lifted my chin with his fingertips and gave me that sexy look that never failed to make me melt. "More time it is. I want your answer by five tomorrow afternoon. You can tell me what you want right after you show me your choices for Miami. For now, I think you need some rest. You've had a rough day."

Turning me over onto my back, he kissed me goodnight, told me he loved me, and laid down to sleep, leaving me with a deadline of less than twenty-four hours to figure out how to say all the things in my heart.

Piece of cake. Right.

Twenty

As the first rays of the sun streamed into our room, I rubbed the sleep out of my eyes and reached for Tristan. I wasn't surprised he was already gone, as it was his usual style, but the envelope on his pillow unnerved me a little. I had hoped to have the day to rummage around my own brain to find a way to tell Tristan what I really wanted, but his letter meant he too would be joining me in my head.

If I didn't know better, I would have sworn he'd left a letter to make sure of that.

I turned the envelope over in my palm and then held it up in front of me to see if I could read what he'd said. Nope. I had to open it, which for some reason filled me with dread. It was just like that first morning I'd woken up and nervously spied his note on the chair.

There was no time like the present.

I slid the letter out of the envelope and unfolded it. My eyes focused on the words as I read them aloud.

Dear Nina,

I missed having our date last night, so after you show me your choices for Miami and answer my question, we'll go to Tony's for pizza. I'm looking forward to it.

Love,

Tristan

I'm looking forward to it. Did he mean my choices, my answer to his question, or Tony's pizza? Jesus. This man was going to drive me mad. Even his letters said little and created more questions in my mind.

There was no point in worrying all day. I knew what I wanted to say. Had to say if I wanted him to know how I truly felt about him. I just had to muster up the courage to say the words.

By four o' clock, I was a nervous wreck. The woman who stared back at me from the mirror in the morning with her bravado had dissolved into a panicky mess. Needing to talk to Jordan but too impatient to wait for email, I snuck up to the attic, evading Rogers' careful eye, and called her for a strong shot of courage.

Every step I took across the attic floor seemed to make the floor creak like it was screaming beneath my feet. If only I hadn't hidden the phone all the way in the corner next to that scary sewing mannequin. I finally reached it and crouched down behind a stack of boxes, just in case my footsteps had been as loud as I thought.

The phone felt heavier in my hand than before, and I quickly dialed Jordan's number, pushing my index finger around in the rotary dialer circle eleven times, all the time questioning how anyone called for help and got it in time before push button phones and 911.

"Hello?"

"Jordan," I whispered into the black receiver. "It's me. I need your help."

"Nina, what's up? Are you okay? How's your head? And can I tell you how great this suite is? That man of yours knows how to live!"

"Jordan!" I whispered as loudly as I could and still be whispering.

"Okay. Sorry. What's up?"

"I need to talk to you about something. Something I need to do with Tristan."

There was silence on the other end of the phone for a long moment. "Nina, what's wrong?"

"He asked me what I wanted after my contract is over. I don't want to make a mistake like I did by saying I love you too early."

"I don't understand. What do you want?"

I said nothing, scared even to say it to her, my best friend. Opening my mouth, I tried, but nothing came out. Finally, I just said, "I don't know."

"Oh, honey. You know."

"You're not helping."

"I know, but I can't help with this one. Think about what you'd tell me if I asked you what I should say to Justin if he asked what I wanted with him."

"I'd like to think I'd be more helpful," I pouted.

"What are you afraid of, Nina?" she asked, cutting straight to the center of the issue. "And don't tell me you don't know."

I let the phone sag onto my shoulder and covered my face with my hands. "I'm afraid that I'm going to let him know exactly how I feel and how much I want to be with him forever and he's going to react just like Cal did."

And there it was. Like a huge cloud of doubt hanging over my head right there in the attic ready to suffocate me.

"Cal was an asshole, Nina. He was a liar and a player and an immature fuckup. You were too good for him from the moment you were born. That he broke up with you after you told him how you felt about him isn't a reflection on you, sweetie. He'd been lying for months. You were just too sweet to see that."

"But what if I'm just not seeing the same thing here?"

"Tristan isn't Cal. I promise you that. I'm not even sure they're both the same species. Tristan has been nothing but incredible, so until he shows you otherwise, I say give him a chance."

"What if he doesn't want as much as I do, Jordan?" I squeaked out.

"Then he's a fool and not the man I think he is. Give him a chance, sweetie. I think you'll be pleasantly surprised."

I wanted to. I really did. But my past and all that hurt felt like it was pressing down on my chest, threatening to crush me.

"Nina, do you remember all those days you stayed in your room crying over Cal and swearing you would never let yourself fall for anyone again? I think if you let this guy go, you're going to be like that forever. I don't want to see you get all hardened over. You're too good a person to be that."

Tears rolled down my cheeks at Jordan's words and the thought of losing Tristan because of my fears from the past. Wiping my face, I sniffled. "I know. I'm just so afraid it's too good to be true."

"You're forgetting my mantra. Remember? Good things happen to good people, and you're the best of the good ones, Nina."

"Okay. Thanks, Jordan."

"Your welcome, sweetie. And don't forget whatever happens, you got this."

I hung up the phone and inhaled a deep breath. *I got this.* Getting up, I walked as quietly as possible across the attic, but I stopped as I passed the trunk with the picture of Tristan and his family. It was silly, but something in me wanted to look at him as a child again. Crouching down, I opened the trunk while I kept my eye on the stairs, just in case Rogers had heard something.

I took out the family portrait and studied the childhood face of the man I loved. He looked so innocent. I wanted to see more—wanted to see what he was truly like as a child— so I sifted through the papers and books to a pile of smaller pictures I hadn't noticed the last time. Together, they catalogued Tristan and his brother's youth and as the pictures clearly showed, the vast differences between the two boys.

Identical in appearance, they were like night and day. All smiles, Tristan seemed to always be so full of life, while his brother stood sullen in the few pictures of him. Tristan was obviously the more athletic, appearing in picture after picture holding trophies, each one bigger than the one before. In the background of one picture his brother stood watching from behind the bleachers as Tristan once again received laurels. Taylor wore the expression I'd seen often in the past weeks on Tristan, a face that told whoever bothered to pay attention that the one wearing it felt the most acute sense of unhappiness. Some pictures showed his mother's pride in her winning son, but none included Tristan's father, except the formal portrait I'd studied earlier. As the boys aged, fewer showed Taylor at all.

I searched the bottom of the trunk to find more images of his brother, but there were none. All I found were papers that appeared to be lists of names and legal documents. Suddenly, a feeling of guilt came over me. It wasn't right that I was snooping up in that attic, even if it was for a silly romantic reason.

Carefully replacing everything as I'd found it, I closed the trunk and quietly made my way back downstairs, tiptoeing each step to avoid being caught by Rogers. It was nearly five o'clock and my time for indecision was over. I grabbed my laptop and headed for Tristan's office, prepared to show off my work on the

Miami suite and praying to God I was ready to answer his question.

I sat in his leather office chair behind his desk and closed my eyes to calm my nerves, repeating my newest affirmation. *I got this. I got this.* A few minutes later, the sound of his footsteps coming down the wood floor hallway told me my time was up.

"You look good behind my desk, Nina," he said in a silky voice that slid over me, enveloping me.

Opening my eyes, I saw him casually leaning up against the doorframe as he loosened his tie, the picture of calm. As usual, he looked incredible. The dark charcoal suit he wore was complimented perfectly by his black dress shirt and red and black striped silk tie.

"You don't look too bad yourself, boss," I tried to say just as casually in an attempt to keep the conversation light.

But he wasn't having any of it.

He walked toward me as he unbuttoned his shirt's top button. "It's five o'clock. I'm looking forward to seeing your choices for Miami and then you answering my question."

"I'm pretty hungry. How about we head over to Tony's for pizza and then get to the work?"

Tristan rounded the corner of his desk and stood next to me wearing a sly grin. "I'm happy to leave the work until tomorrow. You know I don't like doing anything after five."

I stood to leave, but he caught me around the waist and pulled me to him. He looked down at me with a look in his dark eyes so intense I shuddered. There would be no putting him off.

"But the answer needs to happen before we eat."

"Okay." I sat back down in his chair and opened up my laptop. "Might as well get Miami out of the way, right?"

I was stalling for time and he knew it. "As you wish."

Steadying my shaky hands, I presented my choices for the Miami suite, which Tristan easily approved and congratulated me on. I doubted he had even paid much attention to my ideas this time, but there was no point in belaboring the issue.

He closed my laptop and folded his arms across his chest. "I'm glad that's finished."

Unsure what to say, I stared at the desk and meekly smiled. "Me too."

Tristan caressed my cheek with his thumb and then cupped my chin, turning my face to look up at him. "So I believe the question stands, Nina. What do you want from me after your contract is over?"

My mouth became as dry as the Sahara desert. I wouldn't have been surprised if when I tried to speak that sand flew out from between my lips. If ever I needed a drink, it was at that moment. I tried to moisten my lips, but it was no use.

Clearing my throat, I croaked out, "I don't want this to end."

"Are you referring to your job with Stone Worldwide or your relationship with me?" he asked sharply, stroking the pad of his thumb against my jaw.

"Both."

"I can assure you that you have a job with Stone Worldwide as long as you'd like."

"This job?"

He dropped his hand to his side and pursed his lips. "Well, at some point I'm going to run out of suites for you to work with, but I can promise that you'll have a job that will take advantage of your artistic talents."

I swallowed hard, knowing that we'd gone as far as we could concerning the job. Now he was going to want my answer to what I wanted with him.

"But you haven't answered my question, Nina. What do you want from me?"

I closed my eyes and took the biggest chance of my life. Inhaling a deep breath, I said, "I want you. All of you."

There was complete silence as the last word left my mouth, and I feared opening my eyes to see his reaction. I couldn't even hear him breathe as he stood next to me. My heart sank as he continued to stay quiet. What was he thinking? Had I jumped the gun? Didn't he want me to want him?

"Open your eyes, Nina," he ordered gently.

I looked up to see him smiling down at me. My emotions were a jumble, making it impossible to figure out what to do next. I wanted to laugh. I wanted to cry. I wanted to run. I didn't know what to do.

When he continued with his silence, I blurted out, "You know, I hate this thing you do. It makes me uncomfortable. It's rude to stare at someone and not say anything. I know you're trying..."

He cut me off in mid-sentence and took me in his arms, kissing me deeply. As his tongue teased mine, his lips pressed tenderly against my mouth, telling me everything I needed to know.

Tristan was happy.

After the longest kiss I'd ever had, he pulled away and took my face in his hands. "I just hope I don't disappoint now that you'll get everything I am."

Shaking my head, I said, "No way you could disappoint me. Thank you for not freaking out when I said I wanted all of you. A lot of guys might have wanted to."

He leaned in to kiss me gently and whispered against my cheek, "I know I've asked you before, but what kind of men have you been dating?"

As I wrapped my arms around his neck, I answered with the honest truth. "All the wrong kinds."

"Well, I'm happy to be able to help you remedy that."

My emotions were ready to overflow, so before I began crying tears of complete and utter happiness, I whispered in his ear, "What do you say to remedying my hunger with some Tony's pizza?"

He stood back from me and looked at his watch for a long moment before he nodded. "I think it's about time."

We walked toward the car and as he opened the door for me, I said, "I probably look like a disaster. That lump on the back of my head doesn't hurt anymore, but it's like I have a stegosaurus ridge back there."

He leaned in and kissed me. "That will sound great on Page Six."

Page Six. My stomach did a funny somersault. This was the first time he'd ever mentioned anything even remotely related to being with me in public, and the idea was at once thrilling and terrifying. This was everything I'd wanted and now that it was happening, all I could think about were my deficiencies.

I wasn't a tall, willowy, supermodel type whose clothes hung perfectly off her. I had a tendency to make silly comments when I was nervous. For God's sake, there were times I couldn't even get my hair to lay right and not look all flyaway.

Tristan got into the driver's seat and started the car, but one look at my expression and he knew something was wrong. "Did I say something? What's going on?"

"I just remember you saying you never took girlfriends to those events that land you on Page Six, but then you just mentioned it. I'm just wondering if I'm the right type to be on the arm of someone like you."

He cradled my face in his hands and shook his head. "Don't say that. You're a beautiful, intelligent, charming woman who makes me smile. That's more than I can say for anyone I've ever met at those things. If you don't want to go to them, I'm fine with that. But it would be nice to have someone to talk to at them."

"You're trying to guilt me into going?" I joked. "But what about the idea of people seeing you smile? What will that do to your reputation?"

He rolled his eyes and turned to drive. "I hadn't thought about that. Well, then. It's settled. I'll remain

cold and impersonal in public and nobody will know the real me. Except you."

I knew it was selfish, but I liked the idea of the world thinking he was cold. There was something very special about Tristan only feeling comfortable enough to drop his cool facade with me.

We got to Tony's to find the entire restaurant deserted. Peering in through the front window, I saw no one inside. Disappointed, I turned toward him. "I don't think they're open."

Tristan brushed it off and took my hand to lead me inside to a table in the back. A waitress appeared almost instantly to take our order, and as he told her what we wanted, I wondered where all the other customers were.

She walked away toward the front of the restaurant and I asked, "Don't you think it's weird there's no one here?"

He got a strange grin on his face. "No. Not at all."

The lights dimmed throughout the building except where we sat, making me feel there was definitely something odd going on. "Tristan, they're turning the lights out. I think they might be closing early tonight."

I looked around to see where the waitress had gone to and when I looked back at Tristan, he was on one knee on the wood floor next to me and beside him sat a small robin's egg blue colored box. In the palm of his right hand was a smaller black velvet box. He pulled back the top and there sat a gorgeous diamond ring. I'd never seen anything so stunning, and even in the dim light of Tony's, the stone was brilliant.

"It's...oh, my God, Tristan. I don't know what to say." I covered my mouth with my hands and tears began to roll down my cheeks.

"Say you'll marry me."

At that moment, I was sure there wasn't a happier person on the entire planet. As I looked down into those eyes so full of love for me, my heart felt fuller than it ever had before.

"Yes. Yes! I'll marry you, Tristan."

He slid the ring onto my finger and took me into his arms as I cried tears of joy. This was more than I'd ever dreamed could happen in my life. I kissed him right there in Tony's Pizza Heaven and right in front of the waitress, who was standing there with our tray of pizza and crying herself.

The blonde looked down at Tristan with a look of anticipation. "Did she say yes?"

Looking into my eyes, he smiled. "She said yes."

"She said yes, everybody!" the woman yelled toward the kitchen, where a chorus of whistles and clapping exploded. She placed the large tray of pizza on the table and smiled at me. "Congratulations. You're a lucky girl. It's not every guy who arranges a proposal like this."

She left us alone, and I turned toward him. "How long have you been planning this?"

"Since Venice."

I looked down at the dazzling ring on my hand. I guessed the diamond was at least two carets and was set in a platinum setting and band. To say it was gorgeous was an understatement. It took my breath away.

"And you got the people here at Tony's to help you?"

Tristan took a bite of pizza. "I figured it would be easier to get you to say yes if the restaurant wasn't filled with people."

"So you paid to have the restaurant closed to everyone but us?" I asked in disbelief.

Nodding, he smiled. "You sound surprised. Of all the things I've spent my money on, this is the best one. It's not every day a man gets to propose to the woman he loves, and if it costs a little money, that's okay."

I glanced down at the ring sitting on my left hand and back up at him. "A little? I'm not sure I'm ever going to get used to your idea of a little money."

"I've told you before, Nina. I would spend ten times that amount to make you happy. That's all I want."

Leaning over the table, I kissed him sweetly, tasting sauce and cheese on his lips. "I'm the happiest woman in the world because of you. Don't ever doubt that."

With a wink, he smiled and said, "Good. Now eat your pizza before it gets cold."

Twenty-One

Later that night as we laid in each other's arms after making love for hours, I heard the all-too-familiar vibration of Tristan's phone on the nightstand near his side of the bed. In seconds, his mood changed from the blissful happiness we'd shared all night after his proposal at Tony's to sullen and brooding. His shoulders grew tense under my fingers, and in seconds he was gone from our bed to answer that phone I'd grown to hate.

I laid there feeling cold without him next to me and wondering if now that we were planning to be husband and wife did I have a right to ask him what was going on with these calls. Whatever it was that he was dealing with each time that phone rang and it dragged him out of our bed, it tore at my heart that he obviously believed he needed to deal with it alone.

Straining to hear any bits and pieces of his conversation right outside in the hallway, I was able to make out only a few garbled words that meant nothing to me. He was only gone for a few minutes, but when he returned to bed he was visible shaken.

He laid down next to me and moved to take me in his arms as I'd been before. Pulling me close, he was silent but I sensed the tension coming from him in waves. I laid my head on his chest, and he began to coil my hair around his index finger over and over.

After a few minutes, I whispered against his skin, "Tristan, what is it?"

"Nothing. Just work. Let's go to sleep. We have a lot to decide tomorrow."

I knew he was referring to our earlier discussion of what kind of wedding we wanted or if we should just elope since neither of us had much family, but as he spoke of all that now, it sounded like something unhappy to him.

Kissing his neck, I whispered, "You can tell me anything. There's nothing you can say that will change how I feel. I hope you know that."

He sighed heavily and squeezed me to him. "Everyone has something they're ashamed of, Nina. All we can hope for is that the one we love can see past it."

His words were so cryptic they worried me. "I can't believe you have anything to be ashamed of. I'll never believe that. No one who has treated me like you have could have done anything so bad he should be ashamed."

Tristan kissed the top of my head and sighed again. "Sometimes we have to do things because others have done wrong. All I can promise is that I would never hurt someone like others in my position."

I heard the sorrow in his voice and wanted to ask about it, but it didn't seem like the right time. On the night that he'd asked me to marry him, I didn't want to fall asleep after talking about things that made him unhappy. I wanted to make him as happy as he made me.

Snuggling close to him, I whispered, "All that matters is that I love you and you love me. Everything else is out there. Always remember that and we can get through anything."

My words didn't ease his mind, and when he kissed me just before we fell asleep, all I could feel was his sadness.

In the middle of the night, I awoke to Tristan thrashing around in his sleep next to me. He was mumbling something over and over as he frantically shook his head. His body writhed as if he were in pain, and his face twisted into a terrible grimace.

"No! No! Don't...don't do this. Stop!"

I gently nudged Tristan's shoulder to wake him, but he shook his head violently as he pleaded for the people in his dream to stop. Pressing harder into his body, I finally was able to wake him. He stared at me in terror for a few moments before he realized it was just me there with him.

"You were having a nightmare," I said as he took a deep breath. He nodded, and I gently stroked his forehead drenched with sweat. "Are you okay?"

"Yeah."

"What was that?"

He shook his head as he sat up to get out of bed. "Nothing. Go back to sleep."

I reached out to touch his back, and he turned to face me. "Tristan, what were you dreaming about?"

His body sagged and he hung his head. "It wasn't a dream. I have nightmares. I have since the accident. That's the reason I never stay after you fall asleep. I thought I could do it tonight, but..."

I listened as his voice sadly trailed off, so wanting to help fight whatever demons he was dealing with. "Come back to bed. It'll be okay."

"Maybe it would be better if I say in the other bedroom like I always do. They can get pretty bad."

Sitting up, I wrapped my arms around him and pressed my cheek to his back. "I wish you wouldn't. I'm not going to be scared off by a few nightmares. If we're going to be married, I have to know about even this kind of thing."

He took another deep breath and quietly said, "Okay."

Easing back onto the bed, he pushed his hands through his damp hair and closed his eyes. I laid my head on his chest and curled up next to him, hoping my presence helped to calm him. As he usually did when we laid in bed together, he twisted my hair around his finger over and over until just before he feel asleep when he stopped and whispered, "I love you, Nina. No matter what, don't ever think I don't love you more than everything else in the world."

I woke up feeling happy and refreshed, and for the first time ever, I was still in his arms. I vaguely remembered him leaving during the night, and as I focused my eyes, I saw why. On the table near the window sat a glass vase containing an enormous bouquet of my favorite flowers, pink roses. They were a soft pink color and there had to be three or four dozen of them. I inhaled their soft scent and smiled at his thoughtfulness.

Tristan roused next to me, waking up much easier than I did. As soon as his eyes were open, he was wide awake, but there didn't seem to be any evidence of his nightmare now. "I remembered they're your favorite."

Propping myself up on my elbow, I wondered aloud, "Where did you get dozens of pink roses in the middle of the night?"

My question made him smile that gentle grin I loved to see. "I ordered them yesterday. They were delivered first thing this morning."

I shook my head in amazement. "Is there anything you don't think of?"

"Not if I can help it. I guess if you'd have said no my plan with the roses might have been for nothing, but a man should be prepared."

Nuzzling his neck, I said, "Did you think I would say no?"

"You can never be sure. If you had, I would have just had to work harder to convince you that you should say yes."

I climbed on top of him and straddled his hips. "I do love a man with a plan."

"Speaking of a plan, we need to decide on what we want to do about the wedding. For me, I'm all for eloping. I can see us getting married on some island and spending day after day in bed for weeks."

"Are you okay after last night?" I wasn't sure how to approach the nightmare he'd had.

Smiling, he casually brushed the topic away. "It's nothing. I'm told it's quite common for survivors to have them for a long time after an accident. I just hope I didn't frighten you. I had hoped I could go one night without them, especially since last night was..."

I pressed my finger to his lips and shook my head. "You didn't frighten me. I'd rather have you next to me, no matter what, than anywhere else." I didn't believe for a second that it was nothing, like he said, but I hoped when he felt he could talk about it that he'd know he could turn to me.

"Now about that plan."

Rolling my body, I slid up and down his quickly hardening cock. "Mmm...my sister would probably like to be at my wedding."

"Then we can fly her and anyone else to whatever island we choose. Jordan, your sister, her entire family. Whoever you want. But I say we don't wait."

He grabbed my ass and squeezed, exciting me. Sitting up straight on him, I slid the sheet down to reveal the swollen head of his cock. Running my fingers over the soft skin, I said, "Sounds like you're in a hurry. What's the rush? I already live here with you and sleep in your bed."

Licking his lips, he eased his hips off the bed, running his cock through my already excited pussy. "I want you to be my wife. No hurry. I just don't see any reason to wait."

I looked down into his gorgeous face and for the life of me I couldn't find any reason either. Running my fingertips along his hips, I grinned the smile of a woman about to have great sex. "Then I don't either. Name the date and I'll be there."

Tristan focused his gaze as if he were deciding on an appropriate date and said, "December 14. It's a Saturday. All we have to do is pick an island and tell everyone we want there. But first, I can think of something better to spend our time doing."

He pulled me down on top of him and kissed me long and deep as he slid into my body, filling me up. There were better things to do first.

I had the urge for a swim, so I headed to the indoor pool for some relaxing laps before I figured out how I was going to tell Jordan and Kim that in less than two months I wanted them to join me on some island Tristan had in mind for our wedding. I'd loved the pool since that first night he'd brought me here, but I'd only enjoyed it once or twice the entire time I'd lived in the house. A quick swim and then my plan was to have Jenson take me to Jordan's suite by late afternoon.

My hot pink and black striped bikini from two summers ago still fit, thankfully after all the dinners Tristan had treated me to, so I slipped it on in the dressing room adjacent to the pool and got ready to jump in. The crystal blue water felt so refreshing as I descended to the bottom at the deep end. As I swam to the surface, though, I felt something strange on my legs and before I knew it, I had no bikini bottoms on and they were floating six feet away on top of the water.

It was Jimmy Mitchell's pool party in sixth grade all over again, except no one was there to see me, thank God.

I swam my bare ass over to where the fabric bobbed up and down in the water and grabbed my bottoms, happy that the flashback to that summer in middle school was the most embarrassing part of my current mishap.

And then I heard a man's voice and there was a fresh new humiliation. I turned quickly in the water and saw Tristan's gardener before I raced flailing toward the side of the pool to hide myself. I only needed to see his face for a second to know he'd seen all that God had given me. Wriggling into the bikini bottoms, I tried my best to be cool.

"Hi. I didn't realize I wasn't alone. I'm Nina."

He hung back away from the side of the pool and smiled a shy smile. Nearly as tall as Tristan, he was thinner and less built but he looked like he was closer to my age than his employer's. His blue eyes focused on me for a moment before he realized he was staring. Looking away, he stammered an apology and finally said, "I'm Blake."

With my bottoms finally in their rightful place, I relaxed and moved away from the wall slightly. "Hi Blake. I've seen you before in the summer."

He turned his gaze back toward me and nodded. "I'm Mr. Stone's gardener. I didn't know you were in here. I was just cutting through taking a short cut to the back of the house. I'm sorry. I didn't know."

"It's okay. No harm done. Did you work here before Tristan bought the house last spring?"

A look of confusion crossed his face and he looked over my head toward the back wall. "I've worked here for almost two years, miss," he said in a far icier tone than before. "It's nice to meet you, miss."

He walked quickly toward the back door of the pool area before I could say another word. I returned to swimming wondering what I'd done to obviously offend him but with bigger things to think about. Ten laps later, I was ready to begin my day.

I climbed out of the pool and looked up to see Tristan standing on the deck next to the chair where I'd left my things. Dressed in a suit, he didn't look like he was there to swim. "Hey!" I said as I walked toward him to get my towel. "I thought you left for work already. I would have asked you to join me for a swim."

Tristan silently stared at me as I dried off. "I see you met my gardener."

Knotting the towel around me, I nodded. "Yeah. I think I offended him. Sorry about that. I must have said something wrong."

"You should be more worried about offending me."

His tone was cold and matched the look in his eyes. Confused, I shook my head. "What?"

"You heard me."

I couldn't help but feel defensive. He was upset about something, but I had no idea what it was. Trying not to let things get blown out of proportion by either of us, I stood on the tips of my toes and kissed him sweetly on the lips. "I better get going. I have to tell Jordan and my sister the good news."

As I turned to walk away, Tristan caught me by the wrist. "Nina, you can't imagine I appreciate my gardener seeing you swimming half naked, can you?"

"Oh! That's what that sour face is all about." Then I looked around the room realizing what he was saying. "Are you telling me you have cameras in here?"

"You didn't answer my question."

I tugged my wrist from his hold. "You didn't answer mine."

"When you and I began all this, I told you that I'd give you anything to make you happy, but I expect certain things from the woman I'm with. One of them is that other men don't see you like I do."

His words came out like ice cold water dripping from his lips, but I saw beneath his cold facade that he was boiling mad. Part of me was pissed at being recorded doing something so innocent as swimming, and I questioned where else cameras were placed in the house. But another part of me loved seeing him this jealous over another man looking at me.

"Tristan, Blake didn't see anything intentionally."

"Blake?"

My choice of words was unintentional and equally as unfortunate. "It's not what you think. I introduced myself and he told me his name. If it makes things any better, he had no interest in talking to me and left almost immediately."

He cocked one eyebrow. "It doesn't."

Cradling his face in my hands, I smiled up at him. "Tristan, there's no reason for you to be upset. I promise there's no one else but you for me."

His expression remained unchanged, and I saw I wasn't getting through. Without another word, he turned and walked away, leaving me unsure where we stood but sure we could work out whatever it was later.

By three o'clock, I was ready to head out to see Jordan to cruise the bridal magazines and call my sister to tell her the good news too. I searched for Tristan, hoping to tell him I was leaving, but he wasn't in his office or our bedroom. As I walked down the hallway from our room, I heard his voice in the front living room and entered to kiss him goodbye.

One step into the room and I stopped dead at the sight in front of me. Next to the couch we'd sat on that first night, Tristan stood with some woman with gorgeous long, blond hair and legs longer than my whole body. She was standing entirely too close to him and fixing his tie like she'd done it before and felt completely comfortable with her hands on him. I only saw her from the side and hated her.

Then I heard her speak and the hate was purer than anything I'd ever felt.

"Tristan, this tie isn't going to work well. You need something brighter." Her voice was intentionally sultry, like she was affecting a sexy voice instead of using her normal one.

For his part, the man I'd just agreed to marry the night before stood like a statue as she fawned over his collar, but that didn't make it any better to watch. Jealousy coursed through my veins, making my hands ball into fists at my sides.

"Excuse me, am I interrupting?"

Tristan looked around the woman and smiled, but when she turned to look at me, her expression telegraphed loud and clear that, in her mind, I wasn't welcome.

"Nina, let me introduce you to my assistant. Kacey, this is Nina."

I waited for him to explain to Kacey who I was to him, but the words never came out of his mouth. Insecurity mingled with jealousy to create a noxious pain in my gut, and I walked toward them. Holding up my left hand, I said, "I'm his fiancée. Nice to meet you."

She extended her long, skinny arm and shook my hand with her bony hand that had just been fondling Tristan's tie. Her blue eyes slid over me from head to toe and back up again, and I was sure she was judging me.

"My pleasure. We're just getting ready for his interview this afternoon with Executive Homes. They plan to do an entire spread on him and this stunning house of his."

Ours. I wanted to correct her but as she stood looking down at me, I suddenly felt small and insignificant. All I could get out of my mouth was, "That's nice."

Then she asked, "Will you be staying?"

The way she said it made me feel like I was an intruder. I looked at Tristan for some support, but he simply stood behind her looking back at me. His silence was deafening and hurtful. I felt like a visitor in my own home, and suddenly, all I wanted to do was run.

As well as I could, I calmed my anger and said, "I'll leave you to your business. I don't know what time I'll be home, Tristan. Perhaps I'll stay in the city with Jordan. She's been wanting me to go out. I'll let you know."

Kacey looked relieved to see me go and returned to fiddling with Tristan's collar, but I noticed as I turned to leave that Tristan's eyes had narrowed ever so slightly. If he could hang out with his little friend, I could hang out with mine.

I marched out of the living room with my head held high and hoped neither of them saw how shaky my legs were under me. On top of the jealousy and insecurity churning in my stomach, now I was angry. Not only had he never told me his assistant was a female—a stunning one who looked like the actresses who accompanied him to formal events, no less—but he stood there like a statue, never saying a word to let her know how much I supposedly meant to him.

Jenson was nowhere to be found, so I waited outside by the car, preferring to shiver in the late fall weather of upstate New York than stay inside with Tristan and his assistant. It could have been twenty below and I wouldn't have felt the cold I was fuming so badly. The man who had made me the happiest woman in the world less than twenty-four hours earlier now had just let some gorgeous Amazon woman make me feel like an outsider with my own fiancé.

The front door opened and I heard footsteps, but when I turned around I saw it was Tristan. I quickly set off down the drive, but he kept pace with me and overtook me in mere seconds. I so didn't want to have the conversation we were about to have.

"Nina, I think we should talk."

I turned my back on him and stomped off in the other direction. "I don't think so. Go talk to your assistant if you need someone to listen to you."

His hand touched my shoulder and I jerked my body away from him. He wasn't going to get a pass on this one with just a touch or a few sweet words.

"Nina, I'm not going to chase after you," he said as he followed behind me.

"Fine. Don't. It's not like I'm anyone you should be chasing after anyway."

"You're acting ridiculous. You can't be jealous of Kacey. All she did was adjust my tie. It's not like she saw me half naked."

I stopped dead and turned around to see him standing there grinning like some sexy Cheshire cat. So that's what this was all about? Blake and my dropping bikini bottoms?

"Don't even tell me she's not a total bitch who made me feel like I was unwelcome in my own home and you didn't just stand there and let her do it."

"You saw what your jealousy wanted you to see. Sound familiar?"

"So it was just a coincidence that Kacey the blond bombshell was here today after what happened with your gardener? I doubt it. And why didn't you ever tell me your assistant looked like that?"

"I've never told you what any of my employees look like, Nina. They're simply people who do things for me. I don't pay attention to what they look like."

I raised my eyebrows in disbelief. "Is that supposed to make me jealous too?"

Tristan smiled and reached out to caress my cheek. "No. You misunderstood. But perhaps you can see my point from earlier now?"

Sighing heavily, I wilted under the weight of my anger. I hated that I was jealous. I hated that it was so easy for me to feel insecure.

"Tristan, I don't want to do this for the rest of my life. I can't be worrying so much that my husband is having some hot thing with his blond assistant that I go crazy here out in the country and begin to stalk him while he's at work. And I have to be honest. I'm not above the whole stalking thing. It's not my most attractive trait, but I get jealous."

He kissed me and pressed his forehead to mine. "I love you, Nina. Even the jealous you. Maybe we should both remember what happens when we get jealous."

"Okay. I promise no more flashing your gardener," I teased.

He straightened to his full height and laughed. "I wouldn't worry about that. I fired him."

Guilt over Blake's firing made my stomach turn and I stepped back away from Tristan. "Are you kidding? How could you do that? You fired someone for something I did? Do you plan to fire Kacey too since she made me jealous?"

He seemed to consider my idea and reached out to take my hand. "No, but I see your point. I will if you want me to."

I pulled away, horrified at what he was saying. "No fucking way! I won't be responsible for you firing someone twice today, even if it is that snarky bitch. If you fire her, it's because you want to, not because I said to."

"Nina, I want you to be happy. Tell me what would make you happy, and I'll do it."

The petty, jealous me wanted him to fire Kacey, but that was no more right than firing Blake. I understood his jealousy, but we couldn't go on like this. Not if we ever expected to be happy together.

"Don't fire Kacey, but promise me she doesn't ever get close enough to you to touch you again."

With a smile, he took my hand in his and brought it to his lips. "Agreed."

"And give Blake his job back. I can understand you aren't crazy about him working as the gardener since he saw me without my bikini bottoms, but give him another job somewhere else."

Tristan took a deep breath and let it out slowly. "Agreed. Now here's one for you. No staying in the city tonight."

"Agreed." I hadn't planned on staying with Jordan anyway, so it wasn't much of a concession.

"I have to get back to work. That magazine is expecting to tour the house, and I have to be there."

A stab of hurt pushed on my heart and I began walking toward the car. I guess I wasn't allowed to be known as Tristan Stone's live-in girlfriend. "Fine. I guess it's your house, so you should be there."

He grabbed my arm and pulled me back toward him. "Nina, let me explain."

"No need. I understand," I said with a pout.

Spinning me around, he forced me to look at him as he explained, "No, you don't. I didn't think you'd want to announce our engagement to the world this way. I know how private you are, and I love that. I don't need anyone else to know how much I love you as long as you know. But eventually the world is going to find out. I just didn't want it to find out this way."

I couldn't disagree with that. This way, I'd have the chance to tell Kim and Jordan first.

"Okay. I can see your point."

Smiling that warm smile I'd loved since the first night I met him, Tristan pulled me to him and held me tight as he whispered in my ear, "I love you. Tell Jordan I said hi and she's welcome to stay at the hotel for as long as she likes."

God, when he said things like that, I had a hard time remembering that sometimes he really did things that pissed me off. How was I supposed to stay mad at him when he was so sweet and thoughtful to not only me but my best friend?

Hugging him, I said, "One of these days I'm going to figure out how you make me love you so much, Tristan Stone. One of these days."

He pulled away and smiled as he cupped my chin with his palm. "Then that's the day I'll have to figure out a new way."

Twenty-Two

Jordan and I spent hours poring over thick, glossy bridal magazines, oohing and ahhing over the most gorgeous dresses I'd ever seen. Every few pages we'd find another one that we added to the list of "possibles" and fold over the corner of the page so that by the time we were done, the magazines had grown to twice their original size.

My call to my sister went as I thought it would. She couldn't believe her baby sister was getting married and had at least a dozen reasons why I shouldn't marry someone I'd only known for a few months and why they couldn't just pick up and leave to go on a vacation to some island in the middle of December. After her lengthy lecture on how marriage was a serious step that should be taken only after two people knew each other for much longer than six months, I explained that it was an all-expense paid trip for her and her family and if she didn't want to be there, so be it.

Jordan was much easier to convince. I don't think I had gotten the complete story about our island wedding plans out of my mouth before she was jumping out of her chair and racing around the hotel suite rambling about all the things she had to do at work to be able to go. But most importantly, she promised she'd be there, standing next to me as my maid of honor.

By the time I arrived back at the house, the Executive Home people were nowhere to be found. I threw the mail Jenson had picked up at the apartment on the desk in the bedroom and set out to look for Tristan. I found him sitting at his desk in his office looking particularly tired.

"Hey, you. How did your photo shoot go? Did they love the house?"

He looked up at me standing in the doorway and forced a smile. "It was fine. You know how I hate pictures."

"You look exhausted. Tell me what I can do." I leaned over behind him and nuzzled his neck. "A nice massage?"

He hung his head and cracked his neck. "I'd love that. I have to get ready for one of those goddamn events tonight."

My hands eased the tension from his shoulders and neck, which felt like they were twisted into tight knots. "Just remember it's for charity."

Pinching the bridge of his nose, he grumbled, "Not this time. This time it's pure promotion. The Richmont is hosting the release party for some author's new book."

"Why do you have to be there?"

"The board loves to have me at these things. Any time the hotel is featured in some book or movie, they love to build the whole thing up. It's ridiculous, but as the face of the business, I have to be there."

"You mean the hotel was part of the book's story?"

Blowing air out in a heavy sigh, he nodded. "Yeah. It's the setting for a good portion of the book, I guess. Thank God it's not a murder mystery or my lawyers would be suing the poor author for all she's worth."

"Oh. Well, it won't be so bad. You'll have one of the actresses there and you'll be able to practice your looking-like-a-statue skills," I said with a laugh.

He lifted his head. "I have a better idea. Come with me."

"What?"

He spun around in his chair and faced me. "Come with me. It's only a matter of time before we tell the world about us, and at least we won't be the focus tonight. You'll get to see what you'll be facing from now on. I promise to even smile."

"The press will know for sure there's something going on if you smile, Tristan."

"Then it's settled," he said suddenly looking much happier.

I shook my head as the realization of what he wanted me to do settled into my brain. I had no dress to wear to an event like this. I had no practice dealing with

the public or the press. My hair and makeup would need to be done.

Shaking my head, I backed away from him. "No, Tristan. I don't have anything I need to be able to go. I don't have anything to wear."

"No problem. Let me take care of that." Turning around toward his desk, he dialed the phone and said, "Angelo, it's Tristan Stone. I need a gown, red or black, for the same client you handled before and I want to see your choices at my house in Duchess County in an hour."

Angelo said something that pleased him because he smiled broadly as he hung up the phone. I walked to the side of the desk and folded my arms across my chest. "Same client you handled before? I thought you said you picked out all those clothes that day."

Turning on the charm, he pulled me back to sit on his lap. He traced the outline of my lips with his fingertip and said, "I'm guilty. It was a little white lie. I trust Angelo, so it's like I picked them out myself anyway."

"Actually, I think I'm okay with you not picking out my outfits. It has a weird vibe to it and there's something about you knowing that much about women's clothes that I'm not really feeling."

"That's good because other than wanting to tear them off you at times, I don't know much about them. But Angelo does, so don't worry. He'll make sure you have a dress worthy of you."

Worthy of me? Never before in my life had I thought of clothes in terms of anything being worthy of me. If something fit and I liked it, I bought it. Its worthiness or mine was never an issue. A dress worthy of me sounded like another sign that I wasn't ready for this party.

"Are you sure about this?" I asked quietly as he busied himself with shutting down his laptop.

He looked up with a quizzical expression on his face. "Sure about what?"

"Me going with you tonight. I don't want to ruin anything for you."

"Nina, you could never ruin anything for me. You're the woman I love and intend to marry in a few short weeks. Tonight is more for me than anything else. I don't want to go, but at least if you're with me, I'll be happy."

"It's just that..." I stopped myself and then said what was really on my mind. "No matter what Angelo brings for me to wear, I'm not going to look like the women you usually take to these kinds of affairs."

Tristan stood from his chair and wrapped his arms around me, pulling me close. "I don't have any interest in those women. I've told you that. They're picked because they look like the typical type of woman men like me date."

"But that's the point I'm trying to make. I don't look like that type of woman."

"You don't see many of those relationships lasting very long, do you? What kind of man wants to be with a woman who loves the way she looks more than she loves you?"

I looked down to avoid his stare, no matter how much love I knew was in it. "I just don't want to embarrass you."

He gently forced my head up with his hands on the sides of my face so I had no choice but to look at him. His caring eyes stared intently down into my eyes. "I don't ever want to hear you say that again, Nina. I love you for many reasons, but I won't lie. The way you look is one of those reasons. It may not be the only reason or the main reason, but I think you're beautiful. I don't want a stick woman who doesn't enjoy the food I want to buy her or who thinks spending hours doing her makeup and hair is important. I want you because you aren't like them. I can be myself with you. You don't know how much that means to me. I've spent years around women who I had to pretend with. From the first night we met, I didn't have to be anyone but myself. I love that in you."

His words convinced me. I could be the person I needed to be for these events. "Okay. Let's do this."

"That's my Nina. Now go enjoy a nice bath while I discuss something with Jenson. I'll let you know when Angelo arrives."

The bath helped relax me a little, but the reality was that I was terrified of being compared to those other women he always escorted to events. After spending enough time in the water to get pruney, I dressed in the clothes I'd worn that day and fiddled with my hair to get that upswept look like movie stars wore to award ceremonies. Over and over, I twirled and twisted my light brown hair only to have it fall down in a mess around my face. The problem was that Tristan's bathroom had none of the necessary items required to keep my hair like that.

Sure it was hopeless, I stared into the mirror wondering how I'd ever pull this night off. I could probably do something pretty nice with my makeup, but no hair pins meant my sort of straight in parts and sort of curly in other parts look would be the one I'd be stuck with.

Crestfallen, I tried once more only to have the end result be the same, but then an idea struck me. I tore through the house to find Rogers. If there was a hair pin or anything else that might work, he'd be the one to have it. I found him arranging the silverware in the kitchen and as I tried to catch my breath, pleaded, "Rogers, I need hair pins. Please tell me somewhere in this house there's something that can help me look like the women who go to these affairs Tristan attends."

His expression was blank for a long time, and then his long face lifted into a tiny smile. "I think I might know where one or two are, miss. Give me a moment, please."

Thrilled, I nodded excitedly and watched him walk off toward the area of the house he lived in. I waited impatiently, shifting my weight from side to side as he was gone a minute and then five. Finally, he returned with two silver pins that would definitely work.

He handed them to me with a slight bow. "I think these may do the job, miss."

Grabbing them, I turned to race back to the bathroom but turned back as I hit the hallway outside the kitchen. "Thank you, Rogers! You're the best."

The butler nodded and bowed again, deeper this time. "You're most welcome, miss."

The hair pins did the trick and within fifteen minutes I'd transformed myself into a sexy temptress with a gorgeous upswept hairdo and smoky eyes that were all the rage in magazines. Tugging a small clump of hair near each temple out of the pins' hold, I looked in the mirror, pleased with my efforts. I may not look exactly like those actresses Tristan usually had on his arm, but I was sporting a rather sophisticated look, if I did say so myself.

I heard him call my name and found him and a man who I assumed was Angelo in the foyer near the front door. His shopper was thin, immaculately dressed, and expressive, to say the least. He held five dresses in his hand out to the side and almost above his head—all formal gowns that I was sure would look stunning, even on me.

"Mr. Stone, I have five dresses in exactly the young lady's size. Which do you prefer?" he asked with a flourish of his free hand.

"Angelo, I think it would be better to ask the young lady. I pay you to shop for me for a reason."

The man feigned a bow. "As you wish. Miss, which would you like to begin with?"

I turned toward Tristan. "Do we have time for me to try on more than one?"

My question seemed to amuse him. Smiling, he said, "We have as much time as you need. We'll arrive when you're satisfied with the dress. And if you don't like any of these, I'm sure Angelo has more just outside."

I saw a pained look cross Angelo's face telling me he'd brought no more than what he held in his hand. Stepping toward them, I looked through them quickly and picked a black strapless one with a slight bustle in the back. "Let's try this one, Angelo," I said with a smile, hoping he'd see I didn't want to make this job as difficult as Tristan seemed to.

"Black it is, miss."

I tried to take the dress from him, but Tristan ordered him to follow me back to the bedroom with the dresses. Walking back to our room, I heard him attempt to make small talk with Tristan, with little success. As I entered the bedroom, I turned and took the dress from him.

"We'll be out here waiting, Nina," Tristan said with a wink as I closed the door to the dressing room and bathroom.

I soon found that Angelo was just as good with formal wear as he was with my work clothes. The dress fit flawlessly in all the right spots, accentuating my figure and hiding those areas that I'd always stressed over. My breasts looked perfect, and as I twirled around in front of the mirror, I saw the bustle made my behind look incredible.

Looking down at my bare feet, I suddenly realized I didn't have shoes. I flung open the door and before either man could say a thing, exclaimed, "I have no shoes! I can't go without shoes!"

A pair of gold strap stilettos hung from Angelo's hand as he stared at me with a look that screamed he found me silly. "At your service, miss."

Trudging over to him, I took the shoes and slid them on. Just as he'd succeeded with the dress, the shoes were a perfect fit. I wanted to ask how he knew my size, but I figured it wasn't something worth knowing.

I held my arms out and modeled the dress and shoes for Tristan. "Well? How's it look?"

Tristan's expression was serious, and he folded his arms. "Gorgeous. Simply gorgeous."

I beamed at his compliment, agreeing wholeheartedly with his assessment. Turning toward Angelo, he said, "I'll leave Miss Edwards with you for anything else she may need." He looked over at me and smiled. "I have to get dressed, but I'll be back in a few minutes. Whatever you need, tell Angelo and he'll see to it."

He left and Angelo produced a gold choker necklace with diamonds. It looked dazzling merely sitting in his hand. "If you will allow me, miss."

I turned around and he clasped it closed around my neck. Looking down, I ran my fingertips over the necklace, loving the feel of it against my skin. Spinning around to face him, I said, "I love it, Angelo. You have the most wonderful taste!"

"Thank you, miss."

"And not just with my clothes. I love the way you dress Tristan also."

Angelo's demeanor changed ever so slightly and he gave me a genuine smile that made him look almost friendly. "Thank you, miss. If I do say so myself, you look beautiful."

"She does."

Tristan stood leaning against the doorframe dressed in his black tux and looking so incredible I wasn't able to formulate coherent words for a moment. Somehow, that night his tux looked so much better than it ever had in pictures or all those times he'd gone somewhere in it without me. His dark brown hair just barely hit the collar of his stark white shirt and his jacket fit perfectly. Peaking out from beneath it near his wrists were gold and onyx cuff links that seemed to go with my necklace perfectly.

"Thank you, Angelo. You've done a wonderful job. Have a good night."

Tristan's not-so-subtle dismissal of the man made me feel uncomfortable, but Angelo left without another word, and I got the sense that this was how their relationship worked.

"You look incredible, Nina. I want you to remember this whenever you think that you're anything less than anyone. If I wouldn't catch hell from the board, I'd close this door and make love to you for hours like every ounce of me wants to."

I walked over to him and adjusted his bow tie. "After all the work Angelo and I did to get me looking like this?" I teased.

He cupped my nape and pressed his mouth to mine in a hard, passionate kiss that almost took my breath away. My legs felt weak when he snaked his tongue inside my mouth and teased me with the tip of it. He looked so stunning and smelled so good that if he'd told me to strip and tear the pins out of my hair, I would have done so without even a whimper of protest.

Pulling away, he ran the pad of his thumb over my lower lip. "You're right. But tonight when we get home, I'm going to give your pussy what I just gave your mouth. And that's just for starters."

He took my hand and kissed it as he led me toward the car that waited outside. Instead of the usual Town Car or his Jag, we were taken into the city in a stretch Rolls Royce that made the drive feel like we were floating on a cloud. Settled into the leather seats, we talked about the release party and I found out Blake had been given a new job doing work on the rooftop landscaping at Tristan's hotel in the city. And even though I'd wanted Kacey left where she was, within a few days of the Executive Homes shoot and interview at the house she was to be reassigned to the Miami hotel and put in charge of concierge there. I couldn't say I was unhappy, but when Tristan mentioned that her first assignment in her new job was to oversee the placement of my choice of artwork for the Miami suite, I secretly jumped for joy—on the inside, of course.

The whole Blake-Kacey Incident, as I secretly referred to it, had taught me a good lesson. A little jealousy was fine. A lot and it spilled out all over the place and could ruin even the best relationship.

Tristan's hand traced figure eights on my thigh as we traveled down the highway toward the biggest and most prestigious party I'd ever even been invited to, but I wasn't self-conscious or nervous anymore. With every adoring look he gave me, I felt more confident and beautiful than ever before. By the time we arrived, I felt as good on the inside as I looked on the outside.

Jenson pulled up in front of the Richmont hotel and came around to my side to let us out. Quietly, Tristan whispered in my ear as I stepped my foot out onto the street, "Don't ever forget how much I love you, Nina."

Lights flashed all around me before I even could straighten myself and step onto the sidewalk. Thankfully, Tristan was quick to join me and took my arm to guide me into the hotel, poised and cool as if this was second nature to him. Men and women yelled his name and barked out requests to look this way and that way, but he ignored them and held my arm tightly as we walked the red carpet, a private couple no more.

We entered through the glass front doors and the interior of the Richmont hotel nearly overwhelmed me. An enormous crystal chandelier hung from the three story ceiling, reflecting the hundreds of tiny lights that adorned virtually every surface of the lobby. I looked up to take it all in, and in my awe, almost tripped. Tristan steadied me and leaned in to whisper, "Remember, you're marrying the man who owns this. You belong here."

Crowds of people mingled as a string quartet played gentle music meant to provide a background but not disturb the festivities. As Tristan introduced me to members of Stone Worldwide's board and other people he quietly referred to as "people he found worthy of his time and mine," I relaxed into my role as his date and actually enjoyed myself. The author was a quiet woman who seemed out of place at her own event, but I was able to get her to laugh at a story I told when it was just

Tristan and the two of us, and by the time the night had ended, I could honestly say I'd had a good time.

Even more, I could say that Tristan had. As he socialized with the guests, I heard the same whispers over and over. Women and men leaned over to those people next to them and quietly noted, "I've never seen Tristan Stone smile like that." And that was followed by the words, "Is that an engagement ring on her finger?"

That he'd smiled because I was on his arm meant the world to me. I may not have been from his social circle, but I'd been able to make him happy. Me. No one asked if I was his fiancée, but it didn't matter. It was enough to know that for the first time, his picture on Page Six would be of the man I knew with me by his side.

By the time we sat down in the back of the car, I was so wound up I wouldn't have been able to sleep even if I had to. I felt like a girl after her first school dance who wanted to talk about everyone she'd seen and everything she'd done. As I chattered on about dresses and drinks and the best tasting hors d'oeuvres, Tristan merely sat back against the leather seats and listened. We were out of the city by the time I'd realized I'd done nothing but talk for miles.

Shifting in my seat, I played with the end of his undone tie. "I'm sorry. I've been so busy talking, I haven't given you a chance to get a word in edgewise."

"Don't stop. I love listening to you when you're happy like this," he said quietly.

"Well, did you have a good time?" I asked, secretly hoping he did. I wanted this to be something I could believe I made better for him.

He thought about it for a moment and turned his head to look at me. "Yes. For the first time, I can say I did."

Happy to hear those words, I leaned over and kissed him on the cheek. "That means a lot to me that you said that."

Tristan caught my face as I moved to lean back against the seat and kissed me like he had in our bedroom hours earlier. My stomach did a flip and that tiny tug in the pit of my abdomen appeared as he pulled the pins from my hair.

"I want you. Here. Take the dress off," he ordered as he unzipped it and began pushing the fabric from my body.

I protested, if only meekly, "Tristan, Jenson's going to know what we're doing back here."

With my dress in a heap on the floor, he cupped my breast and sucked the nipple hard into his mouth. Looking up at me, he flicked his tongue over the peaked tip and said in a husky voice, "I don't care. He can't see anything, and even if he can, I don't fucking care. I want you now."

He slid my panties off and pulled me onto his lap to straddle him. I felt the hardness between his legs as he lifted his hips off the seat and pushed his cock through my drenched folds. Desperate to feel his body on mine, I undid his pants and zipper and freed his stiff cock. He was so long and thick in my hands, and I stroked the full length of him, loving how my touch affected him.

"God, I want to be inside you," he whispered hoarsely as he slid the head of his cock toward my opening. "I want to feel your tight cunt around my cock as you ride me right here, Nina. Ride me."

He eased into me in one slow push, filling me completely before he began guiding my hips up and down on him. The threat of his driver seeing us thrilled me, and I rode his cock with abandon, loving each time he rammed it inside me. His hands controlled my body's movements, and his mouth sent waves of delight racing through me as his teeth nipped at my breasts. The mixture of the pleasure he gave me with his cock and the pain from his passionate biting was almost more than I could take. I begged him to let me go longer, but that only made him fuck me harder so that I came within minutes of him entering me. Buried balls deep in me, he continued to thrust through my orgasm, wanting release of his own.

My body still quivered from coming, but I wanted him to feel as good as he'd done for me, so I returned to riding his cock quickly. His dark gaze as he stared up at me told me he was getting close, so I rolled my hips with each push down on him, grazing the most sensitive part of his cock with my G spot. He came with a force so powerful I felt like I would drown with each blast inside me. Just then, my own release roared through me for a second time, and I cried out as he pulled my hair sharply to bring my mouth to his as he buried his cock inside my body.

Tristan panted near my cheek as his release slowly subsided, and I looked down to see him touching a reddish mark just above my right breast. He tenderly pressed his lips against my skin where he'd bit me and whispered, "Mine."

"I guess I've been marked," I said as I ran my fingers through his sweat dampened hair.

"I want every man who sees you to know you're mine, Nina. I want them to know even if you were covered head to toe that underneath you bear my mark. That as much as I'm yours, you're mine and mine alone."

Pressing my lips to his forehead, I leaned against him as he held me. "Always."

Twenty-Three

I'd had one of the best nights of my life, and as much as I didn't want it to end, by the time we returned home, I was exhausted. I was spared the embarrassment of having to face Jenson as we left the car since the driver disappeared almost as soon as he turned off the car. The thought that he'd seen this with Tristan before crossed my mind, but I quickly pushed it away with a gentle reminder to myself that I didn't need to doubt how much he loved me and a not-so-gentle reminder to not screw up the great thing we had with my irrational jealousy.

We'd made a mess of each other in the car, so we took a quick shower. As I toweled myself dry, I heard Tristan's phone vibrate on the nightstand and saw his expression instantly turn serious. As if on cue, he picked it up and walked out of the bedroom to answer it.

Curiosity about who was calling and what they said to him to change his mood so drastically played on my mind, and after five minutes of obsessing over it, I made a conscious choice to get into my shorts and t-shirt and distract myself with the mail I'd gotten from Jordan's that day. Junk mail I quickly tore up and a letter from my university about alumni dues took up a few minutes, thankfully taking my mind off what Tristan could be talking about outside.

At the bottom of the pile I found two letters like the one I'd lost that day when Mrs. Phillips' grandson jumped me. Neither had a return address, but they were both addressed to me at the apartment. The envelope of the first one looked like the mailman had dragged it along the street before delivering it to Jordan's mailbox. It was filthy, stained from dirt and what looked like coffee. As I struggled to make out when it had been mailed, I saw the postmark said July 9 and the letter was sent from a post office on the Lower East Side. Turning it over, I saw the hint of a shoe print on the outer edge too.

This letter has been on quite a trip.

I slid my finger under the flap and ripped open the top of the envelope to find the letter inside was in no better shape. Stained from coffee and dirt, it was unreadable, except for one line at the bottom that read in part, "Don't ignore this warning..." I strained to understand the words that came after, but the abuse the letter had endured made it impossible to figure out its meaning through the smeared ink.

Turning the envelope and letter over, I saw nothing more. Sure it was a debt collection letter for some bill I'd forgotten, I dismissed the piece of mail and threw it all in the garbage, along with the alumni and junk mail.

The last envelope in the pile sat waiting for me. I picked it up and examined it, noticing it had the same handwritten address and post office mark on the front of the envelope, but it had been mailed only the day before. At least the mailman hadn't put this one through the wringer. Tearing it open, I unfolded the letter inside and began reading.

The words swam in front of my eyes. *Your father. They got away with murder. Ask Tristan. He knows who's responsible.* My hands began to tremble violently, and I threw the paper away from me. Shaking my head in disbelief, I struggled to hold back the tears.

It wasn't possible. There was no way Tristan was involved in my father's murder. He couldn't be. He didn't even know him.

As I repeated those words again and again in my head, I realized I couldn't be sure he hadn't known him. I knew very little about Tristan before just a few months ago. What if the person who'd written this letter was right?

My head felt like it was beginning to spin, like everything around me was spiraling out of control. My mind raced to find any sign that the accusation made in the letter was correct. Every word he'd said suddenly became suspect, every action confirmation of his guilt.

My stomach tied itself into knots as every moment we'd spent together played out in my mind. Why had he wanted someone like me in the first place? Why had he pushed for me to live here with him? Did the phone calls he'd begun receiving right around the time I should have received the first letter have anything to do with this? I didn't want to believe I was in danger, but for the first time since I'd met Tristan, I was truly frightened.

"Where were we?"

I looked up and saw him standing in the doorway, a look of concern of his face like he always had after taking one of those phone calls. But now he looked different. Foreign.

"Nina, what's wrong? You look like you've seen a ghost."

Staring at the letter that lay near the edge of the bed, I reached over and picked it up. "Tell me you had nothing to do with my father's death. Tell me whoever wrote this letter is simply being cruel."

Tristan's face grew ashen as he stood staring at me, his eyes wide. "What are you talking about?"

"This letter. Someone says you know who killed my father. Do you?" My voice cracked as I pleaded for his answer.

He walked toward me and tried to take the letter from my hand. "What are you saying?"

Jumping to my feet, I pulled the letter from his hold and pressed it close to my chest. "Do you know who killed my father? Tell me!"

"Nina, calm down. Let me see the letter."

I backed away from him, shaking my head. "No! Just answer the fucking question! Do you know anything about who murdered my father?"

His silence was deafening as he remained staring at me, hurt filling his eyes.

"Oh, my God! You do!" I cried. "How could you? Get away from me!"

He followed me and gently touched my arm. "Nina, it's not what you think. Calm down and take a seat."

Pushing his hand away, I screamed, "I will not calm down! Tell me what you know! Who killed my father?"

"Please sit down. I promise you I had nothing to do with your father's death."

Tears rolled down my cheeks as I let him lead me over to the bed. I wanted so much to believe he hadn't been a part of taking my father away from me. Tristan was the man of my dreams and now it seemed like everything we'd had was tainted by this one letter.

I sat down on the edge of the bed and watched him kneel down in front of me, just like he had days earlier when he'd made me the happiest woman in the world. He looked up at me with those brown eyes that spoke volumes even before the first world left his mouth.

He knew. He knew who'd killed my father.

Holding my hands in his, he brought them to his mouth in a kiss. Quietly, he said, "Nina, I never met your father. I need you to believe me. I didn't harm your father."

"Why did the person who wrote that letter say you'd know?" I asked, praying to hear that he knew nothing about my father's murder.

"I need you to understand. Until my father and brother died in that plane crash, I wasn't part of the business. I hadn't found what I wanted to do, but I knew I didn't want to run hotels or anything else they did. I was your typical wealthy kid in his mid-twenties drinking and jamming whatever I could up my nose. I'm not proud of that, but I need you to know I wasn't part of what went on with them."

The man on the floor in front of me seemed so strange now. I'd never known anything about him like that. "Tristan, I need to know what this is all about."

He squeezed my hands and continued in a shaky voice. "When my father and brother died, I was thrust into everything with the business. I had to be that person I'd never wanted to be on top of learning how to run all the businesses, particularly the Richmonts. I had no idea what either of them had done. For months, I found out things about my father and Taylor that I'd never imagined they could do. Then one day I began sifting through documents related to a real estate deal my father and brother had been involved in." He stopped a moment and then said, "I didn't know why, but your father's name was on one of the documents."

Documents? "Why would my father's name be anywhere in papers of your father's?"

Tristan began to speak but his voice cracked and he stopped. "I didn't know. Then when I began digging, I found a slush fund my father used to pay for things he didn't want some on the board to know about. It wasn't until I dug into the money he spent there that I found out why your father would be involved in anything with my family's company. I swear I wasn't involved in what my father did."

"No, don't tell me your father was part of why my father died. Please don't say that."

"I'm so sorry, Nina. He must have been investigating a real estate deal and my father..." He couldn't finish his sentence, so I did.

With a sob, I said the words that broke my heart. "Your father had my father killed because he was getting too close to something he was doing."

Tristan buried his face in my lap and pleaded, "I swear I didn't know. I wasn't part of the business then. If I was, I wouldn't have let that happen. I couldn't get your father's death out of my mind. I wanted to do something to try to make up for what had happened."

I looked down at his head in my lap and realized what he was saying. "It wasn't a coincidence that we met, was it?"

He said nothing but lifted his head to look up at me, and I knew the answer. "No. I was sickened by what my father had done. I needed to do something, so I researched everything about your father and found out about you and your sister. I knew you lived right in Brooklyn and found out you worked at a gallery in SoHo. I just needed to try to fix what had been done, to see if I could help any."

His sorrow touched my heart, but then all my insecurities blew up inside me. "So you thought you'd just come by and see what the child of the man your father had murdered looked like? Maybe throw some money at her to make yourself feel better."

"Nina, I swear I didn't mean any harm. It's all I had to give and I thought if I could help you, then maybe some part of your life could be better."

I pushed him away in disgust and leaped up off the bed. "So that first night you didn't like me or want to spend time with me? You just wanted to take me for a ride in your expensive car and foist some cash on me to ease your conscience?"

He sat hunched over on the floor with his back against the bed. In a quiet voice, he admitted what I already knew. "It wasn't like that. I didn't set out to look for anything romantic. I swear. But then I talked to you as we drove up here and you were unlike anyone I'd ever met."

"So that's what this whole art curator charade has been about? That's why you've been dumping money into my account all these months? To make you feel better?"

Shaking his head, he said, "No. Money's all I ever had to give anyone, so it's what I fall back on. All I wanted was for you to happy."

My heart hurt hearing all of this, but I needed to know everything. "Why did you make up that whole contract thing if you didn't care for me then? Why make me stay here if you didn't even like me?"

He quickly stood and moved toward me, his eyes filled with pain. "That's not true. I did like you and I fell in love with you. I love you, Nina. I'd never do anything to hurt you intentionally. Please believe me."

"But why, Tristan? Why bring me here?"

Letting out a deep sigh, he said, "When my father died, there were still people in the company who had been part of what happened. I realized right after meeting you that they think you have information your father left you that can implicate them. I couldn't stop them from killing your father, Nina, but I could stop them from hurting you. So I came up with the contract and made it a requirement that you live here so I could always watch out for you, either myself or Jenson and Rogers. I figured if I had six months, I could find a way to make sure they knew you had nothing on them."

"And you figured I'd just jump at the chance to live in this great house with you?" I snapped. "Poor, pathetic girl who loved art. It couldn't be hard to convince her to live in a place like this with someone like you, right?"

He cupped his hands against my cheeks. "It wasn't like that. Please listen to me."

"Your father killed my father and you've known every moment you've been with me. How can I believe anything you say to me?"

"Nina, I'm begging you. Listen to me. It wasn't like that. I fell in love with you like you fell in love with me." Tristan's dark eyes pleaded with me as he tried to make me believe him. "This doesn't change anything. I love you. Please tell me you love me."

That was the problem. I did love him. I adored him. If I didn't, then everything he'd just said wouldn't have hurt so much. My heart felt like he was tearing it out of my chest, and the only one who could make me feel better had done the damage.

"Tell me this wasn't some charity thing, Tristan. Tell me that even though I wasn't of your level that you didn't see me like that."

"Never. I never thought of how much money you had or didn't have. It didn't matter."

"Spoken like someone who's always had money. And the test at your penthouse? Why?"

"I can't help who I am, Nina. The doctors say it's probably because of the accident, but I don't trust easily anymore."

"Then why did you return the next night if I obviously hadn't passed your test?" I asked, afraid to hear his answer.

Quietly, he said, "I found out you were in danger. I couldn't let them hurt you like they'd done to your father."

"Did you even like me, Tristan? We slept together that night," I sobbed, the pain of this whole thing settling into my mind.

He leaned down to kiss me, but I turned away.

"I did like you from the moment I began talking to you that night after the art show. You weren't like anyone I'd ever met. I wanted to try to be someone you would want."

"And what about all the possessive stuff? The feeding me. The bringing that couple here for me to paint for you. All that business about you not wanting other men to see me like you do? Was that all because of some faceless people wanting to hurt me?"

He shook his head slowly. "No. I've always been that way. I won't apologize for that, Nina. You're the woman I love, so it's my responsibility to take care of you. It's who I am."

I looked down at the gorgeous diamond ring on my left hand and then back up at him. "When did you love me, Tristan? When did you stop seeing me as someone

you could help or protect and really fall in love with me?"

I let him kiss me tenderly, and he pressed his forehead to mine. "Don't do this to us. I love you. You're everything to me, Nina. Don't do this."

I heard all his words but could only focus on the ones he didn't say. I didn't want to be someone's charity case, even one for someone I loved more than I'd ever thought I could love a man.

Pulling away, I backed up toward the door. "You've lied to me from the moment I met you. How can I believe what you're saying now? How do I know the last six months haven't been about making you feel less guilty for the awful thing your father did to my family?"

In a voice that almost tore me apart, he pleaded, "Nina, don't leave me. I can't lose you."

I couldn't answer him. I needed to get away from all the words he was saying and all the emotions he was causing in me. I heard him call my name as I ran through the house to the garage, unsure of where I was going but knowing that I needed to go.

Four cars sat parked in the garage, but the only choice was the BMW because I didn't know how to drive a stick shift. I'd noticed Tristan kept the keys in the cubby under the dash once and as I climbed into the car, I saw he hadn't changed his habit, thankfully.

I hurriedly started the car, turned the heat up high, and drove away as fast as I could, shivering in the late fall weather in just my shorts and t-shirt. My mind was racing faster than the car was tearing down the deserted dark road that led away from the house. Everything I'd thought I'd found in Tristan had been a lie. I'd let myself believe that a man like him would want to be with someone like me just for being me.

What a fool I'd been!

I looked over at the passenger seat and rummaged through my bag for my cell phone. A swipe of my finger across the screen showed me I still had no service. Tossing the phone back onto the seat, I pressed my foot on the gas, taking the car to sixty and then past seventy.

I didn't know where I was going or how to get there. As much as I wanted to go to Jordan's, it wasn't like there were parking lots or parking spaces all over Brooklyn and I didn't know where I'd park the car. The thought of driving around for hours hoping to find someone going out in the middle of the night was definitely not what I needed at that moment.

The car was equipped with GPS, so at least I was able to find out how to get to my sister's. Kim's house was further away, but I needed somewhere to go and hide out while I tried to figure out what to do about Tristan. How could I ever believe anything he said after what he'd done?

And how could I ever love the son of the man who'd taken my father from me?

The thought of life without him made me feel empty inside, and I finally let out the emotions I'd been holding in. I sobbed uncontrollably as the car flew by the trees and fields near Tristan's home, the tears blurring my vision in the darkness. In one night, all that I'd had and loved had been ruined. My heart felt like it did the night I found out my father had been murdered.

Empty and numb.

I wiped the tears from my eyes as even more continued to flow. A car headed toward me flashed its high beams, startling me, and as I moved my hand from my cheek to the steering wheel, it slipped off. The car jerked into the path of the oncoming car, and I swerved to miss it, sending my car off the right side of the road. Everything flew by so fast and I was airborne before I could do anything to stop it.

And then everything went dark...

Epilogue

Tristan

"Jenson, find out where the BMW is headed. Now!" I ordered into the intercom as I dressed to go after Nina.

"Yes, sir. Immediately."

Pressing on the intercom button again, I barked, "And Rogers, I want all her favorites on the table when we get back."

"Should I order flowers also?"

"Pink roses. I want only the best and dozens of them. Do you understand?"

Rogers understood more than he let on with his simple answer of "Yes." I heard the madness in my voice and knew he did too. He'd been with me long enough to know there had never been anyone like Nina in my life. I couldn't lose her. I couldn't let what my father had done ruin the best chance I'd ever had for happiness.

"Sir, she seems to be headed toward Pennsylvania," Jenson intoned over the speaker.

Her sister's outside Philly. "Get my car out and ready for me to leave in less than five minutes."

It wouldn't be difficult to catch up to her. As fast as the BMW was, the Jag was faster.

As I thought about what I'd say to her, Rogers appeared in the hallway outside the bedroom. "Tristan, may I ask what you plan to do once you find her?"

"Bring her back, Rogers. She belongs here. With me."

Running my hands through my hair, I checked out my look in the mirror and turned to see him standing in my doorway with his arms crossed, as if he were silently judging me. "What is the look you're giving me?"

"I just have to wonder if it's not a better idea to let her go for the night. Chasing her down on a dark road out here might not be your best move. Perhaps she needs time to let everything you told her sink in."

I'd known Rogers since I was a child and knew full well the concerned tone in his voice was more for Nina than for me. My surrogate father, he'd warned me many times since this all began that she'd run away when she found out. That she had seemed to make him even more smug than he usually was.

"I know what you're going to say. You're going to tell me that I should have told her the truth in the beginning. Well, that wasn't an option. How exactly does a person inform someone that his father killed her father and certain people in his own company want her dead? I had to do it this way."

Rogers' frown deepened. "The problem is that she didn't realize this wasn't going to last forever."

"Fuck you. You don't know how I feel about her. I intend on this lasting forever, so get out of my way so I can find her and bring her back where she belongs."

Storming past him, I felt his hand grab onto my forearm. I stopped dead and stared him down. "I'm not interested in a lecture right now, Rogers. The woman I love is out there and I need to get her back."

He nodded and released his hold on my arm. "Fine. But keep in mind that no matter how much money you have, Tristan, it's not about that for her. I've tried to tell you this all your life. There are some people you cannot buy. She's not like the other women you've been with."

"Which is exactly why I love her. Why are you making me the monster here? It was my father and Taylor who had her father killed. I can't help it I fell for her."

"Tristan, sometimes it doesn't matter what you want to happen. For some, trust broken cannot be mended."

"That's fucking ridiculous. She loves me as much as I love her. I didn't kill her father and once she realizes that I was only trying to protect her, she'll be able to trust me again. Now stop giving me platitudes and make sure everything's ready for her when she returns."

I quickly got to the car and drove out of there remembering Jenson's details on where she was headed. If she changed direction, he'd call me, so all I had to do was drive like a bat out of hell and catch up with her.

The memory of our first night together in this very car replayed in my mind making me smile even as my gut churned in pure terror that what Rogers had said was true. Never before had I wanted to be with a woman and not simply have it be a fuck-her-and-forget-her thing. There was something about the way she never pulled any punches that I loved from that first night. For the first time in my life, a woman made me want something other than just a one night stand. She made me want the rest of my life with her.

That wasn't something I planned to let go without a fight.

Now all I had to do was convince her that I wasn't the bastard she thought I was.

I got the Jag up to near a hundred, letting the V-8 open up and slowing down only on the dark curves, but for miles I couldn't see her. Somehow, I couldn't picture Nina driving much faster than the speed limit, if her actions that first night were any indication, so I should have been able to catch up to her.

Tapping my Bluetooth to answer a call, I heard Jenson's voice in my ear. "She's on Longtree Road, sir. You should be able to find her easily. I believe she's stopped."

"Good! Thanks, Jenson."

A quick left and then a right and I was racing down Longtree, but I still had no sign of her. I got ready to call Jenson to see if he'd gotten his directions screwed up and my phone rang again.

"Hello? Is this Tristan Stone?" a man's voice asked.

"Yes. Who is this?"

"Sir, my name is Jacob Nestle. I'm from the New York State Police. A car registered to your name was in an accident tonight. A BMW, sir."

I jammed my foot on the brake, and the Jag skidded to a dead stop. My hands were shaking too much to hold onto the steering wheel. My mind went blank with terror and I mumbled, "The woman driving the car...what happened?"

I couldn't bring myself to ask how she was, dreading the words he might say.

"Sir, she's been taken to Roseland Memorial Hospital with severe injuries."

The man continued to say something, but I didn't hear him. Every part of my brain shut off, except for the part that screamed for me to get to that hospital. I had to see her.

I stood in the doorway to Nina's hospital room where I'd remained for hours watching each labored breath she took. Someone touched my arm and I looked down to see Jordan standing there next to me.

"Tristan, thank you for sending your car to get me. What happened?"

"It was a car accident. That's all the police know so far. She rolled the car."

Her gaze moved over to Nina and I felt her hand squeeze my arm as the first sight of her injuries settled into her brain. Both arms were bandaged because of cuts and scrapes, tubes and wires seemed to be attached to everywhere on her body, and her head was bloody from where she'd slammed into the windshield. Even worse were the cuts and bruises on her face. She looked like someone had beaten the hell out of her.

But it was the internal injuries—the ones we couldn't see—that were worse. A bruised spleen and kidney. Three broken ribs. And a head injury they couldn't say how bad yet.

Jordan covered her mouth and made a noise that sounded like she was going to cry or be sick. I knew that noise because I'd heard myself make it hours earlier when I'd first entered Nina's room. And even now, I felt sick at the thought that she was lying there hurt and unconscious.

"Is she going to be okay?"

"The doctor told me she'll recover, but they don't know how long she'll be in the coma. She's hurt badly," I answered robotically, as I'd done on the phone with Nina's sister.

As she stood there looking at her friend, Jordan began to cry. "What was she doing in the car alone? You never let her go anywhere alone, Tristan. Why wasn't your driver there?"

I didn't know how to answer her questions. I'd spent hours beating myself up over the very same ones. Why didn't I stop her before she left? If I had, she wouldn't be lying there in a hospital bed hooked up to machines to keep her alive.

"I'm going to get some coffee. I want to make sure someone's here with her all the time, so I can get you some, if you like. I'll only be a few minutes."

Jordan grabbed my arm as I turned to leave. "Honey, are you going to be okay? You sound exhausted. Get some sleep. You look like you need it."

Shaking my head, I said quietly, "No. I can't sleep. It's better that I stay up. I want to be up when she comes out of it."

"Okay. Take your time and get some coffee." She smiled at me and added, "Don't worry. She's going to be okay. Nina's tough."

I tried to smile but my mouth couldn't do anything but stay in the frown it had been in since hearing the officer say she'd been hurt. My body felt numb as I went in search of a coffee machine or a cafeteria. My brain wasn't much better. Nothing mattered but Nina recovering, but I couldn't do anything to make that happen. No amount of money, nothing I could say would help her.

By the time I returned, her sister had arrived. Shorter than Nina, she looked like an older version of her. Looking at me strangely, she had no idea who I was as I took my position in the doorway.

"Kim, this is Tristan. He's Nina's boyfriend. Fiancé, I mean," Jordan said as she introduced us. "He's been here since right after it happened."

I stuck out my hand to shake Kim's and mumbled my hello. I didn't want to talk or socialize. I wasn't good with this kind of thing, and talking was only going to lead to having to explain to her why I wasn't with her sister when the accident occurred.

Kim studied me like I was something foreign she'd never encountered before. "It's nice to meet you. Nina told me just yesterday," she said flatly, but I clearly heard disapproval in her voice.

The two women talked about something I didn't care about. I didn't want to hear about the last time Nina visited her sister or how Kim had been planning to drive out to Brooklyn over the summer but never got the chance. I just wanted to be left alone with Nina, to hold her hand and hope she heard me when I told her how sorry I was and how I would make it all up to her.

Jordan seemed to read my mind and led Kim out into the hallway. I slowly crept over to the hospital bed and reached out to touch Nina's brown hair that laid against the stark white pillow. She didn't move when I ran my knuckle softly over her jaw.

I took her hand in mine. It seemed so small as my fingers surrounded her entire hand. "Nina, I'm so sorry, baby. If you can hear me, I love you. Don't leave me."

All I wanted was to see those soft blue eyes look up at me and to hear her say she loved me. But she didn't move.

Bringing her hand to my lips, I whispered, "Don't make me go on without you, baby. Open your eyes and tell me you still love me."

Nina laid in that hospital bed unconscious as I watched nurses do their best to keep her comfortable. The doctors visited every day and seemed to feel the need to constantly explain how it was normal for patients with head injuries to stay unconscious and how her body simply needed time to heal. I didn't want to hear any of their explanations. All I wanted to hear was that she'd be okay and awake so I could tell her I loved her.

Jordan came every afternoon after school and sat next to Nina holding her hand and telling her silly stories about their time in college. Kim left after the first day, but I knew Jordan made sure to call her with updates every day.

After eight days, her face showed what I knew she was thinking. I was thinking it too. What if the doctors were wrong? What if she never came out of it?

Exhausted, but afraid if I left Nina might wake up and I wouldn't be there, I sat slumped in the chair next to her bed as Jordan joked with her about the first time they met in college. My eyes slowly fell closed as the sound of her voice faded away.

"Nina? Honey, you're awake!"

My eyes flew open and I saw Jordan leaning over Nina. She was awake! I leaped from the uncomfortable chair I'd spent so many hours in and stood behind her. The sweet eyes I loved were open and she was speaking.

"Jordan, what happened?" she whispered.

"There was an accident, honey. But you're going to be okay now." Jordan began crying. "Oh, honey! We were so worried."

"Where's my dad? You called him, right?"

Jordan turned to face me and shook her head before she turned back. "Nina, what do you mean? Your father..."

I moved around her and touched Nina's hand. "Baby, I'm so happy you're back."

Nina stared up at me with a vacant look and then looked at Jordan. "Where's my father?"

Nurses swarmed around her to check her vital signs and I walked out to wait for the doctor. Jordan joined me a few minutes later and neither of us said a word. We didn't have to. We both knew something was very wrong.

By the time the doctor pulled me aside an hour later to explain what Nina was experiencing, I knew. All he did was confirm it.

"I've examined her and it's good news. She doesn't remember some things, but she's going to be fine. All her injuries are healing well, and I think she just needs some time, Mr. Stone."

I looked past him and saw her smiling and laughing with Jordan. "She seems to remember her friend, but she thinks her father is still alive. He's been dead for four years," I explained to the doctor, hoping he could help me understand what was happening with Nina.

"As far as I can tell, she doesn't remember anything after right before his death. She remembers her friend because she knew her before that."

The doctor saved me from having to hear the painful words telling me she didn't remember me. After everything we'd been through, she didn't even know who I was.

"I think if you give her time, she'll remember everything. Just give her some time."

He walked away leaving me standing in the doorway staring at the woman I loved who saw me only as a complete stranger. I pulled the engagement ring I'd given her out of my pocket and slid it over the tip of my pinky. Would she ever remember what we were so it would mean as much to her as it did to me?

Jordan tapped me on the arm, bringing me out of a daydream about the night at Tony's when I'd asked Nina to marry me. "Tristan, you should talk to her. Tell her about yourself. I know it's hard, but she needs to know who you are."

"I don't know, Jordan. It might be too much for her. I don't know what to say about her father and I won't lie to her now."

"She knows already. When Kim called, she told her. She doesn't remember what happened to him, but she knows he died. Go talk to her. Don't give up on her."

With a gentle squeeze, Jordan prodded me toward the bed. Nina looked up at me and smiled, like she had so many times before, but I saw in her eyes she was just trying to make me feel welcome.

She didn't know me.

"How are feeling?" The question was lame, but it's what a stranger would ask.

"Jordan says that you and I are engaged."

Nodding, I smiled and pulled the ring out of my pocket. "I just proposed a few nights ago."

"Can I see it?" she asked as she held out her hand. "It looks like a beautiful ring."

I placed it in the center of her palm and smiled as she took it from me. "You liked it when I gave it to you."

She studied it for a minute and then looked me up and down. "I bet you proposed at some fancy restaurant or the opera. Not that I know if I like opera, but you look like the type of man who does."

I looked down at my clothes and couldn't help but smile. Dressed in my suit pants and dress shirt, I'd thought I looked casual without my tie and coat. Leave it to Nina to let me know just how wrong I was.

Lifting my head, I said, "Actually, it was a pizza place called Tony's that we like. I got down on one knee, though."

A sweet smile lit up her face. "I like pizza. That's good to know."

"And roast beef, turkey with stuffing, shrimp scampi, and sausage and peppers."

She was silent for a long time and then finally said, "I'm sorry I don't remember you, Tristan. You seem like a great guy."

I wanted to take her in my arms and never let her go. To do everything we'd done together all over again just on the chance that she'd remember how much we loved each other.

But I couldn't. I wasn't the man she loved. I was just some guy who remembered.

"Can I ask you something, Tristan?"

"Anything and I promise to give a straight answer."

A confused expression crossed her face for a brief moment and then she smiled. "Why don't I remember you?"

I sadly shook my head, her question ripping my heart in two. "I don't know."

Was it because of what I'd told her just before the accident? Had she forgotten everything about us because somewhere deep inside her mind she couldn't forgive me for her father's death?

After two and a half weeks, her doctor pulled me aside as Jordan and Kim visited with an almost healed Nina. Guiding me to a secluded room near Nina's room, he closed the door behind us and I took a seat across from him.

"I want you to know that the good news is that her physical injuries are healing well. She'll be able to go home tomorrow. Her memory loss is disconcerting, however. I had expected her to remember something of her life from the past four years, but I see no signs of that, as of yet."

Listening to him speak, I knew what he was about to say and instantly, my chest tightened.

"Mr. Stone, I just can't say she'll ever remember everything. The human mind is a difficult thing to predict. All I can say is that if you continue to show her what her life was like, she very well may come around."

Extending my hand to shake his, I pressed a smile onto my face. "I understand. Thank you for everything."

I returned to find Jordan and Kim standing outside Nina's room as the nurses did their jobs inside. The time had come to let them know my plans for Nina after she left here.

"Ladies, I'd like to speak to you privately for a moment."

Escorting them to the room where I'd just met with Nina's doctor, I stood as they both took their seats. Jordan looked up at me with wide eyes, as if what I had to say interested her, but Kim wore the same suspicious look she always gave me.

"The doctor just told me Nina will be able to go home tomorrow. I've made arrangements for her to come home with me to our home. You, of course, are welcome to come too and stay for as long as you'd like. I have more than enough room."

"With you? Why would she go home with you?" Kim asked sharply. "She should go home with Jordan."

"She's coming home with me because that's where she belongs. As I said, you're welcome to come stay as long as you like."

"She doesn't even remember you."

Jordan looked over at Kim and then back at me. "I think Kim might be worried that Nina would feel like a stranger in your house." Turning back toward Kim, she continued, "But I've been there and Nina was very happy there, Kim. She and Tristan were...are in love, and he can help her remember their time together."

I looked down at Nina's sister. "I can certainly understand your concern, Kim, but she belongs in her own home. With me."

Kim stood and folded her arms across her chest. "You keep saying belongs, like she's something you own. I'm not some small town rube like my sister. She may think you're something special, but I don't think so. She's not going to stay with some strange man. Not if I have anything to say about it."

"Well, you don't," I said as I crossed my arms.

"I'm not just some fool you can boss around. My husband is a lawyer. You don't think I'll just let you take her without having something to say about it, do you?" Kim asked, her eyes blazing her anger.

Stepping toward her, I smiled. "And I have a battalion of lawyers, all paid to be at my beck and call to do my bidding. You can try to fight me on this, Kim, but you'll lose. Nina is coming home with me. There's no more discussion on that."

"Really? Well, how do you plan to handle Nina's depression, which is sure to rear its ugly head any minute now?"

I knew my face showed that I had no idea what Kim was talking about. Thankfully, Jordan interrupted. "Kim, you don't know that. Nina's been really good for a long time. She might not get down this time."

Kim spun around to glare at Jordan. "Get down? Is that what we're calling it now? The last time she 'got down' she spent months crying holed up in her room. And I think when someone threatens to kill themselves, Jordan, it's a little more than feeling down."

Jordan quickly looked at me for my reaction and then back at Kim. "That's not fair and you know it. Cal broke her heart. And saying you want to kill yourself is different than actually trying to. She never tried to."

"Fine. If I have no say in this, then I have no reason to be here anymore."

Kim stormed out of the room, leaving me with Jordan, whose face had settled into a frown. Standing, she began to explain what Kim might be feeling.

"I don't care. I've heard how she talks to Nina. The woman is lying in a hospital bed, and her sister is chastising her for getting into a car accident."

Jordan nodded. "I know. She's always been tough on Nina, especially since their father's death. And that thing she said about Nina wanting to kill herself wasn't true, Tristan. Nina was just really sad one time and said a few things she didn't mean."

Shaking my head, I said, "You don't have to worry about me not caring about Nina because of that. I understand."

I didn't care that she'd felt depressed and said things about killing herself. The only part that bothered me about that whole thing was that she probably remembered that fucking Cal who'd broken her heart but didn't remember me.

Jordan looked up at me, her green eyes intently staring into mine. "I need to know you're doing this because you care about her. I need to know this isn't some kind of power thing or I swear, Tristan, I might not have all the money to pay lawyers, but I'll make sure she comes home with me. Tell me you're doing this because you love her."

"Have I ever given you a reason to doubt that I'm crazy about her? Have I ever not shown in everything I do that her happiness is the only thing I think of?"

"No, but she's doubted your feelings, so I needed to ask."

I couldn't hide the surprise I felt at Jordan's words. Nina had truly doubted that I cared for her?

"Didn't know she doubted you, did you? Well, she did a few times."

Leaning back against the wall, I shook my head. "Why?"

"Because you're everything she could ever want. It all seemed to good to be true. I don't know what happened the night she got into the accident, but I wouldn't be surprised if you told me you had a fight about her not feeling that she was worthy of being with someone like you."

Quietly, I answered, "No, it wasn't that. But every time she ever said anything like that to me, I told her how wrong she was. I don't care about the money or anything else. I care about her and want her to see that we were in love. Still are, as far as I'm concerned."

Touching my arm, Jordan smiled. "Okay. You've convinced me. Now all you have to do is wait for her to figure it out. She will. As I always tell her, good things happen to good people, and I'm including you in our group of good people who deserve those things."

I wasn't sure I deserved to be in Jordan's Good People group, but from that point on, I planned on doing whatever was necessary to be worthy of Nina and all the good things that came with her.

Nina was sitting up in a chair next to her bed when I finally got back to her room. Kim had likely given her opinion on her coming home with me, but the smile Nina gave me as I entered her room didn't indicate she was upset.

I sat down beside her and thought about what to say. Unsure anything would sound right, I just said what I had to and hoped it came out the way I meant it. "Nina, you're going to be released tomorrow. I'm going to take you home."

She nodded and said, "I hear my sister wasn't crazy about that idea, but I trust Jordan with my life and she says that I'd want to go with you. She's told me everything you've done for me since I've been in here. I guess you're a pretty nice boss if you're willing to take care of all my hospital bills."

"I guess." This wasn't going exactly the way I'd hoped it would.

"I just have one question to ask. Did I move in with you after we got engaged or before?"

"Before. You've lived with me since you began working for me as my private curator."

Tears filled her eyes and she brought her hands up to her face. "I'm a curator? I wish my father had gotten to see that."

I hung my head and said quietly, "I do too."

We sat together saying nothing for a long time, but then she touched my arm softly and said, "I don't know if I'll ever remember our time together, but I hope I do."

I knew it wasn't the perfect situation, but I didn't care. Nina would be coming home and even though she didn't remember everything we were, I had the chance to show her why she'd agreed to marry me while we rediscovered each other. The problems that had threatened to tear us apart still lurked out there, and I'd have to deal with them if I ever expected Nina to be mine again.

We'd been given a second chance. Now it was up to me to prove to her I was the man she wanted to spend the rest of her life with.

TRISTAN AND NINA'S STORY CONTINUES IN

FALL INTO ME

COMING SOON!

Visit K.M. at authorkmscott.blogspot.com, on Facebook at facebook.com/kmscottauthor, and on Twitter at twitter.com/KMScottromance

Made in the USA
Lexington, KY
30 January 2014